He faced danger every day in the wilds of Montana, but this was something he was prepared for...

Awake at 5:00 a.m., Bureau of Land Management Ranger Ryan Taffney would lift his weights for thirty minutes, then it was a shower, shave, uniform, one poached egg, with a single piece of toast and coffee. He would then turn on his computer and link with the office for any procedural or federal statute updates, BOLOs on wanted persons or vehicles, public complaints, specific area violations, and recent crime trends. After that, he would re-fill his coffee mug, kiss his wife goodbye, then head outside to his patrol vehicle. First, came a check of his weapons. Ryan carried a .40 caliber Glock 22 in his belt holster. Inside the Explorer were both a Benelli M-90 twelve-gauge shotgun and a standard .223 caliber M-4 combat rifle. After that came a quick look at the Ford's fluids and tires, lights, emergency light bar, the two-way radio, and, finally, logging on to the computer. When he was satisfied that all of his equipment was in order, Ryan contacted the dispatch center in Butte and advised the female dispatcher that he was in service and enroute to his assigned patrol sector.

"Romeo 16753," Taffney said into the microphone.

"Romeo 16753," answered the dispatcher.

"Ten-eight, 10-98 Trail 79 area via Old Stage Rd."

"Lucky you 167. Drive safe and don't miss you're check-ins."

"Ten-four, but be advised—lots of remote country out there. Not sure I'll have reception everywhere."

"Ten-four, 167. We'll follow on your SAT-NAV. Check in as you can. Have a nice vacation."

"Ten-four, I'll bring you some poison ivy."

"That's a negative, 167."

Ryan clipped the microphone back on the dash as he dropped the transmission into "Drive" and the Ford rolled forward. *It is going to be a hell of a day,* he thought as he drove out onto the gravel road.

He had no way of knowing, of course, that this trip into the northern wilderness of Montana as a BLM ranger would be his last.

It has only been a year since Jason Douglas, a retired thirty-year veteran police detective, narrowly escaped death in the deserts of west Texas. After that harrowing experience, all Jason wants is time to recover from his wounds, both physical and emotional, and to enjoy his retirement as he'd planned. Accompanied by his wife Sonya, he points his RV north to continue their sightseeing travels across the American West. In Wyoming, Jason meets up with two old friends, the three planning a dream fishing trip. Just as metal is drawn to a magnet, suspense, danger, and death are once again drawn to Jason and his two comrades as they make their way into the remote Missouri River wilderness of northern Montana, known simply as "Trail 79."

KUDOS for *The River*

In *The River* by Douglas Durham, Jason Douglas is back, this time in the Montana wilderness on a fishing trip, where he gets caught in a battle between a debtor and his loan shark. Oops. Jason, along with Daryl Jackson and Corey Taggert, are after cutthroat trout, but what they find is danger and violence—and not just from humans. The trio hires a guide to take them in to the wilderness, but after the guide lets them off of the boat at a place called Trail 79, where they plan to hike the river to the best fishing spots, the guide's past catches up with him, when his loan shark's assassin comes to collect his unpaid debt. But humans aren't the only deadly predators in the wilderness, and something out there is pissed off and after blood. Theirs. Like Durham's first book, *Death in the Desert*, this one is a fast-paced, mystery/suspense with our hero battling it out for the good guys against insurmountable odds. It makes for an exciting read. ~ *Taylor Jones, Reviewer*

The River by Douglas Durham is the second book in Durham's *Jason Douglas Mystery* series. This time Jason is on a fishing trip in the mountains of Montana. We are reunited with Daryl Jackson from *Death in the Desert*, the first book in the series, along with FBI agent Cal Johnson, two of my favorite characters. And like the first book, Jason and his cohorts are up against a very skilled and deadly opponent, two of them actually, only one of them isn't human. *The River*, like its predecessor, is fast paced and tension filled. And you never know what to expect. I love it when that happens. This is one you'll want to keep around to read again whenever you're in the mood for a fast, terror-filled trip down a river. ~ *Regan Murphy, Reviewer*

ACKNOWLEDGEMENTS

I would like to acknowledge the following:

My wife Kimberly, who supports my wild ideas; some of my closest comrades in the law enforcement community, including, but not limited to, retired police officers Daryl Dellone and David Griffin; Department of Justice investigator Corey Schroeder; former homicide detectives Todd Fraizer and Soloman Wells (RIP); and the rangers of the Yuma, AZ, Bureau of Land Management field office, all of whom were an inspiration for this book.

I would also like to acknowledge my good friend Art Roberts, who has helped me promote my novels, and the full and part time residents of Yuma, Arizona, who have been so gracious as to purchase, read, and complement my work.

Finally, I'd like to acknowledge Lauri, Mike, Faith, Jack, and all of the other great folks at Black Opal Books, for giving me the opportunity to tell my stories.

Thank you all so much.

THE
RIVER

A Jason Douglas Novel

Douglas Durham

A Black Opal Books Publication

GENRE: MYSTERY/SUSPENSE

This is a work of fiction. Names, places, characters and incidents are either the product of the author's imagination or are used fictitiously, and any resemblance to any actual persons, living or dead, businesses, organizations, events or locales is entirely coincidental. All trademarks, service marks, registered trademarks, and registered service marks are the property of their respective owners and are used herein for identification purposes only. The publisher does not have any control over or assume any responsibility for author or third-party websites or their contents.

THE RIVER ~ A JASON DOUGLAS NOVEL
Copyright © 2015 by Douglas Durham
Cover Design by Jackson Cover Design
All cover art copyright © 2015 *1230*
All Rights Reserved
Print ISBN: 978-1-626943-81-0

First Publication: DECEMBER 2015

Published by Black Opal Books **http://www.blackopalbooks.com**

DEDICATION

As we travel down this road called life, many people we encounter can be called acquaintances, a select few can be called friends, but if we are truly lucky, one or two can become "best friends." This second novel in the Jason Douglas series is dedicated to one of my best friends.

I arrested Mark Odwin Williams, when he was fifteen years old, for a petty juvenile crime. I was a brand new cop, twenty-one years of age, but instead of taking him to Juvenile Hall, I took him home and released him into his father's custody, which was a fate much worse than anything "the hall" could dish out. From that day on, Mark and I were destined to become closer than brothers. On many occasions, particularly as we sat around a campfire in the Sierra Nevada Mountains, Mark encouraged me to write about my adventures and experiences in life, "because you are a damn good story teller" he would say.

Mark and I shared many hunting, fishing, off-road ATV, and camping experiences together, not to mention our daily interactions and telephone calls. Tragically, Mark was taken from those of us who loved him in 2008, leaving a large hole in my heart. Not a single day passes that I don't think of him, remembering his laugh, his love of motorcycles and music, and his contagious smile. Not a single day passes that I don't curse him for not being here with me any longer. The River is dedicated to you, buddy. I'm sorry you're not here to read what you inspired me to write.

GLOSSARY OF TERMS

420: A slang term for marijuana or marijuana smoking.

ARTICLE 15: US Army non-judicial punishment for infractions of regulations.

ARVN: Army of the Republic of Vietnam (South Vietnamese Army)

ATV: All-Terrain Vehicle, i.e. Jeep, quad-runner, etc.

AWOL: Absent without leave.

BILGE: The rounded portion of a ship's hull forming a transition between the bottom and the sides. The lowest inner portion of a ship's hull.

BLM: Bureau of Land Management (federal).

BLOOPER: Nickname given the M-79 40 mm grenade launcher, carried by US Forces, due to the "Bloop!" sound it made when fired.

BOLO: Be on the lookout.

BOLT: Steel or aluminum shafted crossbow arrow.

BULKHEAD: The inner wall of a boat from bow to stern.

CAMELBACK: A pouch like backpack for carrying drinking water with a rubber tube over the shoulder for drinking directly from the pack without taking it off.

CONSIGNMENT: A retailer sells your item for you, taking a percentage of your asking price for doing so.

CV JOINT: Constant Velocity joint. A rotating, flexing steel coupling connecting a vehicle's axle to the back side of the wheel mounting hub.

DAK TO: A village in the Kon Tum Province of South Vietnam, made infamous by a November 1967 battle between US and North Vietnamese forces.

DEA: Drug Enforcement Agency.

DEADLINED: Taken out of service.

DOJ: Department of Justice.

EMD (Easy-Moderate-Difficult): Ratings given to four-wheel drive trails/roads.

EOD: Explosive Ordinance Disposal.

FLETCHING: Stabilizing "feathers" at the rear of an arrow or crossbow bolt.

FMJ (Full Metal Jacket): The name given to a bullet

where the entire bullet is sheathed in copper with none of the lead core exposed.

FNG: Slang/derogatory term for a new man, i.e. "Fucking New Guy."

GP MEDIUM: A very large single-room tent used by the US military.

GPS (Global Positioning System): A satellite-based navigation system made up of a network of twenty-four satellites placed into orbit by the US Department of Defense. GPS was originally intended for military applications, but in the 1980s, the government made the system available for civilian use.

GREEN CARD: Temporary legal alien document, allowing the holder to live and/or work in the United States.

GUNWALE (pronounced "gunnel"): In simplest terms, this is the top edge of the boat's hull, the portion extending above the deck, so called because that is where the holes for the guns used to go.

HEAD-STAMP: The end of a firearm cartridge casing, on which the caliber and manufacturer are embossed.

HQ: Slang for headquarters.

HRT (Hostage Rescue Team): The name given to the

FBI's (Federal Bureau Of Investigation) special unit, which is dedicated to counter-terrorism. It was formed in 1983 to fill a gap in federal counter-terrorism capability.

HUEY: A nickname given to the Bell UH-1 Iroquois Utility helicopter

HMMWV (High Mobility Multipurpose Wheeled Vehicle): The US Army's main four-wheel-drive, all-terrain utility vehicle. Commonly referred to as a "HUM-V" "Humvee," or "HUMMER."

ICM Ignition Control Module: The small computer that controls fuel and air flow to the cylinders of the engine.

INS (Immigration and Naturalization Service): A division of the United States Department of Justice authorized to handle all the legal and illegal immigration and naturalization issues of non-US citizens within the borders of the United States.

IRS (Internal Revenue Service): The government agency charged with collecting taxes for the federal government.

JESUS NUT: Nickname given to the assembly that connects the main rotor hub to the driveshaft of a helicopter's engine, i.e. "If the nut fails, you get to meet Jesus."

LIFT KIT: Longer vehicle springs and shock absorbers to allow for additional ground clearance on a vehicle.

LZ (Landing Zone): US military slang for the actual point where aircraft, especially helicopters, land to take on or let off troops.

M-4: Standard assault rifle in 5.56 mm caliber (.223) used by the US military and federal law enforcement.

M-60: A belt fed 7.62 caliber machine gun that was the main light machine gun of the US Army for many years.

MH-53: Large search and rescue helicopter used by the army. Also known as "Jolly Green Giant" and/or "PAV-LO" depending on the configuration.

NCO: (Non-Commissioned Officer): A military officer who has not earned a commission, i.e. corporals and sergeants. Non-commissioned officers usually obtain their position of authority by promotion through the enlisted ranks, as opposed to commissioned officers who generally hold higher ranks and have more legal authority.

NSA (National Security Agency): An intelligence organization of the US Government responsible for global monitoring, collection, and processing of information and data for foreign intelligence and counter-intelligence purposes.

NTSB (National Transportation Safety Board): Federal agency charged with investigating plane crashes.

OIC (Officer in Charge): A military term generally used to describe the person who has authority over a specific situation or mission.

OXY: Short for OxyContin, a powerful pain killer in the opiate family.

OCU (Organized Crime Unit): A unit of law-enforcement personnel charged with investigating organized crime or mafia-related crimes.

PHU BAI: A village in the Thua Thien Province of South Vietnam.

PTSD (Post Traumatic Stress Disorder): An anxiety disorder that can develop after a person has been exposed to one or more traumatic events, such as soldiers fighting in a war.

REMF (Rear Echelon Mother Fucker): Slang/derogatory term for the officer in charge.

RICO (Racketeer Influenced and Corrupt Organization): An act created by congress to help law enforcement fight organized crime.

ROV (Remotely Operated Vehicle): A remotely operated underwater vehicle.

SAC (Special Agent in Charge): An acronym for an FBI special agent who is in a supervisory position.

SAR (Search and Rescue): The search for and provision of aid to people who are in distress or imminent danger.

SNO-CAT: A tracked vehicle made for carrying passengers and equipment over deep snow.

SPETSNAZ: Russian special forces soldiers.

STEEL POT: Nickname given the older style steel helmets worn by the US military.

STICK: Slang term for the cartridge magazine of any auto-loading firearm.

SWAT (Special Weapons and Tactics): The name given to specialized law enforcement teams who generally handle difficult situations most law enforcement personnel are not equipped to deal with, such as hostage situations.

TELEMEX: Mexico's national telephone company.

THE HAGUE: A city in southern Holland, known for world court trials of war criminals.

THE POINT: Nickname for West Point a US Army military college.

TOPO MAP: A topographical map, in color, showing land contours and elevations, along with roads, trails, rivers, and streams in great detail.

USGS (United States Geological Survey): A scientific agency of the US government that studies the landscape of the US, its natural resources, and the natural hazards that threaten it. The USGS is a fact-finding research organization with no regulatory responsibility.

WEAVER STANCE: One technique of firing a handgun from a standing position, developed by Jack Weaver, a Los Angeles County Sheriff's Deputy in the 1950s.

WILLIAM CLARK: The "Clark" of the Lewis and Clark expedition of the early 1800s.

CHAPTER 1

DREAMS

Whop! Whop! Whop! Whop!" The popping sound of twin rotor blades attached to the main rotor hub of a Bell UH1-D Iroquois helicopter slicing through the air was distinctively unique. To anyone who had ever served on one, or simply just spent time being ferried in one as I had so many times over the past ten months, it was a sound that was never forgotten.

The sound was visceral and could literally be "felt" miles away and easily identified as a "Huey" long before the helicopter ever came into view. Inside the machine, when in flight, particularly with its doors locked open to allow the ugly fluted snouts of the M-60 machine guns mounted on each side to protrude, it was a maelstrom of engine noise, wind, and vibration, coupled with the stink of canvas, aluminum, hydraulic fluid, and JP-5 exhaust. Attempting to talk without a headset, such as that worn by the crew, was an exercise in futility.

I'd spent hours in these "birds" and was now so accustomed to the noise and smell that none of it really registered anymore. Sitting in the centermost of the five aluminum framed canvas seats bolted to the floor at the rear of the cabin, I was resting the back of my head against the thin, and mostly useless, sound insulation padding attached to the rear bulkhead. I was absentmindedly staring out through the front windscreen between the pilot and co-pilot. Both my hands rested on my Colt M-16A1 combat rifle upright between my knees. The weapon had a full thirty-round "stick" inserted into its magazine well, but there was no live round in the chamber. It was a well-known fact that this particular pilot wouldn't even let his own gunner chamber a round in his '60 until the need came to actually fire the weapon.

The story passed around was that this pilot had been on his first tour of duty when he was assigned to fly a load of Eleventh Cavalry troopers to an LZ out near Dak To. As the bird prepared to lift off, a young soldier sitting in a seat, just like the one I now had my ass parked in, had accidently discharged his "Blooper" grenade launcher inside the helicopter. The blunt rounded tip of the 40 mm fragmentation grenade had punched its way through the cabin roof and exited out the top where it was immediately struck by one of the spinning rotor blades. Fortunately for all concerned, the grenade's passage through the cabin ceiling and the strike from the rotor blade kept the projectile from spinning the required number of times to arm itself, thus it did not detonate on impact with the whirling aluminum. It was simply knocked through the swirling dusty air in a high arch like a well-hit baseball, falling into the red Vietnamese dirt 300 feet away where it lay still, like the menacing deadly little green egg that it was.

It was an accident in every sense of the word, of course, but that didn't change the situation, nor aid the young trooper with his misfortune. The helicopter's engine was shut down and the operation was quickly handed off to another unit. EOD was called out to dispose of the grenade, and the damaged helicopter had to be deadlined, pending repairs. The soldier was given an Article 15 and quickly transferred to a rear area support job. The incident made a zealot of the pilot when it came to loaded weapons on board *his* aircraft.

Can't blame him I guess, as I thought of the story and snorted, shifting my position in the seat. Sitting as I was, I was not comfortable. My steel-pot-style helmet was wedged upside down between my legs and jammed tightly under my crotch. The endless vibration made the ride miserable as the helmet chafed the inside of my thighs and my groin, but it gave my genitals a small measure of protection against any potential ground fire.

Granted, the thin steel of the helmet would do nothing to stop a heavy caliber anti-aircraft round, should it burrow its way up through the aluminum floor and out the roof taking my balls with it, but it was certainly more protection than the seat canvas or the thin fabric of my jungle fatigues.

"Yeah you prick, I'm wearing jungle fatigues," I mumbled out loud to myself as I looked down now at the mottled camouflage pattern of my pants and shirt with the name *DOUGLAS* embroidered in black lettering above the slanted right breast pocket. My thoughts strayed to my recent conversation with this new jerk-off of a second lieutenant named Momus Savage. I snorted again. *Momus...Jesus spare me,* I thought as I recalled his first name. This black FNG was shiny new and straight from "The Point." Several days earlier he had taken me to task, telling me, "Military Police are not authorized to wear jungle fatigues, troop!"

I, of course, answered him with a snappy "Yes, sir!" and a perfect hand salute. I knew well how to play the game, but I had no intention of taking them off. They were way too comfortable, compared to standard-issue fatigues. This guy had been in-country for only three weeks. He didn't know shit and didn't want to listen to those who did. I'd be surprised if he was alive in two weeks, much less two months. Most importantly of all, he wasn't *my* lieutenant. "Kiss my honky white ass," I remembered mumbling as he'd walked away satisfied I would bend to his will and obey his order. Race relations were not good in the US Army in 1971. I chuckled softly. *Fuck that guy* was my final thought on the matter as I turned my attention back out through the windscreen to the checkerboard pattern of green rice paddies and red dirt passing beneath the helicopter.

There were six of us inside the noisy, smelly machine today. A flight crew of three, two MPs, including myself, *and* the prisoner. We were fifteen minutes away from landing at the headquarters of the XXIV Corps at Phu Bai. The prisoner was another black soldier who had deserted from an airborne infantry battalion, bivouacked just outside the nearby city of Hue, two months before. He'd been living in the Cholon district of Saigon, shacked up above a combination bar and whorehouse with an attractive half-French, half-Vietnamese prostitute, one of hundreds in Saigon.

When the bar's proprietor confronted the soldier over his not paying for the girl's services for a week, he'd told the man to fuck off. The bar owner promptly called the Saigon National Police, or "White Mice," as they were known, due to their small stature and white uniforms. It took six mice to drag the kicking, flailing, cursing soldier out of the bar, where they turned him over to the US Army Military Police in Saigon. It was soon discovered that he had been listed as AWOL from his unit. The Saigon MPs shipped him to the army stockade at Long Binh to await court martial.

Holy shit. I shook my head thinking about that one— *LBJ, the notorious Long Binh Jail. No place I'd want to be.*

At some point, some REMF OIC decided the imprisoned soldier should be sent back to XXIV Corps HQ for special court martial as opposed to standing a general court martial in Saigon. HQ Saigon probably didn't want the publicity, race relations being what they were. My accompanying MP partner and I had been detailed to pick the prisoner up and escort him back to our small holding facility to await trail. *Someone must want his ass out of Saigon ASAP to detail a chopper instead of having us just take a jeep or truck*, I thought. I was looking at his hand-cuffed wrists, his wrinkled uniform, and his tired, yet still hostile, black face when he noticed me staring at him.

"FUCK YOU HONKY PIG! I AIN'T IN YOUR CRACKER ARMY NO MORE!" the prisoner shouted at me above the noise.

The MP sitting on the other side of him jabbed his rifle butt into the prisoner's ribs, hard, doubling him over. I just shook my head. *Curse me all you want, boy*, I thought, *you're the one that's in deep shit now.* He was right about one thing, though. He would be given his discharge from the US Army. I was certain it would read "Dishonorable." Since he'd been AWOL for longer than thirty days, he was now classified as a deserter. They'd hand it to him as they put him on a plane, under guard, bound for the confinement barracks at Fort Leavenworth, Kansas. The army took a dim view of soldiers who were convicted of desertion in the face of the enemy in times of war. That's exactly what the charges read on the warrant paperwork in my pocket.

Legally, the army could even hang this soldier for such a conviction, but that hadn't happened since Private Eddie Slovik in the second world war, and it certainly wasn't going to happen to this guy.

Hell, when it's all said and done, they'll probably just kick him out as undesirable and give him a bus ticket back to whatever ghetto shithole he was drafted out of.

I shook my head again. Leaning closer to him, I looked directly into his hate-filled eyes and shouted back, "CONSIDER YOURSELF LUCKY, ASSHOLE! IF ARVN WAS FLYING YOU BACK OUT HERE, THEY'D HAVE THROWN YOUR BLACK-ASS OUT THE DOOR FOR MOUTHING OFF LIKE THAT." I smiled, gestured my thumb toward the open door, then added, "THEN THEY'D HAVE WRITTEN IT UP AS 'KILLED DURING AN ESCAPE ATTEMPT!'"

The prisoner glared at me, but he knew it was true. The South Vietnamese Army was not fond of most Americans at this late stage of the war, but they *particularly* didn't like Black American soldiers shacking-up with their women, even if they *were* prostitutes.

"FUCK YOU HONKY MOTHER-FUCKER!" the prisoner shouted back at me, which earned him another blow to the ribs.

One dumb son-of-a-bitch, I thought as I shifted my gaze back to the windscreen between the flight crew. *Fuck him too.*

I was anxious to land, dump this guy into what passed as a stockade at the firebase, take a shower, and go have a few warm beers at the NCO club.

Sitting as I was, I could see a good portion of the many dials, gauges, and switches that surrounded the two men piloting the aircraft. Suddenly, as if responding to my gaze, a small yellow light in the center of the control panel began urgently flashing. By the pilot's reaction, I instinctively knew that it was flashing a "you may be about to die!" message. The two warrant officers piloting the aircraft had, just seconds earlier, been relaxed in their seats, discussing over their helmeted headsets the difference between women's breast sizes and which golf club was best to tee off with. Now they both suddenly sat up straight and began paying very close attention to the array of gauges and controls in front of them. I could not hear what they were saying to each other, but it was plain that something was seriously wrong. The co-pilot turned toward me in his seat, shouting to me over the noise, "CHECK THAT LITTLE ROUND VIEWING GLASS IN THE BULKHEAD BEHIND YOUR HEAD!" I gave him a questioning look, but un-fastened my lap belt and turned in my seat so I could see what he was pointing at. Sure enough there was a small round viewing glass, about an inch and a half in diameter, right behind my head. The glass was stained dark, however, and I could see nothing.

"WHAT AM I LOOKING FOR, SIR?" I shouted back.

The flight engineer turned from his machine gun on the right side, as if trying to decide if crawling across everyone to assist me would accomplish anything. He finally decided to just reach across and hand me an "L" shaped green army issue flashlight that had been clipped to his flight suit.

Shouting above the noise, he instructed, "USE THIS AND SEE IF YOU CAN SEE THE FLUID LEVEL!"

I took the light from him and shined it into the small porthole. Turning back to the co-pilot, I shook my head and yelled, "I DON'T SEE SHIT IN THERE, SIR!"

The flight engineer finally decided he needed to see for himself and crawled over to me, grabbing the light from my hand and shining the beam into the glass. He turned to the co-pilot and drew his right index finger across his throat as he spoke into his headset. This set off an immediate reaction. The co-pilot turned quickly, relaying that information to the pilot, who swiftly began to move the cyclic stick between his knees, the pitch/throttle control on his left side, and the foot pedals all at the same time. This combination of movements put the helicopter into a steep and fast decent toward a dry rice paddy.

"MAKE SURE YOU'RE STRAPPED IN AND HOLD ON!" the flight engineer shouted to everyone as he clawed his crawled his way back to his own outboard seat behind his machinegun, taking the opportunity to place his left knee squarely into the balls of the prisoner as he did so. As he buckled his own lap belt, he turned to me a winked. He was a southern boy, from Georgia, he'd told me, and he had zero tolerance for mouthy blacks. I shook my head and grinned to myself as I quickly re-fastened my own belt. I didn't know much about the mechanical workings of helicopters, but having turned wrenches on cars a good portion of my early life, I was well aware that when it came to any powered machine, if there was *no* fluid where there *should* have been fluid, bad things happened. This was particularly true in a flying machine hurdling through the air at 120 MPH, three thousand feet from the ground. I quickly examined the prisoner's lap belt. As an afterthought, I un-handcuffed his hands, which were in his lap. The other MP partner shot me a

questioning look then just shrugged. The guy wasn't going anywhere. He knew that, if he tried to escape, one of
us would crack his skull with a rifle butt—or just shoot
him.

The pilot was now struggling to get the machine on
the ground before it stopped flying. He almost made it.
We were still fifty feet in the air and moving fast when
there was a loud "BANG!" from over our heads, and the
helicopter lurched hard to the right.

The transmission had seized due to loss of fluid.
When this occurred, the jarring collision of gears had
caused the large bolt attaching the "Jesus Nut" of the aircraft to sheer off. In theory, this was supposed to allow
the ungainly aircraft to auto-rotate to the ground under
the pilot's control. In this instance, the entire assembly
failed, allowing the main rotor hub, along with the blades,
to separate from the body of the aircraft. When that happened, Mr. Gravity made his presence known.

In the blink of an eye, the Huey fell the last forty
feet, slamming into the ground belly first, still moving
forward at fifty MPH. Both landing skids immediately
snapped off and the fuselage bounced high into the air
like a fatally injured bird attempting to fly once more. It
violently crashed back to the ground, flipped onto its left
side, and slid to a stop, pieces of the tail rotor blades flying through the air in every direction like deadly scythes.
Both doors blew off on this second impact and joined the
broken skids and rotor hub, all cartwheeling away. Dirt,
sticks, rocks, broken Plexiglas, papers, helmets, weapons,
ammo cans, and anything else that wasn't bolted down or

strapped in flew around the inside of the cabin. We might as well have been in a blender, being beat to shit as we were. Finally, the heavily damaged fuselage of the helicopter settled to a stop on its left side in a cloud of dust and smoke.

Stunned speechless, I was trying to grasp what had just happened. *You've got to be shittin' me! We crashed?* I asked myself as I hung painfully sideways in my seat, held there by my lap belt. Blood dripped from a multitude of scrapes and abrasions on my face, head, and arms. My M-16 was nowhere to be seen. I was still trying to get my wits about me when the pilot shouted, "GET OUT! WE GOTTA GET OUT OF THIS FIRE TRAP!" *Fire? FIRE? Oh shit!*

I flipped off my lap belt. The others in the cabin did the same, which resulted in all of us falling into a heap, against both the left inside wall of the chopper and the hard packed ground which now filled the void left by the open door. Cursing and yelling, the four of us in the main cabin struggled to untangle ourselves from each other as all six of us began to claw our way up and out of the right side door openings, now pointing skyward.

My own instincts for survival took over then, as I had absolutely no intention of burning to death in this aluminum coffin. I crawled up and out onto the right side of the fuselage which was now ten feet from the ground. Closing my eyes, I tried to let my body go limp as I rolled off, waiting for another jarring impact. I landed hard on my right side.

I was puzzled. *Strange, that didn't hurt at all.* I

opened my eyes a second later. I couldn't comprehend what greeted me. It was not the hard red dirt and dry stubble of a long abandoned Vietnamese rice paddy that I'd expected. Instead, I found that my face was pressed into...*carpet*?

CHAPTER 2

REUNION

J ason? Jason? Are you okay? *Jason, wake up!*" My
wife Sonya was on her knees, bending over the edge
of the bed, looking down at me, her hands on me,
shaking me awake.

My eyes finally focused and I could see the concern
in her face. *What the hell?* I could now see I was wedged
between the bed and the closet doors in the bedroom of
our RV.

"You were dreaming," she informed me as I attempted to sit up. Not an easy task for a six-foot-tall, 200-
pound—okay, okay, a 230-pound—man in the tight space
I now found myself wedged into.

"Dreaming?" I asked, still confused.

"Yes, you were." Her expression changed, from one

of concern, to one of obvious irritation, now that she realized I was actually okay. "I was sound asleep and woke up thinking you were having a heart attack or collapsed or something. Then you started shouting something about getting out of this fire trap. Scared the shit out of me!"

My wife liked to wake up slowly and peacefully. She was not happy at being ripped from her own dreams—which I'm sure involved Tom Selleck and her, naked on a white sand beach somewhere—so abruptly.

"Sorry babe," I mumbled as I struggled to pull myself from the tight space.

"Uh-huh," she mumbled back as she tried her best to, once again, wiggle her toes in the sand and twirl her fingers in Tom's chest hair. I couldn't blame her for being a bit peeved. Fire is not to be taken lightly by people who travel in RVs, or in our case, *live* in one, as we'd been doing for the past three years since my retirement as a detective from a large California police department. We were now part of the American "snow-bird" class of nomads. Sell everything and go. Winter where it's warm, and summer where it's the most fun. It was a great life style, or I should say, it *had* been until a year ago when I'd let myself get talked into helping out a West Texas Sheriff's Department in solving a couple of murders. That little diversion had damn near gotten me killed, leaving me badly injured. I looked at the red LED digital numbers of the clock on the dresser. They read 5:42 a.m.

Sonya closed her eyes again, but alas, Tom wasn't to be found anywhere so finally she asked, "I thought you didn't have those dreams anymore?"

"I haven't had in a long time," I replied.

"Well, I sure hope they're not coming back. I don't want to go through all that again," she said, a hint of despair in her voice.

"One-time deal I think," I replied as I shook the cobwebs out, trying to clear the heavy sleep from my head.

Sonya decided there was no need in pursuing the matter further so she changed the subject. "Do you have your alarm set?"

"Yeah, it's set." *I sure-as-shit hope the dreams are not starting again,* I thought, briefly recalling the episodes, sometimes even embarrassing *public* episodes, of reliving those bad days in a far off land. *I don't want to go through that again either.* It had taken years for me to get past them. Back in 1971 no one had ever heard of the term "PTSD," which is so readily tossed about now.

I pulled myself up and looked at the clock a second time. *Screw it—no need to go back to bed now, though, I guess. Have to pick him up at the airport at seven thirty. Guess I'll make some coffee.* I moved to our small kitchen. *What's it been now...a whole year since I've seen him? Damn—a whole year.* One hour later, I was driving into the early morning sun to a reunion with an airplane and the man flying it.

The shiny two-tone orange and white Mooney M-22 Mustang smoked the tires ever so slightly as it touched down on the single paved runway on the outskirts of Buffalo, Wyoming. Although I'd been looking east for the plane with my binoculars—listening for it as well, the white color of its head-on profile, coupled with the early morning sun behind it, had made it virtually invisible to me. The first I saw of it was when it dropped out of the sky near the end of the runway only a few hundred feet from touchdown. The plane's forward momentum slowed quickly as the Lycoming six-cylinder engine idled back. It was a graceful-looking flying machine in the air, but blunt-looking to me as it turned off of the narrow runway onto the taxiway, rolling toward me where I stood next to my parked truck.

Being the small private airstrip that it was, there was no control tower, only a single story house inside the fenced perimeter where the female caretaker, who also doubled as the airstrip manager, lived with her husband. I had introduced myself when I'd knocked on their door thirty minutes earlier.

"Jason Douglas," I'd told them, apologizing for the early hour and explaining that I was there to pick up a friend who was flying in that morning. After a short but nice conversation with the middle-aged woman, she gave me permission to pull my truck out by the row of small aircraft hangars where the taxiway ended. It was there I now stood, watching the plane approach. The Mooney rolled toward me, the twin-blade prop spinning just fast enough to keep up its forward momentum. I could now make out the solo occupant behind the tinted Plexiglas windscreen. The man was wearing a crumpled baseball cap and "aviator" style sunglasses. He waved to me as the plane came to a stop twenty feet away. The engine died and the cockpit door opened as I walked up. I grinned, walking around the left wing. It was great to see Daryl Jackson's smiling face again.

"Hey stranger," I said as Jackson climbed out. I extended my hand. He did likewise and we shook hands, but after a brief few seconds of uncertainty we disregarded the handshaking and embraced tightly as men sometimes do. We had been total strangers a little over a year ago. Now we were as permanently bonded and as close as real bothers.

I'd known this feeling before. It was the heart-felt bond of men who have faced life-threatening events together and survived. The two of us stood there in an awkward silence for a moment, looking each other up and down, then both of us started talking at once. The words spilled from our mouths in an incoherent stream as we tried to ask and answer questions at the same time. Giggling like schoolgirls at this incoherent exchange, we finally calmed down enough to engage in sensible conversation.

"Damn, it's good to see you, Daryl! How the hell are you?" I asked as I helped him push the plane to the parking tie-down rings embedded in the asphalt.

"I'm good," he replied, throwing a canvas cover over the engine cowling. "I don't even limp much these days." He chuckled and gently slapped his upper thigh. "Oh, there are days on occasion I still long for the 'Oxy,' but I threw away my last half bottle six months ago. That shit was starting to scare me, it was so good. Thought later I should have sold it and made some money."

"Yeah, right," I replied, rolling my eyes, "Daryl

Jackson, drug dealer. Somehow I don't see that happening."

"Now days, I don't take anything stronger than ibuprofen when the need arises. Can't be a junky and get a flight doc to punch your ticket." Jackson looked up and down my reasonably muscular six-foot, 230-pound frame. "You look good Jason—looks like you've been working out some?"

"Some," I replied as I struck a ludicrous bodybuilder pose. "I might be getting old but I hate looking like it. Been pushing some weights when I can and biking some. Knees won't take the running any more, though."

"I hear that—bitch, getting old," he said.

I was wearing short pants. Jackson looked down, pointing at the large jagged purple scar on my right shin, nodding at my right side at the same time.

"Hurt much?" he asked.

I also lifted my shirt for him to see the small dark-pink-colored circular scars on my rib cage, then I shrugged. "Good days, bad days," was my only reply as I allowed the shirt to fall back into place.

"Yup." He nodded his understanding and took an overnight bag from the plane's cargo hold.

"I'm so happy for you—flying again I mean," I said to him. "I know how important it is to you. What about the job? Still flying for the computer chip company?"

"Nope. They won't let me fly the execs for pay anymore. Don't want the liability, I guess, so they offered me a choice between a spot grounded in the front office, or a severance package. I took the package. That, coupled with my retirement from the airlines and my investment stuff, means I get to do what I want, when I want. I mean, I miss the job at times, but not *that* much. I was basically just a flying limo driver anyway."

"And a new plane I see," I said, eyeballing the Mooney nose to tail.

"Yeah, well not brand new, but I found a smokin' deal on it and couldn't resist. I sold the Cessna. With what I got for it, and part of my severance money, I bought the Mooney."

"Like it?"

"What's not to like?" he replied. "Lots of room. Enough power. Handles like a sports car in the air. A bit cramped for guys your size but not for me."

I looked the plane over again. "I guess I'll get to see for myself tomorrow, eh?"

He smiled as he closed the cargo storage door.

"So what about your other hobby?" I asked him

"I assume you're referring to my old quest to rid the modern day world of the scourge of coyotes?"

"*Old* quest?" I asked, puzzled.

Jackson watched another small plane land on the runway. Just for an instant, a troubled look flashed across his tanned face, then vanished just as quickly. "To tell you the truth, Jason, I haven't been hunting since I got out of the hospital. Oh, I still go to the range and shoot my rifles once in a while—pistols too—and I kept all my hunting gear because I keep telling myself I'll start hunting those prairie wolves again someday, but I always seem to make excuses as to why I can't go, and just like

that old Creedence song goes, 'Someday never comes.'"
Jackson looked around me at my truck. "I thought you
said your cop buddy was going to joins us," he said, seeing no one else inside the cab.

"You mean Corey Taggert? I *think* so. We agreed he
was going to have to make his own plans to get there,
though. Had some family stuff to do, so I gave him all the
information on where and when, and the coordinates,
both to this place and the place we're going. Hopefully,
he can pull it off and meet us somewhere. Coming from
two different states as we were, it was just too hard for
him to coordinate an exact meeting place—oh, and he's
not a cop, not in the traditional sense, anyway. He's a
DOJ crime scene guy. We worked together at Vista, doing the same kind of work but he's a state big shot now.
You'll like him, so I hope this plan all comes together.
The guy knows how to fly fish, a real expert in the sport,
and he loves it."

With the plane properly secured, we climbed into the
cab of my truck. "This should be all I need for tonight,"
he said, holding up his overnight bag. "I'll leave everything else here and we'll load the rest of your gear in the
morning."

I nodded. "That'll work." After a few seconds
passed, I added, "I understand, you know—you not wanting to drop the hammer on living things anymore. I was
that way for a long time after 'Nam. I still am to some
degree."

He frowned for a brief moment, then his smile returned, and he quipped, "I picked up another hobby,

though, you know. Something to go along with the flying, which is why I'm now into *fly* fishing, get it?"

I rolled my eyes. "Dumb joke"

"I thought it was clever." He smiled at his own humor. "That's why I flew all the way up here to the middle of bum-fuck nowhere so you can show me how to catch some of these cutthroat trout I keep hearing about."

He changed the subject yet again. "So how's Sonya?"

I grinned at him, "I'm just tickled it worked out. I was pleasantly surprised when you said you wanted to come up and fish with me. She's fine."

He made curving motions with both his hands. "Yes, she is. You are one lucky man." Then his expression returned to the serious side. "You ever hear from Sanchez or Olsen?"

I shook my head. "Not lately. An occasional e-mail from Olsen. They're both doing fine, though, he says— healed up. Both still on the job."

Jackson nodded in response. "So what about you, Jason? You're still traveling, I see. You still keep up *your* shooting skills?"

I shrugged. "Not as much as I should," I replied. "I try to go out occasionally, but with this liberal anti-gun bullshit agenda making ammo so hard to get and expensive, I've been reluctant to shoot up my supply much."

Jackson sighed and shook his head. "Fuckin' politicians—they're *all* so full of shit. Hey, not to change the subject, but is the fishing up where we're going as good as you say it is?"

I didn't answer. I just looked at him and raised my eyebrows.

"That good huh?" he replied. "Where we going?"

I nodded at a range of mountains out on the northern horizon. "Over those—northern Montana on the Missouri River, near Glasgow. A feeder creek near a place called 'Trail 79.' Heard great things about it. If you believe the stories, the trout are as big as your leg, though not as big as my middle leg, I don't believe."

Jackson rolled his eyes.

"We'll hook up with our river guide at some place called Sand Wash," I continued. "He'll boat us in on the Missouri to the feeder creek. Should be a hoot, but it's about 450 miles from here. Your new plane make that in one jump?"

He grinned. "Oh yeah—it's got a range of about 1200 miles give or take. It'll cruise at 180 knots, so it'll take us about three hours to get there. I've mapped it all out. When we fly out, we'll have to land in Helena and get fuel to get back, though. So, you treating Sonya right?"

"She's still with me, so I must be doing something right, and since we'll be staying over tonight before we head up to the high country, you'll have a chance to see for yourself. Besides, she needs an ugly bastard like you to come around so she can appreciate my rugged good looks and manly charm."

He snorted. "Yeah, right. What she sees in you I'll never figure out."

"Sonya insisted on seeing you, actually," I told him.

"That's why we didn't just gas up your plane and leave from here."

"Good! I want to see her, too, and grab a few winks before we get up there. Those mountain drafts can be tricky, as can a dirt landing strip, and I don't want to fly up in there when I'm already beat, unless of course, you don't care about possibly becoming a red stain inside a smoking hole in the ground?"

I struck a thoughtful pose and rubbed my chin. "Nah, think I'd like to stick around for a bit longer. I'll let you get some sleep before we wing into the wild blue yonder."

The drive back along the Wyoming interstate took us through green rolling hills dotted with several large herds of antelope. Smaller groups of both white tail and mule deer were occasionally visible, also.

"Damn," Jackson commented as he noticed the animals' proximity to the freeway. "Didn't realize there was so much game up here."

I nodded. "Yeah, we didn't either. I figure the antelope must be smarter than the deer, though."

"How's that?"

I pointed out a large red stain with patches of brown fur stuck to the concrete of the center lane as we passed by. "Rarely see dead antelope on the roads here, just dead deer—a lot of dead deer."

Forty five minutes after leaving the airstrip, I tuned the truck under a sign that read *Deer Park RV Resort*.

"Nice place," Jackson said as he noted the golf course that wound its way around the outer edges of the resort, the tall pine trees, several small ponds, and the colorful well-kept flower beds near the clubhouse and pool.

Sonya was waiting for us as we pulled up. Walking up to Jackson's side of the truck, she grasped him in a hug as soon as he stepped out. Tears were running down her face.

Somewhat embarrassed at his own watering eyes, Jackson put his arms around her and both stood there, embracing in silence for almost a minute, memories of the previous year flooding in. No words were necessary—that would come later.

She turned and pointed to two cups of steaming black coffee sitting on the patio table, a small shot glass filled with dark brandy sat next to each.

"Sonya, you look great and you are one great woman. Why don't you leave Jason and fly away with me?" Jackson quipped.

"It's tempting sometimes, but then I'd miss all this luxurious living," She waved her hand at the RV.

"Well then, let's just have an affair," Jackson replied.

"Mmmmm, I'll put you on the list," Sonya fired right back.

I shook my head as I dumped the brandy into my coffee. "I already told Sonya that if she wants to get some strange, it has to be with someone rich, who can support *both* of us."

"I'm rich…well, sorta," Jackson responded.

"Not rich enough, sweetie. If I'm gonna let anyone else pet this kitty, Jason gets a '65 427 Cobra out of the deal," Sonya told him as she patted him on the side of the face.

I nodded and took a sip of the hot liquid. "An original, mind you, not a kit-car. She's right, you're *not* rich enough."

CHAPTER 3

MORAL COMPASS

As a nation, Yugoslavia began to come apart almost immediately, when its authoritarian dictator Josip Tito died in 1980. Even the powerful Soviet government, with all its military might, couldn't stop what was to come. By 1991, what remained of the country exploded into conflict. Three main ethnic groups—the Serbians, the Bosnians, and the Croats—began to fight over control of the territories. It was not long before the Bosnians and the Croats joined in a coalition to defend themselves against the more powerful Soviet-backed Serbian army. The Bosniak-Croat faction desired three separate nation-states. The Serbs wanted control of the entire nation, or so they claimed, and this was true to a degree, but theirs was an age-old hatred, a blood feud, which manifested itself into what some called a civil war but, in reality, was rapidly escalating into genocide. The Serbs were obsessed with either driving all of their enemies out or killing them, and they would stop at nothing until the purge was complete.

Serbian by birth, there was never any question that Jospair Yakif would fight on the side of the Serbian Army, also known as the "HVR," against the Bosniak-Croat forces of the "ARBiH." He was eighteen years old when war broke out in the split nation of Bosnia-Herzegovina. Jospair killed his first man that year, one of several Bosnian soldiers guarding a small village. It had been a swift and silent death, the Serb using a compound hunting crossbow provided to him for just that purpose. Jospair was one of those men who had that rare gift of incredible accuracy when firing any type of weapon.

Upon stealthily making his way to within fifty feet of the Bosnian soldier in the moonlit darkness, he had hit the man in the left eye with the razor-sharp, broad-head-tipped bolt. The shaft passed almost completely through the man's skull leaving just the fletching visible in the man's eye socket, killing him instantly and dropping him silently to the ground.

Jospair's entire life had revolved around brutality and death. As a young child, he had been raised on stories told to him by both his grandfather and his father, of the brutality of the Russian Cossacks and the Czar, then of the iron-fisted occupation of the Nazis, and finally the slaughter of Russians themselves by Stalin. In his own lifetime, he'd seen the heel of the Soviet boot. The rule of their dictator Tito was tame and even enjoyable by comparison. Jospair had killed many since that first Bosnian soldier. Killing came easy to him now. He was good at it, and he liked it. He felt no pity, no compassion, no remorse. Behind his back, the other soldiers began referring to him not by his name or rank, but simply as "Ajkola," or "Shark." In retrospect, maybe Jospair's murderous destiny had been unavoidable. His father had been killed in combat with Croat forces on Jospair's nineteenth birthday. Had Jospair been raised with any moral compass at all, any trace of it was erased forever the day he witnessed his mother decapitated in the front yard of their small house by an 81 mm Croat mortar shell. He would never forgive the Croats for either of these deaths, or the Bosnians for being Croat allies. For three years now, he and his platoon of men had fought, burned, raped, and murdered their way across this small country. Jospair's utter ruthlessness, as well as his tactical mind and skills as a natural leader, soon caught the eyes of his superiors. He rose quickly to the rank of senior sergeant. The Russian "Spetsnaz" military advisors had trained him well. Jospair was naturally gifted and a quick study. The "Shark" now commanded a platoon of thirty hand-picked men. He was an uncompromising leader, demanding and receiving obedience and loyalty from those in his charge. Like most sociopathic killers, when any human being became a difficulty to him, or even just an obstacle in his path, he simply killed and discarded them without hesitation, much as a child would throw away a broken toy. This included his own men, which he had demonstrated on two occasions, when his orders had not been immediately obeyed.

Jospair *did* make exceptions, however—or maybe "stays of execution" would be a better term. Rape was common on both sides during the conflict. The HVR, however, used gang-rape as a terror tactic. Those poor souls unlucky enough to be seen as reasonably attractive to Jospair and his platoon of men were used to satisfy their combined torturous sexual lust. It mattered not if they were male, female, child, or adult. Many times these assaults would last for several days. When their victims were no longer of any sexual interest, most were killed and their mutilated bodies put on public display as a warning to others to flee, should the Serbian unit return. However, a select few were allowed to live, always with scars of their capture, so as to take the story of their brutal ravaging back to their villages, friends, and relatives.

Jospair once offered a rare explanation to his men, accompanied by an even rarer smile. "It will be difficult for our reputation to strike fear into the hearts of others, if no one is left alive to tell of it."

Jospair was many things—a good soldier, a remorseless killer, a brutal rapist. One thing he was not, was stupid. As the Americans and the British, and to a lesser degree the French and the Germans, began their involvement to end the war by deploying their own considerable military might, Jospair took note. He recognized the inevitability that the combined armed forces of these countries *would* indeed put an end to his war. He also realized what would happen to his country when the fighting was forcibly brought to a close. More importantly, Jospair knew what would happen to *him* and those like him. They would surely be deemed "war criminals" by the intervening powers and tried for their crimes at The Hague. He needed a way out before the end came, which would be soon.

Over the years, Jospair had kept in close contact with his favorite uncle on his mother's side. The man had fled Yugoslavia years before, immigrating to America, and was now living in San Diego, California. Prior to the fighting, they had written regularly and even talked on the telephone when time and money allowed. His uncle's criminal exploits as a young man in Yugoslavia had helped him to prosper in America. The man was now the owner of an up-scale restaurant in some place called "La Jolla." Jospair had no idea where that was, or even how to pronounce it, but he did know his uncle had amassed a great deal of wealth in a short period of time and was an important figure in the local Serbian community. Jospair, now forced to rapidly make plans to escape Bosnia, would enlist his uncle's help. With some luck, he too would slip into America. It would be a difficult distance to travel, and the cost of bribing government officials and purchasing false travel documents along the way, would be high, but he had heard that once he made it to Mexico, the actual crossing into America would be easy, due to the ridiculously loose southern border security. The high cost of getting to America was not of much concern to Jospair. He would pay for his passage with the large sum of jewels, gold, and silver looted from his victims, which he had buried in a location known only to him. All Jospair needed to do was slip away from his men, retrieve his loot, and, with the help of his mother's family, contact his uncle.

Just before dawn, one week before the forced cessation of hostilities, as his own platoon of men lay sleeping in a small clearing, Jospair quietly slid out of his sleeping roll and moved into the tree line. It was there he ran into his first of what would become many "obstacles" in his journey to the West. One of his own men was on guard nearby, standing between Jospair and his freedom. Why the young soldier had moved to this particular spot to stand his watch perplexed Jospair. This man had been assigned another quadrant. He quickly decided he would have to dispose of him as he had so many others The Shark was a black shadow as he crept up behind the man—a private he. knew well. Jospair had deliberately chosen the youngest and most inexperienced of his soldiers for guard duty this night, just in case this situation might present itself. It was 4:20 a.m., that time of the twenty-four hour cycle when humans are at their worst. The young soldier's head bobbed. It was obvious he was fighting sleep. Jospair came in low—behind the man in a silent crouch—then, in one quiet swift motion, he stepped up behind the soldier and harshly clamped his left hand over the man's nose and mouth, jerking his head violently to the left, while, at the same time, kicking hard into the back of the private's left knee. The effect was immediate. The young soldier was thrown totally off balance and into a slump. A well-trained hand-to-hand fighter with more experience would have rolled with the blow to the knee in that direction and possibly dislodged Jospair's grasp, but this young private had neither the training nor that experience.

Shocked at the sudden undetected attack from the rear, the man's instinct was to try to regain his balance and yell out, but Jospair's hand was clamped firmly in place, preventing all but a small muffled "mmmmmfh!" sound from escaping the man's lips. In his right hand, Jospair grasped the grooved cork handle of a ten-inch-long double-edged K-bar combat knife. He drove the tip of the blade into the soft spot at the base of the man's skull, burying the blade nearly to the hilt, then he violently twisted the blade in a half turn to the right. There was a scraping "crunch" as the brain stem was severed. It was as if a switch had been flipped. The man crumpled like a deflated balloon.

Jospair knew it had been a swift merciful death. In all probability, the only thing the young guard felt was the sting of the initial knife's penetration, then nothing at all. As the guard collapsed in his arms, Jospair grabbed the man's AKM assault rifle to keep it from making any noise as he silently lowered both the rifle and the young limp body to the ground. Wiping the knife blade on the man's coat, Jospair paused, listening, then turned and, once again, became a silent shadow moving into the darkness of the forest.

Making his way several miles across familiar country in total darkness, Jospair retrieved his looted money and jewel stash. He then shed his uniform and all of the other trappings of his life as a "solider," keeping only his knife. In civilian attire, he began his quest for America.

It took five long weeks of covert travel by train and on foot through southern Europe, where he boarded a tramp steamer bound for Buenos Aires. From here, he made his way on land up through Central America and southern Mexico. With his gold, silver, and jewels, and his knowledge of the workings of the criminal under-world, Jospair had been able to purchase false travel documents and also to bribe the border guards and immigration officials in several countries not to look too closely at them. It had always amazed him that, on any given day and with the right amount of money, most people can be "persuaded" to look the other way on just about every issue.

He'd laughed out loud on several occasions, thinking about the fact that this was the way American politicians operated *every* day. There had been one close call along the way, though. In Prague, an honest uniformed police-man had shown too much interest in Jospair's false documents. When the cop didn't answer his radio, his comrades searched for him. They found him dead in an alley the next morning, surrounded by a large pool of blood, a gaping hole from a thick-bladed knife visible just above his larynx.

On Tuesday of week six, Jospair found himself standing in the small town of Los Algodones, Mexico, only a few miles from Yuma Arizona, near the point where Mexico, California, and Arizona all come together.

Pay telephones were all but extinct in the United

States by the late '90s, what with everyone carrying cell phones, however, in this small Mexican town not everyone could afford a cell phone, thus Telmex, the national telephone exchange of Mexico, still maintained a few payphones, including two that were located in front of a bright purple painted liquor store on the Mexican side of the US border crossing. Jospair walked into the liquor store and purchased a bottle of Mexican tequila and a phone calling card, since the phones outside didn't take coins. The tequila was merely a prop. He wanted to appear as of the many "*turistas*" that visited this small town daily, to buy the inexpensive Mexican liquor.

Walking to one of the payphones, Jospair lifted the receiver began dialing. It took him several minutes to make himself understood to the operator and to get the charges accepted with the card. The operator spoke English, however, both she and Jospair had very different and difficult accents. Completing what became a lengthy verbal exchange with the operator, Jospair was finally successful in making a call to his uncle's cellular telephone in the United States. After a brief conversation with the man, Jospair hung up and got into the line at the Andrade, California, US border crossing station, carrying his bottle of tequila in a purple plastic bag. This would be the final hurdle and Jospair was both excited and nervous, emotions *he* rarely experienced.

The blue tactical uniforms and the SIG .40 caliber side arms of the American border agents standing near the line of tourists looked impressive, as did their Malinois K-9 police dogs, their handlers directing the animals to sniff both the people standing in the line and the cars exiting Mexico on the adjacent roadway—more so, the latter.

Finally, it was Jospair's turn and he was waved into the building and up to one or several inspection counters. Expecting to be riddled with questions from the agent sitting behind the computer, he was pleasantly surprised to see that after swiping his forged passport through the border security computer's reading pad, the bored-looking US Customs and Border Security Agent gave him only a cursory glance, then asked him why he had been in Mexico. Jospair smiled and presented the bottle of Tequila. "Sightseeing and liquor. I—" Jospair had prepared and rehearsed a long explanation, but before he could get any of the rest of it out, the sour-faced agent gave him an unsmiling nod of dismissal and waved the next person in line forward.

"Good bye. Have a nice day," Jospair said to the agent as he walked away from the counter.

"Uh huh," was the only reply.

Apparently the information Jospair had received about the low morale of these American border agents had been accurate. They didn't seem to care who walked into the United States, as long as you didn't look Mexican, didn't have on a shirt that read *Terrorist*, and weren't trying to smuggle dope. He suddenly became alarmed. *Was this some kind of trap,* he thought as he covertly looked around for signs of additional agents closing in on him. *Trying to lure me into complacency?* Jospair saw nothing out of the ordinary as he walked toward the exit.

Can it really be this easy to enter America? He exited the chain-link-fenced corridor into the warm sunshine on the American side of the border and smiled at his good fortune, yet shook his head in his amazement.

How could a people as complacent and lazy as these Americans hold onto all their power and wealth for so long?

"*Neverovatno*—unbelievable," he muttered to himself. Just to his left he saw a very large parking lot for the automobiles of tourists. Jospair marveled and the number of people walking to and from their cars, carrying the purple shopping bags similar to the one he now held. From what he could see, most of the cars in the lot bore license identification plates from Canada, though there were also many Arizona- and California-plated cars. *This will be an excellent place to hide in plain sight,* he thought as he sat down on the curb to wait. Here at this border melting pot of people, he was just another "gringo" tourist.

With time to kill, Jospair removed the liquor bottle from the bag and looked it over. "*Herencia de Plata Reposado* 100% agave," he read the label out loud. He'd never heard of it, but then he'd never tasted tequila before. *What the hell is agave?* he wondered. *Must be some kind of plant—cactus, maybe?* Shrugging, he opened the bottle and took in a mouthful of the amber colored liquid. The liquor was warm and burned some as it slid down his throat, but the flavor was better than expected, especially compared to the homemade swill he was used to drinking. He looked at the bottle again then took another swig.

"I could come to like this," he said to no one in particular as he took a third mouthful.

The bottle was nearly empty four hours later when his uncle's white Cadillac Escalade pulled into the parking lot.

"Uncle," Jospair said, greeting his elder relative as he slid into the seat of the luxury SUV.

"Jospair—It is good to see you nephew," the man said and slapped Jospair on the shoulder. He leaned over and both men exchanged a brief kiss to both cheeks as was the custom in their country. "It smells like you have discovered Tequila. You crossed the border without difficulty, I see."

Jospair grunted and nodded to both statements. "Surprisingly, the border crossing was the easiest part of the journey. It has been a long trip for my ass, from sitting in the soil of our homeland to sitting in the seat of this automobile." He examined the inside of the luxury SUV. "I see life is treating you good uncle."

"And how are things in Serbia?" his uncle asked. He was just making small talk. He was well aware of the chaos that had engulfed his nation.

"Not good. The meddling Western powers have put an end to our taking out the trash. I fear we will never be able to return, and, if we ever did, we will find that our land has been divided up between the Croat and Bosnian scum."

His uncle nodded. "Well, you are now in America and no longer need to worry about such things."

Jospair looked around a second time at the inside of

the Escalade then at the expensive clothing and jewelry his uncle was wearing. "I see you have made good in America."

His uncle shrugged. "I have seen some success with my business ventures."

"Ventures? Plural? You have other businesses besides the eating establishment?" the Jospair inquired. He had not known of this.

"Oh, yes." His uncle nodded again. "My restaurant does well but it is my other business that pays for all of...this." He waved his hand around, indicating his material wealth. "Although it is a business that is not for public knowledge. The authorities would frown upon it. In fact, it is in *that* field of endeavor that I intend to employ you. You will be needing a job now and you have, shall we say, a particular set of skills that make you a prime candidate for the line of work I have in mind, and it pays very well. I have a good contact at INS and he owes me a very large favor. I will be your sponsor, and he will provide you a "green card." Seeing the confused look on Jospair's face, his uncle laughed. "A temporary visa to stay in this country." Jospair nodded his understanding now so his uncle continued. "To the authorities, you will simply be my nephew who lives with me and, by the way, works as a waiter in my restaurant."

"Mmmmm, this INS man owes you a favor—he owes you money, perhaps?" Jospair saw his uncle twitch.

"You were always the bright one in our family," his uncle replied and changed the subject. "Are you still comfortable with your false passport?"

"Yes." Jospair nodded. "I have had no troubles using it."

"Give it to me. I will need it for my INS contact." He reached out his hand. Jospair handed him the small brown folder. His uncle continued. "In your travels, or in our homeland, for that matter, were you ever fingerprinted?"

"Yes," Jospair answered. "Prior to the war, I was arrested by our local village *politsiya* for a minor crime, but that was long ago when I was fifteen. The police station is now in ruins."

"So there was no chance that Interpol has a record of your fingerprints?" his uncle pressed

"I don't see how they could. My transgression was a local matter. Myself and several of my friends decided it would be a good idea to steal a neighbor's horse for a few days. He was quite upset about it and called the constable." Now it was Jospair who changed the subject. "You loan money." It was a statement.

"Yes," his uncle replied, smiling at his nephew's perceptiveness. "Sometimes a great deal of money."

"You need me to collect delinquent payments." It was another statement

"Among other things."

"Those things being?"

"Most times, it is just about reminding individuals that payment is due, along with what one might call a...um...motivational talk, shall we say, regarding paying one's debts on schedule. Other times, it's about collecting the respect."

Jospair knew exactly what his uncle wanted from

him. "Isn't that a bit self-defeating?" he asked. "Killing the person who owes you the money, thus losing your investment in those instances?"

His uncle paused, thinking, then replied, "A businessman such as myself must look at the larger picture. I must take whatever actions necessary to stay…oh, what is the expression the Americans always use?…ah, yes, to stay at the top of the food chain. Mine is a risky financial business and, as such, there are times when I lose money—but only temporarily. In the long run, the lost revenue can be regained with a substantial profit from *future* customers who understand they must abide by their agreement by paying back their loans with substantial interest. For my business to thrive, it is necessary for all of my clients, both current and future potentials, to understand that repaying their loan, even with the highest of interest, is much better than the penalty for nonpayment. Establishing a reputation to that end is an absolute necessity. If I lose money in the short-run doing so, I must consider it just the cost of doing business."

Jospair looked at his uncle. "How much does this line of work pay?"

"Ten percent of all normal collections and fifty percent of any collections you can obtain from accounts I have…um…written off so to speak"

Jospair shook his head. "No, Uncle. I want *twenty* percent of all normal collections, and eighty percent of anything from an account that you have written off." His uncle began to protest but Jospair held up his hand. "Let me finish, Uncle. As far as the latter is concerned and as a bonus to your 'reputation,' I will still kill them, even if I get them to repay the money. You can publish the fact however you wish. Also, *you* Uncle, will pay all expenses, including equipment and travel costs—oh, and any legal fees, if necessary."

His uncle thought a moment. "Fifteen percent and sixty-five percent, and I will pay all of your *legitimate* expenses, but only when you are working a job for me. I will not pay for whores or your liquor. If you have trouble with the police while on one of my requests, I will pay your legal fees. If you get into trouble on your own, you are on your own. I will not be responsible for it. Also, you should know, I do not, under any circumstances, condone any drug use. We have not seen each other in years, Jospair. Do you take drugs of any kind?"

Jospair though a moment then nodded. "Your proposal is acceptable, and, no, I take nothing stronger that aspirin." The two men then shook hands in agreement, laughing at their bargaining skills as the Escalade pulled into the parking lot of his uncle's restaurant.

"Now let's eat. You are hungry, Nephew?"

"Famished," came Jospair's reply as he opened the door of the Escalade to step out.

"Yes, come, we will talk more about business while we eat," his uncle said.

That first meal in his uncle's restaurant was now several years in the past. Jospair's side of the business, that of collecting money, had thrived. His talent for intimidation—and murder, when the situation called for it—had been put to good use many times since.

CHAPTER 4

THE RIVER

We're gonna land on that?" I said into the small black foam windsock of the microphone in front of my lips. For the past ten minutes, Jackson had been piloting the Mooney over a valley of dark green pine trees mixed with the lighter greens and tans of sage brush and a few small meadows. The Missouri River was visible to the north of us, snaking its way through northern Montana's mixture of bare rocky canyons and heavy forest. Directly in front of the plane's propeller now loomed the sheer steep cliff of a sage-covered plateau. A thin tan colored ribbon of dirt, the airstrip on which we were to land, was visible on the top of the escarpment leading away from us at the bluff's edge. It was an airstrip in name only, resembling more a rough dirt road than anything that was made for aircraft to land on.

"Right where it's supposed to be," Jackson answered as he glanced down at both his Garmin 496 and Avmap IV aviation GPS mounted side by side in the dash. The strip looked to be approximately three-quarters of a mile long, sage brush choking both sides. To my untrained eye, it appeared as if there was no room for the wingspan of the Mooney, and the closer we got, the rougher and narrower the long narrow cut in the brush looked. I switched my gaze from the approaching cliff to Jackson and back again.

I was as nervous as a dog shitting peach pits, as the old saying goes, but it was comforting to see the total lack of concern on Jackson's face.

Four hours earlier, the two of us had bid Sonya farewell, piled my fishing and backpacking gear into the Mooney next to his, and lifted off into the cloudless cobalt-blue Wyoming sky. It turned out to be a wonderful day for flying over some of the most beautiful scenery in the nation. Yellowstone National Park had been briefly visible off to the west, and we'd passed directly over the Little Big Horn battlefield where George Custer had met his fate a hundred plus years before. None too soon, we would be traveling several miles up-river on a boat, with a guide, to the point where he would drop us off.

And we would be on foot and on our own, camping and fishing along the feeder creek, immune to all save the excited yell when one of us hooked one of the large cutthroat trout that inhabited the waters there. *Providing we survive this landing*, I told myself silently.

"Macho guy stuff," Sonya had called it the night before we departed, wrinkling her nose at the thought of
wearing the same pair of underwear for days on end.

"Not a problem," I'd told her. "You wear 'em for
three days, then turn 'em inside out and wear 'em for
three more. Saves room in my pack and, as a bonus, I'll
come home with that macho-man musk smell you love so
much. You'll be so turned on, you'll want to jump on me
right then."

"Gross!" She stuck her finger down her throat in a
mock gag. "The minute you get back, you'll be throwing
those underwear away and taking three showers before
you even *think* about getting that thing near me," she'd
replied with distaste as she'd pointed to my crotch.

Smiling to myself as that brief memory crossed my
mind, I now repeated my question to Jackson, looking out
at the rapidly approaching narrow strip of dirt. "You sure
we can land on that?"

"No sweat," Jackson replied. "I'm going to make one
pass off to the right, get an up-close look at the strip and
see what the winds are doing. The tricky part is the up-
drafts off the bluff there at the end of the runway, especially on a warm day like this. We'll check it out, then
turn back out, and come back around to land. Probably
cross the edge at a hundred feet or so, give or take.
Should be plenty of room providing—"

I cut him off. "Should be? Providing? Providing
what?" My concerned and doubtful tone made him
chuckle.

"You didn't want to live forever, anyway, did you, Jason?" he asked, smiling.

"Not funny, asshole! As a matter of fact, I *do* want to live forever. In fact, forever isn't long enough." I hesitated but then mumbled, "But I guess there's worse ways to die."

Jackson grinned. "Have a little faith baby," he said, maneuvering the Mooney parallel to the swath in the sage, his concentration now on the surface of the strip, a faded orange wind sock attached to a steel pole thirty yards to the left of the runway, and the instruments in the panel in front of him. The windsock stuck out stiffly from the pole like some bizarre giant orange erection. It moved around the points of the compass every few seconds with the ebb and flow of the wind. The plane bucked and jumped as we crossed over the edge of the bluff at a thousand feet.

On this first pass, Jackson banked the plane slightly to improve his view. When he was satisfied, he applied power and climbed, turning back out over the valley. As he did so, I noticed a weathered metal aircraft hangar at the far end of the airstrip. Large white letters painted on the roof spelled out *BLUFF*. Another small plane was visible, parked near the hangar, sunlight glinting off of its spinning propeller. It looked to be a high-wing Cessna or something similar. Just for an instant, as we turned away, I saw the bright white reflection of the sun off of the plane's windscreen as it started to move.

"You see that plane parked over there? It's rolling," I commented.

"Yeah, shit. I got a little complacent. I should of squawked three miles out but didn't think anyone would be around this remote strip—and *that's* just the kind of thinking that gets you killed," Jackson replied, sounding irritated with himself.

I should have known his quick eyes hadn't missed the potential danger.

"Better late than never," he mumbled. "I need to let him know our intentions." He quickly glanced at the display on the Mooney's digital radio screen to be certain the glowing green numerals read 122.7. He then spoke into his headset. "Mooney 729 November on final at Bluff, runway 165 from the Southwest at two miles."

The answer came back instantly. "Cessna 421 Bravo holding at the line, Bluff runway 165."

"Atta boy," Jackson said softly to himself.

"No need to worry about leaving the plane parked here I shouldn't think," I chirped. "This is God, guts, and gun country. No one messes with other people's stuff out here."

Jackson didn't answer me. A glance at his face told me he was now concentrating on his approach, which was my clue to shut the hell up and let him do his pilot thing. The Mooney crossed the edge of the bluff at a scant one hundred feet of altitude. The timing seemed to be just right with no unexpected thermals catching him by surprise. He'd said there was plenty of clearance, but it still looked to me like we were going to scrape the undercarriage on the edge and my butt cheeks involuntarily tightened, as did my grip on the "Oh shit!" hand-hold in front of me. As soon as the edge of the bluff passed under the plane, Jackson throttled back and the Mooney settled. When the landing gear finally made contact, the plane bounced hard, jumping back into the air several times, swerving back and forth toward the sagebrush on both sides, and throwing up a huge cloud of dust. The wings dipped first one way and then the other. Jackson advanced the throttle and the plane's wings leveled.

My knuckles were white as I now gripped the straps of my chest harness with both hands. *Holy shit*, I thought. *I don't expect to live forever, but I really don't want to die today!*

Jackson finally got the bucking airplane straightened out and rolling in a stable taxi on the rough surface.

"Damn!" he blurted out as the plane rolled toward the hangar. "Sorry about that crappy landing. Surface of the strip was a lot rougher than it looked—lots of moguls and dips I couldn't see from up high."

"No problem," I tried to say, in my best nonchalant voice, then added, "but I will need some help getting this seat cushion out of my ass. That landing had a sphincter factor of about 9.5, buddy!" I let out a silent sigh of relief now that we were back rolling along on terra firma where humans belonged.

"Had it under control the whole time," Jackson said grinning as he swung the Mooney wide around the second plane and on toward the hangar

"Yeah, right," I chided him. I knew he actually did.

No sooner had the Mooney rolled passed the Cessna than its engine revved to a loud angry buzz. The pilot gave us a wave and a smile, apparently unfazed by Jackson's breach of approach etiquette, then announced his intention to take off over the radio as he turned onto the runway and accelerated in his own dust cloud.

Jackson, satisfied now with the Mooney's position near the hangar, chopped the throttle, and the propeller stopped spinning.

It was only then I noticed a man walking toward us from the open-sided hangar. It was my friend Corey Taggert, the California DOJ investigator.

I opened the door and climbed out, greeting him and shaking hands. "Good to see you, bro. Been a long time. Didn't see you as we taxied up. Wasn't sure if we were gonna be able to time this right, but it looks like it worked out well." I gestured at the retreating Cessna in the distance. "That plane was yours, I take it?"

Corey nodded. "Yeah, got here about an hour ago. I waited over there until you chopped the throttle." He waved at the hangar. "I wasn't about to walk up close to your spinning prop, after that one guy—you remember, don't you?"

"Oh, yeah, I remember.

Corey was referring to a call he'd been on years before when we'd both been working nights at Vista PD. The pilot of a private plane had landed late at a small local airport. After taxiing to a spot near the pilot's lounge, the man got out of his plane, leaving the engine idling, intending to run inside to relieve himself. In the darkness, he proceeded to walk face first into his own spinning propeller. It had definitely ruined the guy's day.

Corey glanced at the retreating Cessna. "The pilot hung around and made sure you guys made it."

"That was nice of him."

"Yeah, he was nice, but not that nice. He charged me fifty bucks an hour to stay. Said time was money. Glad you showed up when you did."

Jackson climbed out of the Mooney and I introduced the two. They exchanged handshakes.

"You're one of the guys involved in Jason's deal last year?" Corey asked

Jackson's mouth pursed into a frown, then he nodded. "Still trying to forget it."

"I don't know the whole story," Corey said, looking back and forth between Jackson and myself. "Maybe you guys can fill me in on the particulars when we're out there?" he asked, waving a hand in the direction of the Missouri River.

"We'll see," was my only reply.

With Corey's help, the three of us pushed the Mooney near the open end of the hangar, tied it down, and secured it. There was too much debris on the floor to roll the plane inside, and we didn't want to waste time cleaning it all up. I repeated my comment to Jackson about the safety of his plane and, this time, he nodded his acknowledgment. Corey rounded up his gear from the hangar floor where he'd left it. Jackson and I did the same from the plane and, together, the three of us began our hike down the well-worn three-quarters of a mile long deer trail between the top of the bluff and the river.

We marveled at the terrain surrounding us—a mixture of steep canyon walls, tall pine and cottonwood trees, alpine meadows, and sage-covered hillsides. The hike down was fairly easy. With nothing else to do but walk, I decided to relate the previous year's incident to Corey in detail. Jackson filled in his role, as well as those parts I didn't remember, for obvious reasons.

When we'd finished, Corey looked up from the trail at us both then just shook his head. "Damn."

"Yeah," Jackson replied

It took the better part of an hour to hike the path, which ended at a flat sandy beach. The letters on a small wooden sign nailed to a tree near the water read, *Sand Wash*. We dropped our gear on the ground. I looked up and down the river. We'd expected our guide to be waiting for us.

"Sure hope this guy shows up. Hate to have to hike outta here," I said. The others nodded. A quarter of an hour had passed when we heard the approaching sound of a boat motor. Within minutes, a twenty-two-foot aluminum drift-boat, powered by a large outboard motor, came into view around a brushy bend down river. Our guide had finally arrived as promised. We greeted him as he nosed the high prow up onto the sand and jumped out, introducing ourselves as he did so.

"John Kimber," he replied. "Sorry I'm late. Had a bit of eye trouble."

"Eye trouble?" a skeptical Corey asked.

"Yeah, couldn't see—couldn't see getting up any earlier." The guide guffawed at his own joke.

"Lame," Corey mumbled.

Kimber then directed us as to how he wanted us to load our gear and to sit in his boat. As we climbed in, I couldn't help but notice the stainless steel Mossberg Mariner twelve-gauge pump-shotgun clipped to the gunnel next to the steering pedestal.

"Our trip on up the river to our drop-off point won't take long," the guide said as he backed the boat away from the shore line.

The boat, powered by what I could see now was a big Mercury 150 HP outboard, parted the clear greenish-blue river water with ease at a respectable 45 MPH. Not near speed the boat was capable of, I was sure. As if reading my mind, when Kimber saw me looking at the throttle position and the speedometer, he explained that, at this time of year on the river, there were drifting logs and floating snags of brush to dodge. Either was capable of ending our trip suddenly and most unpleasantly if we were to hit one at top speed.

The river itself wound its way through steep canyon walls of red, tan, and brown sandstone. Along the river's edge were groves of pine and quaking aspen, separated by patches of tall brush or old rockslides from the cliffs above. Deer were easily spotted if you knew where to look. The river began to narrow, its rocky bottom becoming visible in places. As we rounded one of the final bends in the river, our guide John slowed our forward progress, pointing out the stone and wood remains of several small buildings on the north bank.

"That used to be a small ranch, back in the late 1800s," he told us. "Belonged to a settler family named

Clark. Rumor was they were related to William Clark, as in Lewis & Clark, but I don't know if that's true or not. Story goes that, five years after they settled here, they starved to death one particularly bad winter. Don't know if that's true either 'cause no remains were ever found."

"Maybe they just said 'screw this' and packed up and left?" Jackson mused.

"Probably more like it," Kimber answered. "Had to be hard life."

"So there's another way in here besides boat?" I asked, a bit surprised looking up at the steep red canyon walls. "Seems so remote."

"Yeah," John said. "There's a jeep trail behind the cliffs, not far from where I'm dropping you off. Goes right behind Sand Wash, actually. You guys had to walk right across it, and you're not wrong, by the way. It is *very* remote in here. That rough jeep trail is the only way in here, other than by boat or plane to the plateau, but the trail is a stone-cold bitch. Has an EMD rating of five. No one uses that road, except an occasional hunter, and then not too many of them, 'cause you gotta carry extra parts with you in case you break down. One place on the trail, there's a half-mile uphill climb on a rock face that's gotta be a forty-degree incline—hairy as hell. It's called 'Chicken Rock' by the locals, for obvious reasons. Traveling in here by boat is my preferred method. If my boat breaks down up here, I can always just drift back down river." He looked up at the colorful but incredibly jagged cliffs on both sides of the river, shook his head, and mumbled, "Christ, I'd hate to have to hump it outta here."

All three of us grunted our agreement.

Our guide slowed the boat and picked a small patch of gravel that separated the water from a stand of quaking aspen and pine trees. With the boat at a near idle, he eased the prow up onto the shoreline where the keel kissed the gravel with a soft "crunch." I jumped out and secured the bowline to a tree. Several doe mule deer bounded away noisily through the aspen grove, startled by our arrival.

"Any Elk down in here," I asked John as we hefted our gear out of the boat.

"Might be, but I've never seen any. Lots of deer, though. Oh, and a bear or two," he added as an afterthought. "That's why I keep this handy." He pointed to the Mossberg. "Mostly black bears. They are shy, for the most part anyway, and, most times, will go the other way or skinny up a tree if you don't screw with them or leave your food out. You should know, though, that every so often, grizzly have been spotted down here by the river. You need to keep a close eye out for one of those unpredictable bastards and, if you come across one, be very, *very* careful. They can be unpredictable and dangerous as hell. You guys are armed, right? Or at least brought some bear spray, like I recommended?" the guide asked.

"Both for me." I gestured at my pack, then I looked at Jackson and Corey with a raised eyebrow. Jackson nodded.

"Pinocchio have a wooden dick?" was Corey's answer as he patted his pack.

"Good," John said, "but remember, never shoot a

bear, any bear, and *especially* a griz, with a pistol, unless it's your last resort. Most of the time, it just pisses them off. Use the bear spray. They hate that shit," He looked up at the canyon walls again. "Bears aren't the big danger up here. The big danger here is falling and getting hurt, or doing something else stupid, so, you know, *don't*. You guys are experienced so don't take any unnecessary risks. I want you to have a great fishing trip and come out of here in one piece. Let's see, what else?" He tapped his chin with his finger. "The creek water is drinkable, but I'd still either boil it or use your filter. There's lots of fish here so if you're any kind of a fisherman at all, you won't starve to death. I usually come up river every couple of days so you can flag me if you have a problem. Guess that's it unless you guys have any questions?"

We looked at each other then collectively shook our heads.

John hopped back into his boat. "Give me a shove off."

I lifted and pushed the bow of the skiff off the gravel. The current immediately caught the boat and it began to drift rapidly away from the shore.

As an afterthought the guide added, "Keep your fishing licenses and ID's in your pocket, just in case a game warden comes along. Don't carry your wallets in your pants, in case you fall in. Have fun! See you in a few days."

And, with that, he started the big outboard, backed the boat out into mid-river, waved, and applied power. In less than a minute, the boat had vanished around the bend and, several seconds later, the sound of the Mercury faded altogether.

Near-silence returned again to the river, the only sound being the swish and gurgle of the water's passage and the whisper of wind through the aspen leaves behind us.

After a few moments of enjoying the quiet solitude of this remote place, the three of us picked up our gear and began our trek up the feeder creek to find a suitable place to set up camp before dark. An hour's hiking found us in a small flat meadow of alpine grass. The wide creek wound its way through the center. Red cliffs rose on both sides, protecting the meadow from the wind. Heavy groves of pine, aspen, and cedar ringed the edges of the clearing. There was an abundance of dry firewood to be found, in the form of downed limbs and snags. It looked just like an Ansell Adams photograph.

Jackson looked around and raised an eyebrow at me.

"This is it, boys," I exclaimed happily. "Heaven with a fishing rod for the next seven days!"

We all dropped our gear on the soft ground and began to set up camp.

"What pistol did you bring," Jackson asked me as I began to set up my small Coleman tent.

I reached into my pack and handed him a Model 29 Smith & Wesson .44 magnum revolver.

"Wow! Nice. You had it magna-ported?" he asked, referring to the two angled slits cut near the end of the four-and-a-half-inch barrel, one on each side of the front sight.

"Nah, I bought it that way from a retired sheriff's deputy in California. He'd had it done. Really reduces the recoil from this short barrel. Doesn't do anything for the flash and noise, though. In the dark or twilight, it's like looking at the sun and having someone hit you in the forehead with a rock at the same time." I chuckled as he handed the gun back. "What'd you bring along?"

"My Glock 27 .40 cal. Nothing trick on it though," he replied. "How about you, Corey?"

Corey held up his short-barreled Ruger SP101 .357 magnum revolver.

"Well, between the three of us, we should be able to handle just about anything that comes our way," Jackson said cockily as he turned back to his pack.

It was a statement that would come back to haunt us.

CHAPTER 5

SOLO UNIT

The Ford Explorer was white, with the exception of those areas on the outside of the fenders covered with dried reddish-brown mud. On both front doors of the four-wheel-drive SUV were large yellow-and-blue-colored decals in the shape of a shield. Words in the center of the decals read *US Department of the Interior Bureau of Land Management*. Larger letters beneath proclaimed, *Law Enforcement*. Four-inch-wide brown stripes were painted along both sides of the vehicle and, across the rear tailgate just beneath the windows, large letters proclaimed *RANGER* with the same brown color incorporated in the center of each stripe.

The door decal design was nearly identical to shoulder patches and the gold-colored badge pinned to the dark-green jumpsuit-style uniform of BLM Ranger Ryan Tafney.

By definition, Ryan was a federal law enforcement officer, but to police officers and sheriff's deputies, and even agents of some fellow federal law enforcement agencies, BLM rangers weren't *real* cops. They were just glorified park service employees. This, of course, was nonsense. Ryan was as much a real cop as any of them— more so, in some ways. BLM rangers in some areas had to patrol thousands of square miles of wilderness, the majority of the time as a solo unit with no one around to help them, *or* come to their rescue should they encounter bad trouble. Lately, there seemed to be plenty of that to go around.

To many Americans, The Bureau of Land Management was a detested branch of an oppressive and intrusive federal government. This was especially true after the confrontation with a rancher over grazing rights on federal land in Nevada. Snickers and comments about BLM rangers by other cops didn't bother Ryan, however. Well, not much, anyway. He'd heard it all and he really didn't give a shit what other cops thought. What *did* bother Ranger Ryan Tafney was the distrust and, at times, downright hatred he saw in the eyes of normal Americans he came into contact with daily. When he'd started his career, Ryan very much wanted to be a caretaker of the special lands of America. Now he questioned his career decision every day. He had not signed on for a war against his own countrymen.

These were confusing times.

Ryan had started his law enforcement career right out of college, first as an officer in a small police department on the northern California coast, where he'd worked for five years. Desiring a bit more action, he soon applied for and was accepted by a nearby larger city's police department, where he advanced to the rank of sergeant after another five years had passed. *Onward and upward*, were his thoughts then but, down deep, he really didn't have any aspirations to promote any higher up the chain.

Growing restless once again, Ryan had heard through the police grapevine that the government was recruiting for both BLM and National Forest Rangers. Ryan was an avid outdoorsman who loved America's wild lands and unsettled country. He much preferred wide-open spaces, as opposed to the cramped city life he'd been working in. *What the hell,* he'd decided one day, *I'll apply and see what happens.*

To his surprise, he was hired almost immediately by BLM. His first choice had been National Forest Law Enforcement, but BLM needed men and women badly, so they got the first shot at him. The Federal Law Enforcement Academy in New Mexico came next, then his first posting to Montana, where he was now in his second year.

Ryan and his wife of seven years had bought a house in Helena and had settled in just before the first snows of October. Being California raised, Ryan was in no way mentally prepared for his first Montana winter and, by January, he'd begun to have real doubts about his ability to stay in this part of the country during winter, but he stuck it out and, after making the adjustment and learning just how much fun it was to get around in the back country on a "Sno-Cat" or a snowmobile, he decided he loved what he did now more than ever.

Ryan was technically assigned to the Butte, Montana BLM office, but he actually worked out of his home, most of the time, only having to drive the sixty-eight miles to the office once a week, weather depending, to turn in his paperwork. He would make an extra trip to transport a prisoner to the main jail there, when the occasion called for it, although this didn't happen all that often. Most of Ryan's encounters with law-breakers resulted in the issuance of citations, not arrests, and that was just fine with him. Driving to and from Butte ate up almost the entire shift, particularly when combined with any office duties he had to perform while he was there.

Ryan had just completed his computerized morning briefing. *Nice to be able to go to a briefing in your own living room*, he thought as he closed his laptop and refilled his travel mug with coffee. He began each day with the same routine—awake at 5:00 a.m., lift his weights for thirty minutes, then it was a shower, shave, uniform, one poached egg with a single piece of toast, and coffee. He would then turn on his computer and link with the office for any procedural or federal statute updates, BOLOs on wanted persons or vehicles, public complaints, specific area violations, and recent crime trends. After that, he would refill his coffee mug, kiss his wife goodbye, then head outside to check his patrol vehicle, which doubled as his secondary office. First came a check of his weapons. Ryan carried a .40 caliber Glock 22 in his belt holster. Inside the Explorer were both a Benelli M-90 12 gauge shotgun and a standard .223 caliber M-4 combat rifle. After that came a quick look at the Ford's fluids and tires, lights, emergency light bar, the two-way radio, and, finally, logging on to the computer.

When he was satisfied that all of his equipment was in order, Ryan contacted the dispatch center in Butte and advised the female dispatcher that he was in service and enroute to his assigned patrol sector. *She has a nice voice*, Ryan thought, *not harsh and bitchy like some. Wonder what she looks like*. He conjured up an imaginary picture in his mind to go with the soft, breathy voice. This made him smile. Then a second harsh and bitchy image popped into his head which made him wince, shake his head, and mutter, "Oh, man, woof!"

Ryan quickly shook off *that* mental picture and looked down at the USGS topo-map in his hands. Today's work would be different. He would be driving into a remote area he was not familiar with—an area simply called "Trail 79," located in the back country on the Missouri River. His map showed several roads in the area, but he knew they were roads in name only. They were all either four-wheel-drive roads or very rough Jeep trails. The one he would be using was the only Jeep trail into and out of that area and, from what he'd been told, it was a rough one. Folks who frequented that part of the country, hunters and fisherman mostly, did so by boat on the Missouri. Neither the BLM rangers nor state fish and game went into that area by vehicle much, unless called for, but Ryan's boss wanted someone to "show the colors" in the area at least once every season, just to let people know that it was patrolled.

And, since Ryan was the closest, he was assigned the duty.

The time it would take to get into the wilderness area, do any kind of patrol at all, and come back out, meant it would be a two- or three-day trip, thus Ryan had brought some basic camping gear and extra food and drink, in addition to his regular equipment.

He perused the map again. "Shit! A class five trail," he said out loud to himself.

After seeing that designation on his map, the ranger had doubts about how far in his Ford Explorer would take him. Granted, it had a lift kit, oversize tires, and a 12,000-pound Warn winch mounted in the heavy front bumper. But, for all that, it was still *just* an Explorer. He shrugged. "I'll only go as far as I can. I sure as shit am not going to break down out in the middle of nowhere," he mumbled, tossing the map into the front passenger seat. Ryan wasn't about to tear off a fender—or, worse, break an axle and have to hike out of there.

The sun was rising on the eastern horizon now. The day was clear and shaping up to be a nice one. *Big sky country*. He smiled inwardly as he thought of the old phrase.

He turned on his GPS then turned the ignition key. The Ford's engine rumbled to life.

"Romeo 16753," Ryan said into the microphone.

"Romeo 16753," answered the dispatcher.

"Ten-eight and ninety-eight, Trail 79 area via Old Stage Rd"

"Lucky you, 167. Drive safe and don't miss you're check-ins."

"Ten-four, but be advised, lots of remote country out there. Not sure I'll have reception everywhere."

"Ten-four 167. We'll follow on your 'SAT-NAV.' Check in as you can. Have a nice vacation."

"Ten-four. I'll bring you some poison ivy."

"That's a negative, 167."

Ryan clipped the microphone back on the dash as he dropped the transmission into "Drive" and the Ford rolled forward. *It is going to be a hell of a day,* he thought as he drove out onto the gravel road.

He had no way of knowing of course, that this trip into the northern wilderness of Montana as a BLM ranger would be his last.

CHAPTER 6

BIG SKY COUNTRY

Smoke belched from under the tires of the Bombardier-Aerospace CRJ700 commuter jet as the rubber kissed the concrete runway of the regional airport in Helena, Montana. The ground guide crossed the orange wands in his hands, bringing the Canadair operated plane to a halt in its assigned parking spot near the terminal. The twin GE CF-34 engines spooled down and the portable staircase was rolled up to the front passenger cabin door of the aircraft. Passengers began to retrieve their carry-on bags from the overhead compartments and move forward up the narrow aisles of the plane's cramped interior.

When he finally stepped out through the oval cabin door into the early morning sunlight, Jospair was somewhat surprised at the noise level, as flying machines taxied nearby and baggage trains darted to and fro, creating a cacophony of sound. The sun was shining, yet the temperature was quite cool and the stiff breeze made him hunch his shoulders involuntarily. The wind carried the heavy smell of jet exhaust to his nostrils as he descended the staircase. He wished now that he had followed his first instinct and put on his coat instead of just draping it across his arm, but it was not worth the effort now as he was holding his carry-on bag in his other hand and he would be inside the terminal building shortly. Jospair followed in line with the passengers ahead of him, all of them making their way across the rubber-and-kerosene-stained concrete to the single glass door at the terminal gate.

Once inside, he approached one of the terminal information and directory kiosks. Looking it over, he soon discovered what he needed. Turning, he walked swiftly to one of the three car rental desks located near the baggage claim area. Producing a false California driver's license for the woman behind the counter, Jospair paid cash for five-days' rental of a red four-wheel-drive Jeep Grand Cherokee. The false identification had been made for him by one of his uncle's associates. Jospair was certain he would only need the vehicle two, maybe three days at most. However, after his work was complete, he didn't want anyone looking for it right away. Hence, the five-day rental.

"This model has the GPS?" he asked the woman behind the counter.

"Yes, sir. It's the type that is built into the dash. It's the top-of-the-line model," she said.

"Excellent, thank you," he replied.

Jospair didn't give a damn whether it was a built-in model or a dash-top model, as long as it worked properly. Like everyone else with a smart phone, he used "Google Maps" constantly, but that program was only good as long as he got a signal from the cell towers. It would be of no use to him in the mountain area he was seeking. He needed the satellite-broadcasted GPS signal to keep track of his location and destination.

"The instruction booklet on how to use it is in the glove compartment with the owner's manual. Please keep your rental agreement in there, also, because that acts as your vehicle registration identification should you get stopped."

Living in a former communist country all his life where identity papers were required to go anywhere, this statement alarmed Jospair. "Why would I be *stopped*?" he asked, a little too aggressively.

The woman, taken aback by his tone, stammered, "I—I—I didn't mean you specifically, sir, I just meant anyone—like for speeding or something."

He smiled at the woman. "Ah, yes, forgive me. I'm a bit tired from my travels."

"Oh, that's okay. I know how it is, flying these days. I hate it," she replied

Upon completion of the necessary paperwork and obtaining the keys, Jospair asked the woman if he could look at her local phonebook. Smiling, she agreed and handed him the thick paper book. He found what he was looking for in the yellow pages. Borrowing a pen and paper, Jospair wrote down the name and address of a large and well-known local sporting goods outlet, aptly named "Montana Outdoor Sports." He handed the book back to the woman, thanking her, and turned toward the double exit doors.

"Excuse me, sir?" the woman called after him.

"Yes?"

She gestured to Jospair's hand. "You have my pen."

"Oh, yes, sorry," he said to her and reached to hand the pen back.

"Oh, never mind."

She smiled as she took in Jospair's muscular six-foot frame and not-un-handsome face. She did notice his eyes seemed somewhat vacant, however. She then nodded at the Atlas Rent-a-Car coffee mug on top of the counter, which was full of pens. "You keep it. I've got plenty."

Stupid cow, Jospair thought as he slipped the pen into his pocket and walked outside to the car rental parking lot. He found the red Jeep and unlocked the door. Just before he climbed in, he slipped on a pair of thin black leather driving gloves.

He knew the gloves would draw no unwanted attention due to the chilly weather. With a turn of the key, the engine started and Jospair turned out onto the main highway toward the location of the sporting goods store three miles away.

He spotted the store while still a half-mile distant, due to the thirty-foot-long metal facsimile of a Winchester lever-action rifle mounted on the roof. He parked the Jeep and walked through the double glass doors.

"May I help you," the elderly sales clerk behind the gun counter asked.

"Yes, I am from California and am visiting a friend here. We are to go camping in the back country. and I would like to purchase pistol for protection from wolves," Jospair told the clerk.

The man chuckled. "Not many problems with wolves around here, son. Oh, there's a few out there. I suppose if they were hungry enough they might try for a person, but they are pretty smart. They figure out pretty damn quick that people carry guns."

Jospair winced inwardly. He had read that wolves were a menace in Montana and Wyoming since they had been reintroduced into the wild back in the early '90s. His ignorance in this matter may have now exposed him.

"It's all right, son," the clerk continued, smiling. "Most of you folks from California usually have all the wrong ideas about our part of the country. Some folks even think Bigfoot is roaming around out there some-where." He chuckled again.

What is a Bigfoot? Jospair wondered.

"That being said though, it's always good to carry a gun in the back country. You never know what, or who, you might run across out there, but really the only thing you need to be careful of here is the occasional Griz-zly…well, that and the mules."

Now I have to watch out for this Bigfoot thing AND also deadly donkeys? "Why would donkeys be danger-ous?" he asked the clerk.

"Hawwww! Ha, ha, ha!" The clerk slapped his leg as

he laughed out loud, shaking his head. "You gave me a good laugh with that one, son. Drug traffickers, son, drug traffickers. Ain't you never heard that term 'mules' before? They hike across the Canadian border with backpacks full of ganja. Kids mostly, hired by the Mexicans to hump it across the strip."

First a Bigfoot and mules, now this ganja, and someplace called the strip? Jospair was very confused and his face must have shown it.

Seeing his bewildered look, the elderly clerk patiently explained. "You must've lived a sheltered life, son. See, there's too much border to guard up here." He pointed to a map of the Montana-Canadian border on the wall behind him. "So the Feds have clear-cut large strips of land along the border, kinda like a no-man's land, see? Bet they didn't tell those fuckin' Greenpeace or the Sierra Club hippies about that, wadda ya think? Now they can use their goddamn drones to watch out for ganja. Marijuana, son. They look for smugglers and illegals, but mostly smugglers now, though, since this jerk-off we call a president lets every illegal Tom, Dick, and Harry into the country for free these days. We're gonna pay the price for *that* one day, you mark my words, son."

Jospair smiled about the ease of his own border crossing, thinking, *If you only knew, old man, if you only knew.*

"Son, I'm sorry to tell you, but since you are not a resident of Montana, you can't buy no pistol. You can only buy a rifle or a shotgun. Gotta live in Montana to buy a handgun. I've got some good rifles and shotguns here I can sell you, and the good news is there's no waitin' period on anything, but I do have to run a quick background check in the computer."

"I see," Jospair said as he paused to think about this problem.

He'd known, of course, that he could not fly in an airplane with a firearm, so he'd planned to purchase one here and he desired a handgun for its concealability. From what he'd read, he'd been under the impression anyone could just walk in and buy a pistol in Montana. Now he was faced with a dilemma, since he'd not even considered a long gun due to its awkwardness and lack of concealability.

Finally he spoke. "Since I am going to be hiking a lot, I was hoping for something smaller and lighter than a rifle or a shotgun."

Seeing that he might be losing a potential sale, the clerk quickly spoke up. "You know? Come to think of it, I *do* have a gun here that might just be what you're looking for. It came in on consignment. It's used but in great shape. We shoot all of our used guns and check them over thoroughly when they come in, because we offer a lifetime warranty on *all* our guns. Hang on one second."

The clerk turned around and removed a short, unusual-looking firearm from the rack behind the counter. Holding it up for Jospair to see, he continued. "I'd never seen one before but the owner told me they were popular in the '70s. It's called 'The Enforcer.'"

Jospair immediately recognized the weapon as a custom shortened version of a .30 caliber M-1 carbine of

WW II fame. The weapon hadn't been "customized," in the aftermarket sense. This was a factory-manufactured weapon, only eighteen inches long with a stubby barrel and a hand grip instead of a shoulder stock.

The clerk droned on. "My boss said they quit makin' 'em years ago but there's still a few out there. Latin American armies loved 'em. Not many left, though, in the states 'cause .30 caliber carbine ammo is getting expensive and kinda hard to find." The clerk pulled the bolt back to make sure the chamber was empty then handed it to Jospair.

"I can buy this?" Jospair asked.

The clerk nodded. "Technically, it's classified as a rifle, so no waiting period and no problems about being a non-resident, but you better check before you take it back into California with you. Your state's getting real shitty—whoops, excuse my language, getting real twitchy about guns these days. It accepts a twenty-round magazine. This one came into us with three mags, but we do have a few new thirty round M-1 mags for sale also. Not much call for 'em, so I can make you a deal on 'em if you want 'em."

Jospair handled the weapon. He liked it. *Not as concealable as a pistol, true,* he thought. *Have to get close but I'd have to do the same with a pistol, and the extra firepower of having twenty or thirty shots might come in handy. Not too heavy either.* "I'll take it. I'll be wanting three additional magazines for it, the thirty-round ones you say you have, and ammunition also. You do have ammunition?"

"Sure thing, pal," the clerk said, "but, like I said, the ammo for that thing ain't cheap." He pointed to the shelves behind him. "How many boxes you want? Comes twenty rounds to a box."

"I'll take all you have."

This took the clerk by surprise. "I have, like, 500 rounds. You sure you want all that?"

"Yes, I plan to do some shooting at the range before we go."

"Okay, you're the boss," the clerk said, smiling. *Wow, this guy didn't even ask the price of the gun or the ammo!*

The clerk quickly pulled the price sticker off the rifle, adding in his head an additional fifty dollars to what the sticker read. This had turned into quite the sale, after all.

"You'll need to fill this paperwork out and let me see some form of identification. You're California driver's license will be just fine if you have one."

Jospair had noticed the quick removal of the price tag on the weapon and was sure the clerk was going to gouge him on the price, but he didn't care. He wasn't paying for it out of his pocket. He produced his falsified license to the clerk and began to fill out the single page federal firearms purchase document. When it was complete, the clerk advised him that it would take about twenty minutes to run the background check through the federal firearms database.

Jospair nodded and turned away from the gun counter to walk the store and shop for other equipment and clothing he would need for spending several nights in the Montana backcountry.

Forty minutes later, Jospair was back in the Jeep. It was now time to find the man who had borrowed seventy-five thousand dollars from his uncle and skipped town. Jospair looked down at the slip of paper in his hand, on which were written a name and a location. The man he was looking for owned a river guide service on the Missouri River near a town called Glasgow. The name written on the paper was John Kimber.

CHAPTER 7

GUIDE

John Kimber had grown up in Moab, a small town in central Utah located on the Colorado River. He was quite young when his mother had been killed by a drunk driver while returning home from visiting a friend in Mexican Hat, another small town some 80 miles south. John had been raised by his father, a local mechanic. In the 1980s, Moab had been discovered as one of the premier vacation spots for outdoor enthusiasts. The influx of tourists with their mountain bikes and backpacks, their rock climbing gear, their rafts and kayaks, and most important of all, their money, had finally brought prosperity to the town. Every type of motorized transport, both on land and in the water, needed mechanics who could repair them. John's father had finally been in the right place at

the right time and he made a good living turning wrenches. The downside for his new-found prosperity was that it
left little time for raising John. When vacation season hit,
John was pretty much on his own.

From a young age, John hung out with the older men
who guided rafting trips on the Green and Colorado rivers. He was a quick study, and by the time he was a senior in high school, John Kimber was one of the best
guides and outfitters in Moab. As soon as he'd turned
eighteen, John obtained the proper guide certification to
allow him to take the multi-day rafters through the con-
fluence of the Green and the Colorado and on through the
Grand Canyon—no easy task. He thought about starting
his own company in Moab, but there was still a lot of the
big wide world to see. The large rafting company he'd
worked for treated him well. The work was fun and paid
well, especially considering the tips he raked in, in the
form of both cash and the attention of teen-age daughters
of tourists, but John had never been one to save enough
of his money to start a business. He spent his money as
fast as he made it, but he didn't care. He longed to see
what opportunities and adventures were waiting for him
outside Moab.

John's twenty-third birthday found him on the
beaches of Los Angeles County working as a lifeguard.
He was a natural at it and he *loved* this job. The pay was
just okay, but there was a bonus, and that bonus was
sex—a lot of sex. With his handsome tanned face, his six-
foot-two-inch height, dark hair, and green eyes, and his
six-pack abs, John had no trouble at all bedding any girl

he wanted. His looks and body had even landed him a bit-part in a pornographic movie as—what else?—a horny lifeguard. That role led to three other triple-X films, and those side jobs had paid *very* well, however, the County of Los Angeles took a dim view of his amorous endeavors. When his *face* was finally recognized in one of the films and his bosses discovered that the rising porn actor "Richard Long," was, in reality, lifeguard John Kimber, the county "suggested" to him that he would be much happier working elsewhere, lest he have to put a termination on his resume, so John once again moved on.

Las Vegas was the next stop. John was an intelligent man and, after becoming certified in one of the many small Las Vegas dealer's schools and gaining recognition at the top of his class, he was recruited to work as a black jack dealer at the Venetian Casino on the Las Vegas strip. It was here that Kimber got into real trouble—he began to gamble. Casino rules made it impossible to gamble in his own place of employment and, like so many others, he started small, shooting craps or playing at the roulette table on the other side of town at places like Boulder Station, or Sam's Town. John loved the bright flashing lights, the noise, and the action of the Vegas casinos, and of course, the women. It wasn't long before he was gambling in those same casinos every spare minute of his time, spending more money than he was making, which was a considerable amount. John won some sure, but he lost more—the Las Vegas story.

John loved to gamble, but he was no dummy. Soon he realized that his gambling habit was out of control. He had not only spent all of his own money, but had also borrowed a *lot* of money from, what in the old days had been referred to as a "loan shark." Of course, in this modern day and age, they referred to themselves as "financial consultants," or "short term loan advisors,"...a rose by any other name. In this case, John had been told that his benefactor for his most recent "loan" of over seventy thousand dollars was a man out of San Diego.

He was also warned that the man was Serbian and not prone to forget those who did not pay back their debts. John was warned that it would be wise to promptly pay the loan back with interest as stipulated in the agreement. If not, the results *would* be most unpleasant. John had not gambled away any of the money yet. Save for a few dollars spent on impressing a large set of blonde-haired tits one night, he still had the sizable sum in his possession.

He thought about giving the original loan back and trying to re-negotiate the interest payment, but he doubted the loan guys would go for it. There were no installment plans with these types of loans, and one could not just give back the money without the additional accrued interest, which John did not have. *Since I haven't spent that much of it, maybe I can just drop off what's left and skip town,* he thought, *or keep the money and go back to Moab. If I'm lucky, they'll figure it's not worth the trouble of finding me.* John was kidding himself and he knew it. He was worried and needed a good plan to get out of Sin City with his skin intact. Unfortunately, as it turned out later, the plan came late one night in the form of a phone call from his old friend Toby, from his high school days in Moab.

Toby and John had been high school "420 buddies," sneaking off together between classes to get high on weed, but John had always been more of a "work-out-in-the-gym" kind of guy than a "sneak-out-and-smoke-pot-behind-the-gym" kind of guy, so soon he and Toby had drifted apart. Toby had never changed his ways, however.

During the catch-up conversation about their lives, Toby told John about how much money *he* was currently making smuggling marijuana from Canada into the United States across the Montana/US border. Several of the drug Cartel leaders in Mexico, being the ruthless yet shrewd business men that they were, had realized months before that the legalization of marijuana in several states was inevitable. Now they were on a real push to get as much of *their* product into the US as they could before this happened. They paid handsomely, especially to people with special abilities, such as John's river guiding skills. The phone conversation with Toby was making John a bit nervous, considering all the recent news stories about cellphone monitoring by the government.

"Relax," Toby told him after hearing John's concerns. "No one listens to this shit. Besides, I'm on a burner that can't be traced so you know, *fuck the NSA!*" Toby emphasized the last three words.

Toby talked and John listened. Toby told John he could hook him up with the right people if he was interested. John *was* interested and the more he heard, the better it sounded. A plan began to form in his head. If John could get out of Nevada alive and up to where Toby was, he would use the remainder of his "loan" to start his own legitimate river guide service on the northern Missouri River, taking just enough fishermen and hunters into the back country to keep up the façade, all the while making some real money smuggling pot. With a bit of luck, he could make a bundle from the dope runs, pay back his loan, then drop out of that trade and continue doing what he liked best, guiding on the river. *Hell I might even move back to Moab and open an office there. Wouldn't that be something?* As he talked to Toby, John decided to keep the loan money and disappear north. Ah, the best laid plans...

After agreeing to meet with Toby and discuss the details in person, John hung up and began to put his plan into action. The next morning, John packed his bag and headed to McCarran International Airport. Halfway there in the taxi, he changed his mind and told the driver to take him to the Greyhound Bus station. He didn't want to risk having his carry-on bag X-rayed at the airport. When the taxi dropped him off, John went inside, stepping over the sidewalk drunks and homeless as was the norm at a bus station. He walked up to the ticket counter where he purchased a one-way ticket to Helena, Montana, his $75,000 dollars, less the price of the airline ticket tucked securely in his day-pack.

Two years had passed since John had stepped on that bus in Las Vegas. His business had flourished, from both his legitimate guide clients *and* the marijuana trade. John had a lot of money in his pocket and finally had money in the bank, though he had to hide most of the cash in his house to keep the IRS off his back and the DEA from becoming suspicious. The winters were harsh this far north, and that killed the guide service during the cold months, but the marijuana continued to flow in, as did the money, which greatly aided his "retirement account," as he liked to call it.

Paying with cash, John had bought a new boat and a nice four-wheel-drive Dodge Ram truck to pull it with. He was still single, by his own choice, for one simple reason. Between his money and his good looks, John was *never* short on female companionship. "Getting more ass than a toilet seat," was a term bantered about by some of his drinking buddies.

As John pulled out of his driveway that morning, headed for the river, he was thinking that life right now was pretty good. He launched his aluminum drift-boat then parked his truck and trailer. After consulting a map of the river, he turned the key starting the 150 HP Mercury outboard. Satisfied that the engine was warm and running smoothly, John accelerated out into deep water.

The wide and smooth Missouri River was actually more of a lake at this point, and John was able to open up the throttle and let his boat run at top speed—a respectable 70 MPH. His job this morning was on the legitimate side of his business. As he sped along through the cool morning air, his thoughts were on the three fishermen he was to transport into the backcountry by boat. The men had flown in for a few days of trout fishing. A guide never knew what type of clients to expect when he was hired.

Will they be totally ignorant in their knowledge of hiking and camping in the backcountry? Or will they be the experienced outdoor types? he wondered. An hour's run over the blue/green water brought him to a small beach area simply named "Sand Wash." John nosed his boat into the soft sand. The three men, who'd arrived via the deer trail down the side of bluff from the airstrip on the plateau, were waiting for him

After greeting and talking to the men, John was pleased to see that all three seemed to know what they were about. The first thing he noticed was that they had the proper gear, food, and clothing for an extended stay in the woods. He was also pleased to see that all of their belongings looked used, yet well cared for. Nothing the three men had with them looked like it had just come off the shelf yesterday at Cabela's. A few minutes spent greeting and conversing with the three confirmed his observation that these three would not need babysitting. John showed the men where in the boat to stow their gear. Once they were in and seated, John helped one of the men lift up and push on the bow of his boat, freeing it from the grip of the sand and hopped in. Starting the big Mercury for the second time that day, John backed the boat away from the brushy shoreline and continued his trek downriver. It wouldn't take long for the quartet to reach their destination, as it was only another nine miles on the waterway to a small creek that fed into the Missouri. The creek and its tributary, and the surrounding area, were listed on maps simply as "Trail 79."

When the bow of the boat once again touched the

shore, the three men jumped out and John handed out all of the packs and equipment. With a few last-minute words of caution about bears here in the backcountry, John let the boat drift out into the current, then he put the outboard in gear and accelerated back up river, leaving the three men standing on the shore, the small waves from his boat's wake lapping at their feet.

CHAPTER 8

PREDATOR

Her sides were a beautiful dark-tinted silver-blue, while her back was a shade of green so dark it was almost black. Small black spots ringed with green were scattered everywhere along her entire twenty-five-inch long body, from just behind the gills all the way back to her five-inch-tall powerful tail. Only her belly was plain. A brilliant white without any other markings. One bright orange colored "slash" one-half inch wide was visible on the underside of her throat from gill to gill. Both her lower and upper jaws were lined with an abundance of sharp teeth nearly a quarter of an inch long. The female cutthroat trout was raw power, her body nearly all muscle meat, thick, hard, and solid. She was a deadly predator—the lioness of her watery environment.

Silently, the large trout hovered just above the bottom of the stream in the shadow of a submerged boulder. Her coloring was the perfect camouflage from above and below. Her pectoral and abdominal fins, along with that powerful tail, moved constantly, keeping her in place against the slow moving current.

The trout's size, power, and speed made her the dominant hunter in this section of water and, as such, she had claimed the most lucrative food producing spot in the stream. Now she was hungry and on the hunt. Small sensory organs in her head and sides, along with her excellent eyesight and sense of smell, constantly fed signals to her primitive brain. Therefore, she did not fail to notice the one-inch-long Caddis fly as it kissed the water overhead. It wasn't much of a meal by itself, of course, but her instincts told her that if she could catch enough of them, they would provide ample nourishment.

The trout didn't move, preferring to wait until the insect completely settled on the water, but then suddenly it disappeared. She returned to her silent waiting routine. Fifteen seconds passed and the Caddis fly was back. All of her interest was now focused on the bug, but again it just kissed the water and quickly disappeared for the second time. The trout had infinite patience. She could hover for *hours* in the same spot, waiting for a food source to come her way.

The Caddis finally returned for the third time and this time it *did* settle on the water. Had she the ability to reason, the trout might have wondered why the exact same insect would return to the exact same spot on the stream three times in a row, a guaranteed fatal mistake in the world of predator and prey, but she possessed no such reasoning capability, just insatiable hunger and the instinct to feed. She started to rise slowly from the bottom up toward the small morsel. The fly lay still on the surface and the trout held its place a foot beneath, watching it. Her brain registered an abnormality with the action of the insect and her instincts told her something wasn't right.

Bugs on the water were rarely still for long. Some flitted their wings as they absorbed the needed moisture, others flipped, twitched or crawled in their attempt to escape the surface tension of the liquid. She watched the fly for a few seconds then began to drift back down near the bottom, yet never taking her eyes off of it. Finally the Caddis twitched and jerked as any water trapped insect would. The sudden movement immediately triggered her strike reflex. The trout launched a full body length out of the water in the violence that was her strike.

The Caddis fly should have passed right down into her gullet, but instead it hung up on her lower jaw as she fell back toward the safety of the stream. She felt an unfamiliar sting and a tugging she had never known before. The trout panicked then, shaking her body violently in an attempt to rid herself of the Caddis fly along with the pulling and dragging she now felt on her jaw. She dived for the safety of deep water then swam swiftly upward. She jumped clear of the water and twisted in mid-air, again and again, fighting to free herself from her unseen antagonist of hook and line.

"Holy shit! I've got Moby-Fucking-Dick here!" I shouted to my two companions as I saw the huge fish break the water and take the fly.

Jackson was upstream a good forty meters, while my fly fishing mentor, Corey was the same distance downstream. Corey had been the one to assign us our fishing spots along the stream, based on his expertise in reading the water, though had I been left to my own devices, this very spot would have caught my eye as I was no novice to stream fishing. White water cascaded over boulders to my immediate left, and again, farther down to my right. In between was a bed of river rock submerged under four feet of the crystal-clear, slower-moving liquid, which then flowed through and around a large deep hole adjacent to the far bank. It looked like perfect trout water to me. Although I was an experienced trout and bass angler with other types of tackle, this was my first real fly-fishing experience.

"Keep your rod tip high and don't do that set-the-hook bass thing or you'll jerk that small hook right out!" Corey shouted as he splashed my way through shallow water in his waders. "Is your drag set right?" he called and I nodded. "Then let him run if he wants, but don't let your line go slack or loop on him. Keep light pressure on him and reel him in slow." Corey was standing beside me now. "Work him—work him to you easy, don't jerk him. Tire him out." He extended his cotton fly fishing net. "I'll try to net him fo—Holy shit!" It was Corey's turn to exclaim at the size of the fish as it broke water again in an attempt to escape.

"I told you he was a whale," I said excitedly. It took almost ten minutes of playing the large fish before I could work it into the net Corey was holding.

I smiled when he had to use both hand to hoist the fish clear of the water. "Eat your heart out," I told him

"This thing has to be at least eight pounds—a female I think!" Corey said, jealously admiring my catch. "I'm supposed to be the one catching the big fish, not you."

Turned out the big cutthroat was just over ten pounds in weight.

"If she's okay and just lip hooked, turn her loose," I told Corey, "after we take a picture or two of course."

"She looks okay. You sure?" he asked, removing the small fly hook from the trout's jaw.

I nodded. "Yeah, let's try to catch something smaller for supper. There's no way we could eat that much fish in one sitting and we've got no way to keep the rest. It'd just be a waste to kill a fish that marvelous if we're not going to eat it."

"Okay, bro, your call," he said.

I had him snap a few pictures with my iPhone, then he slipped the exhausted fish back into the stream. She didn't move for a good minute, save for her gills which were pumping much needed oxygen back into her body. Then with one flick of her powerful tail, she was gone.

"Guess I taught you too well," Corey mumbled as he walked back downstream, shaking his head.

As it turned out, that was the *only* fish I caught. Corey ended up being the provider that afternoon. The shadows were growing long and the air had a chill when we finally got out of the water. Jackson had hooked four or five but couldn't keep them on the line. I was just lucky I guess. Corey returned with three perfect size fish for dinner. He had turned another half dozen larger fish back into the stream.

"I'm no novice when it comes to fishing, but you're truly the master of this fly fishing game," I told him, admiring his abilities.

"How'd you manage to do so well?" Jackson asked him as the fish fried in the pan over our campfire. "I couldn't get even one into my net today. Kept flipping off right when I got 'em close."

Corey chuckled. "Today I taught you guys everything you know." He looked at me, grinned, and winked. "But I didn't teach you everything *I* know."

"Kiss my ass," was my reply.

He laughed out loud at that one but followed it with, "Hey, don't complain. You caught...what was it you shouted when you about pissed yourself?...oh yeah, "Moby Fucking Dick.""

"That I did, and I've got the pictures to prove it," I said, proudly holding up my iPhone.

Corey shook his head. "Can't believe you brought your phone."

"It's my main camera now days," I replied

Night descended on us quickly, as it always does in the high lonesome. Our meal of fried trout had been delicious. I passed around a flask of brandy as we talked in low voices, so as not to disturb the silent forest surrounding us. The crackling of the fire, as it consumed the wood

I'd added, seemed so very loud in the stillness. A slight breeze made the boughs of the trees whisper, and there was a chill in the air. The heat from the campfire was soothing. Smoke swirled up through the trees and, like kids, we played the beams of our flashlights upward into it. Millions of bright stars and planets dotted the indigo black sky. The sight was majestic.

Jackson stared into the flickering yellow and orange flames and yawned. "Must be getting late," he said in a low voice.

Corey and I looked at each other and started laughing.

"Look at your watch," I told him.

"I don't have it on," he replied

I held up my phone so he could read the time. The digital face read 7:14 pm.

"Damn! I coulda' sworn it was ten o'clock," Jackson exclaimed. "When it gets dark, you just natur—" He suddenly stopped talking. In the distance we heard the sound of two spaced shots, accompanied by the echoes through the canyons, "BOOM!—boom." "BOOM!—boom."

"Didn't sound that far off," Corey offered.

I shrugged. "The mountains can fool you. Could be one mile or three miles. Just can never te—"

This time it was my turn to be cut off by a rapid succession of shots, followed again by their echoes. "POP! POP! POP! POP!—pop, pop, pop, pop."

It was obviously a different weapon than the first we'd heard fired. The shots repeated themselves. Suddenly a *third* weapon joined the fray with rapid-fire progression, accompanied by the echoes. "CRACK! CRACK! CRACK! CRACK! CRACK!—crack, crack, crack, crack, crack."

The reports from these last two weapons repeated themselves for at least a minute, then stopped with the second weapon we'd heard firing the final few "POPS!" The echoes died away.

"Holy shit, boys, someone's having a friggin' war out there in the dark," Jackson muttered as we continued to stare off into the darkness.

Corey looked at me. "Can't be hunters, I wouldn't think."

"Poachers more like, after dark like this. Bear parts bring a pretty penny these days, especially in China," I offered.

Jackson snorted. "Yeah, crazy fuckers think snortin' ground up bear claws or eatin' dried and fried bear balls gives 'em hard peckers or some silly-ass shit like that." The three of us sat in silence, listening.

"I sure don't know of any hunting season going on this time of year," I continued. "It's gotta be someone poaching or just shooting—maybe to scare something off?"

In the darkness we could see nothing outside the ring of light provided by our fire, yet unconsciously, the three of us stared in the direction of the shots.

"Not pistols, that's for sure. First one could've been a shotgun." Corey was thinking out loud.

I nodded my agreement, reaching under my coat to fondle the butt of my big Smith & Wesson revolver. The hard black rubber Pachmayer grips were comforting.

"Maybe we ought to kill the fire," I said softly. "It can be seen from a long way off and since we don't know who's out there..." I let my thought hang in the air.

"Oh man, what are you sayin'?" Jackson asked, looking at me.

I knew what he was thinking. In my own mind, a little voice was saying, *No way, not again.* Butterflies began to flit around in my stomach.

I tried to quell their uneasiness as well as my own. "Relax, guys. It's a long way off and the odds of anyone coming our way are pretty slim, but if someone *is* poaching out there—" I nodded at the darkness. "—we know there are at least three of them and we don't want them to know we're here, right? Killing the fire is just a precaution until they move on."

"Never heard of poachers firing that many rounds at anything, except maybe each other," Corey mumbled softly. Both men looked at me with concern etched on their faces, then nodded again. In unison we stood and kicked the fire down to glowing coals as we spoke in hushed, nervous tones about a possible run-in with poachers in this wilderness. Our nervousness at the thoughts of such an encounter, however, would have instantly changed to fear had we been aware that, at this very moment, we were already being watched by eyes that shined yellow-green in the starlight. Eyes that were the size of tennis balls and set in a massive skull covered with long brown fur.

The huge black shape moved like a shadow with sur-

prising silence, despite his size and weight. On large pad-
ded paws, the animal moved to within thirty yards of the
smoldering campfire. Armed with massively strong jaws,
wielding three-inch-long canine teeth, with seven-inch-
long claws, and a *real* bad attitude, the thousand-pound
animal was tremendously dangerous when provoked. He
had absolutely no fear of men—or anything else in his
domain, for that matter. He was fully prepared to drive
interlopers from his forest or kill them. His muscles had
tensed for a charge when the sudden sound of the gunshots brought him up short. The beast raised his nose into
the air attempting to identify this new threat, but he could
smell nothing, save the scent of the three men he was
now stalking.

The loud report of the shots now made him unsure.
This feeling confused him as it was not one he was used
to. Instincts developed over thousands of years of evolu-
tion prompted the animal to err on the side of caution. He
turned away and, just as silently as he'd approached, re-
treated through the heavy timber, leaving the three men
unscathed. The only sound of his passing was a quiet
"huff" he made as he swiftly moved back into the safety
of the forest.

Forty-five minutes had passed since the last shots
had been fired. Our worries were slowly fading and the
three of us used our small headlamps to ready ourselves
for an uneasy night's sleep.

"Guess whoever was doing the shooting must've
moved on," I said, once again attempting to quell our
concerns, as we crawled into our sleeping bags. I slid

down into my mummy bag in just my underwear, the blue steel of my Smith .44 pressing cold against my naked thigh. I wrapped my fingers around the grips. It wasn't a particularly comfortable way to sleep, but I sure as hell wasn't going to have to fumble around in the darkness, trying to find it, should the need suddenly arise. I would much rather suffer the slight discomfort of sleeping with the revolver jabbing me, and the cold steel would warm soon enough. I didn't ask, but I was certain that Corey's Ruger, and Jackson's Glock were similarly located. We continued to talk quietly for a short time, listening to the night sounds of the deep forest and hoping we would hear no other shots—we didn't.

Sleep finally overcame us, one by one. We were blissfully unaware of the fur-covered death on four paws that had passed us by.

CHAPTER 9

CONFRONTATION

Ryan stood outside his patrol unit on top of the bluff near the airstrip, overlooking Sand Wash. He was holding a set of Nikon eleven-by-fifty-power binoculars to his eyes, "glassing" the wash below him. Ryan hadn't originally planned to drive up the trail to the airstrip, but had changed his mind as his patrol day wore on. He was tired of crawling along at a snail's pace for the past five hours over the rough four-wheel-drive road that led into the wash . When he'd remembered being told about the airstrip and hangar up on the plateau, he decided that the hangar would make an ideal spot to spend the night.

Ryan finally located the access road that led out of the canyon and up the side of the bluff to the strip. Soon after he reached the summit, the ranger discovered that he could see not just down into the wash, but also the river in both directions for nearly a mile. He'd immediately noticed the red Jeep Grand Cherokee parked in the wash three-quarters of a mile below him. The ranger stopped, climbed out, and grabbed the binoculars from the case in the seat next to him.

The sun was setting, but now he was curious about the red Jeep. Although this was his first time on patrol in this particular area, he knew this was not the type of vehicle one normally encountered in such a remote area. *Broke down perhaps? Abandoned? Stolen? A poacher maybe? The possibilities are endless,* he thought. Using the powerful binoculars, Ryan visually searched the wash and any nearby open patches of ground within sight. Movement at the very edge of the lens caught his eye. *There! Someone is down there!* The ranger focused on a man standing near the water's edge looking up river. As he watched, the man walked back to the SUV and retrieved something off the passenger front seat. *Shit! That's a gun!* But Ryan had never seen a gun quite like it. It was very short, like a sawed-off rifle or shotgun. Ryan made an adjustment to the focus wheel on the binoculars. He could see the weapon clearly now, and it didn't really look like either a rifle *or* a shotgun. As he watched, the man walked into the brush near the river, once again disappearing from Ryan's view. The ranger decided he needed to check the man and the weapon out.

There might be nothing about either that would need further attention, other than just a routine check. After all, this was the Montana backcountry. *Hell, everyone is armed up here*.

Ryan looked around. The light was fading fast. Tempted as he was just to let it go and go fix his camp for the night, he decided that he still needed to check the guy and his little gun out. The ranger was halfway back down the access road when he attempted to call it in. He reached for the microphone.

"Romeo 16753." There was no reply so he tried again. "Romeo 16753." The radio remained silent, mocking him. He tried a third time but it was no use. The results were the same. After these repeated attempts to contact his dispatch, he replaced the microphone in the dash clip. *Too far down the canyon I guess*. As was his habit in these situations, Ryan quickly scribbled a note of the vehicle's description as well as the man's clothing description on the top sheet of his notepad.

The sun was behind the far ridgeline now and twilight had settled over the river, the cliffs on the far side casting purple shadows on the water. The ranger was driving with no lights showing, using only what was left of the natural light to see the trail. He also worked at keeping his patrol vehicle's engine near idle so as to not be heard in his approach. He knew the rushing sound of the river would cover the sound of his vehicle to some degree, but he still needed to be cautious, wanting to remain undetected until he knew more about what the armed man in the Jeep was doing.

It took almost thirty minutes of very slow travel over the approximately four miles of rough trail to a wide spot he'd picked out with his binoculars from the bluff above. He was certain that, parked here, his vehicle would not be spotted from Sand Wash, concealed by large boulders and brush. From here, Ryan would quietly approach the wash on foot. After shutting his engine off, the ranger stepped out of his SUV and stood listening in silence. When he was satisfied that his presence had not been compromised, he removed the M-4 rifle from its rack and began the short hike to the wash. Ryan slowly made his way over the rough ground. It was full dark now, but the trail cut a swath through the dark timber, so it was actually easy to follow. Ryan just needed to be careful about his footing, lest he make noise and lose the element of surprise. He stopped and cocked his head. Hearing what sounded like an outboard motor, his heart began to race as another thought popped into his mind. *Drug runners!* Soon he got close enough to hear a man's voice.

Ryan reached the upper edge of the wash, hiding behind the rear fender of the red Jeep. It was then he saw the large drift boat at the river's edge and heard a second male voice. The ranger listened intently but could not hear all of the words spoken between the two men, only bits and pieces of conversation. He could however see the silhouettes of both, his eyes now fully adjusted to the dark. One of the men stood on the shore thirty yards from the boat, partially concealed in the brush. A second man stood next to the boat itself. *What have I stumbled onto?* Ryan wondered. He cocked his head once again, straining to hear the conversation.

The man standing in the brush said something Ryan

couldn't quite catch, but he did hear the words "money" and "drugs."

The ranger decided it was time to make his presence known before he was discovered. He'd obviously never heard that old saying, "Confidence is what you feel just before you truly know the situation." Maybe Ryan was thinking about the commendation he would get for bringing down this obvious criminal enterprise, or maybe he just had the misplaced confidence that the M-4 rifle he held in his hands and the words *Federal Officer* printed on the badge he wore would intimidate the two men.

Whatever his thoughts at that moment, Ryan did something not commensurate with his years of experience. Something his instructors at two different police academies had told him time and time again *not* to do. He broke cover and stepped out from behind the steel protection of the Jeep

Raising his rifle to his shoulder, Ryan shouted, *"Federal officer. Stand still. Drop your weapons and let me see your hands."*

Law enforcement officers rarely, if ever, were confronted by highly trained, highly motivated, and well-armed criminals, terrorists, or soldiers. It was Ryan's very bad luck this night to stumble upon Jospair Yakif, a man who was *all three.*

The first two shots were suddenly fired by the man near the boat and they took Ryan totally by surprise as he hadn't even seen a gun in the hands of *that* man. The ranger's focus had been primarily on the man he knew was armed and standing in the brush. Ryan had assumed, by the small amount of conversation he'd heard on his approach, that the man near the boat was about to become a victim. In the darkness, the ranger hadn't seen the Mossberg shotgun leaning against the hull, nor had he seen the man at the boat dive for it. Ryan now swung the barrel of his M-4 in the direction of the boat.

Jospair didn't hesitate. In one swift movement, he swiveled at the hips and opened fire, first on the man diving and rolling into the sand near the boat, then on the ranger. Even firing from the hip, Jospair's accuracy was deadly. One bullet struck the man diving for the boat. Five bullets struck the ranger, two in the stomach, two in the chest, and one in the throat. Ryan's bullet-proof vest, had it been on him and not laying in the back seat of his Explorer, would have saved him from the first four bullets, but would have done nothing for the fatal throat wound. To his credit, the ranger *was* able to return fire in the general direction of his assailant before he fell, two full bursts, but it was ineffective as Ryan's body was already shutting down—he was literally dying where he stood. He collapsed to the ground, his rifle clattering beside him, the sand drinking up his blood as it spread beneath him.

His heart stopped beating seconds later and his brain function soon followed. In under a minute, BLM Ranger Ryan Tafney was dead.

CHAPTER 10

ADRIFT

John Kimber knew he was shot. He didn't know how much damage the bullet had done inside him or how badly he was bleeding, but he could feel the warm life liquid oozing down his side. In the dark, he couldn't see his wound and he dare not turn on a light. He felt for it with his fingers and soon found the damage.

It had been three hours or more since he'd dropped the three fishermen off. Kimber had then motored up river several miles to check out the water conditions. It had taken longer than he'd thought, and now the sun had set. John realized he wouldn't be able to make it back to the boat ramp and his truck tonight. He didn't want to navigate the river in the dark unless he had to, but he knew he could make Sand Wash just about dark and would spend the night there. Kimber turned the boat back down river, arriving at the wash just as night settled in. The river guide always carried a sleeping bag in the boat for just this situation.

The moon was just a sliver, but it provided enough soft blue light that John could see well enough to nose the prow of the boat into the sand of the wash. As Kimber jumped from the bow into the sand with the bowline in one hand and the Mossberg in the other, he noticed a darkened vehicle parked at the other end of the wash, obviously having come in via the rough four-wheel-drive trail. Although he couldn't see it well in the low light, it looked like a wagon type SUV, maybe a Jeep Cherokee Not the type of four-wheel drive typically seen in this rugged backcountry. *Hunh!* S*urprised that damn thing even made it in here over that trail*, he thought as he tossed his sleeping bag onto the beach. John leaned the shotgun up against the hull, near at hand. He looked around for the owner of the darkened vehicle but, seeing no one, he shrugged.

Probably a backpacker, or maybe another fisherman, he thought.

John began to unroll his sleeping bag.

"You will move from the shotgun my friend." The voice came from the edge of the wash behind him.

John froze, then turned slowly and saw the dark shape of a man standing in waist-high brush thirty yards or so from him. He could tell the man held a weapon of some type near his hip and John assumed, correctly as it turned out, that the weapon was pointed at him. Kimber's brain kicked into overdrive as adrenaline flooded his system. *Who the fuck is this?* His heart raced. John's immediate thought was that this was an attempted drug rip-off by someone who knew about his side business.

Shit, kill me and take over my operation? he wondered.

John noticed this guy had a weird European accent. "I don't have any bales with me, if that's what you're looking for. I do have a small amount of cash and you're welcome to it," John offered

"Bales?" the man asked, confused at first, but then stated his understanding. "Oh, you think I am here for your drugs, my friend?" He clucked his tongue and laughed. "Such is not the case, I assure you. As for the cash? How much? You left Las Vegas owing my employer seventy five thousand dollars, plus interest. That is, most likely, more than the small amount of pocket change you have on you, no? I am here to collect what you owe—or what remains of it. Oh, and to kill you, of course." The man chuckled again, shaking his head. "I thought you would have been smarter, my friend. I have been waiting for you several hours and thought I would have to hunt for you here in this place. I was actually prepared to hike up this river to find you, once I knew where you had gone. You could not have made it easier for me to find you. Your stopping here for the night was most considerate of you, and fortunate, yes? Well, for me anyway. Not so much for you, eh?"

John's mind raced as he stalled for time. "How did you find me?" He had already decided to take a chance and make a grab for the Mossberg, which he was inching toward, hoping the low light and the distance between the two was such that the man wouldn't notice.

"It is of no concern to you, but it wasn't hard. As I said, a man in your line of work should be smarter, or at least more careful. It only required asking the right questions of the right people. Oh, and a bit of...persuasion, shall we say?...for your friend Toby. Or I should say your former friend. He was most cooperative after the proper motivation was introduced." The man raised the muzzle of his gun and now John could see it was indeed a shortened rifle of some type. "I don't blame you for trying for the shotgun, my friend. I would do the same, were I in your shoes, but you will never make it."

Damn, John thought, *he noticed.* "Still, as they say, it is better to die as a bull in the ring, than a steer in the slaughterhouse, is it not?" *Damn, damn, damn!* John was fairly certain this would be his last day walking this earth. He closed his eyes, waiting for the impact of the bullets that would end his life, when unexpectedly, a third man made his presence known in the wash near the rear of the Serb's parked Jeep.

"*Federal officer. Stand still. Drop your weapons and let me see your hands!*"

John could not see this second man clearly, but by the sound of his voice and the commands he gave, John knew he was some kind of a cop. John could not see the M-4 pointed at him, but he figured the guy had to have a gun out and ready. Out of his peripheral vision, John saw sudden movement as Jospair, the man who'd been sent to kill him, swung his weapon toward the new arrival. John saw his opening and made his move. Time stood still as he dived for the sand, snatching up the shotgun in mid-air, firing twice in Jospair's direction, not looking to see if he'd hit him. The man in the brush was quick, however, and reacted faster than John thought possible. Diving out of the way of the deadly buckshot, the Serb came up firing his stubby rifle, first at John then at the cop standing next to the Jeep.

John never felt the impact of the single bullet that struck him in the side as he dived into his boat—his adrenaline level was too high. The two men on shore were exchanging fire with each other now. Sand Wash lit up with the bright flashes from the muzzles of their rifles and the sound of the shots echoed through the canyons up and down the river. Fortunately for John, he had not had the time to secure his boat to the shore with the bowline. When he threw himself over the gunwale near the stern, the momentum and his weight raised the prow off the sand and the current did the rest. As the boat drifted out into the river, one of the rifles on shore fell silent.

After a brief pause, the other rifle continued to fire and two small holes appeared near the top of the port gunwale just above John's head. He heard two more bullets strike the engine cover.

Fate is a quirky mistress. Sometimes the simplest things can change your life—or save it. Things like arriving at the airport too late to catch the flight that later crashes in a Nebraska cornfield, killing all aboard, or making a last-minute decision to stop at that bar for a beer on the way home from work, thus avoiding being right behind the semi-trailer hauling five thousand gallons of gasoline on the interstate that jack-knifes, rolls, and explodes, incinerating the cars on all sides. In John Kimber's case, the simple thing was a cloud briefly moving in front of the moon. Darkness became total, cloaking John's boat long enough for it to drift out of range of Jospair's deadly short-barreled carbine. It was only then that John finally felt the fire in his side and the warm sticky wetness of his own blood soaking his shirt.

He reached up to the steering podium, without exposing himself too much, and turned the ignition key. The big Mercury coughed as it tried to turn over. The sound drew more fire from shore, but the bullets fell short, raising small geysers of water fifty feet from the stern. After the third attempt, the engine caught and started, but ran very rough. It too was wounded, it seemed.

John knew he would never make it the forty miles to the boat ramp and his truck. He would either bleed out, or the engine would stop, and the results for him would be the same. He needed help. John tried to think. *Wait! The fishermen I brought up river are only nine miles away! Closer actually if they hiked to where they told me they were going.* It was his only hope.

John grabbed a large towel and shoved it against his side. The pain made him groan and suck air through his teeth. He spun the wheel and advanced the throttle, once again pointing the boat upriver towards Trail 79, hoping that the boat would make it *and* that he could find the men in the darkness before he bled to death.

CHAPTER 11

FLAMES

It was a deadly game of hide and seek that Jospair had played many times. He had silenced the unexpected intruder's rifle fire with his last long burst then turned and fired the remaining rounds in his magazine at the darkened drifting boat. He knew he had hit both the river guide and his boat, though he wasn't sure how much damage he'd done to either. The boat and his quarry within were at least 100 yards from where he stood. He looked down at his right leg. In the moonlight he could see several small red stains on the front of his right pant leg.

"So you did score a point in the game, my friend," he said to himself.

Jospair turned, wincing at the discomfort of the buckshot in his calf. He slowly crept up on the prone form lying on the ground near the rear of the rented Jeep.

In the moonlight, Jospair could see the dead man's shoulder patch. It read, *Department of the Interior—Bureau of Land Management—Ranger*.

Jospair shrugged. To him, the killing of the lawman was of no concern. He would be back in San Diego long before the body was found, *if* it was ever found. What *was* a concern to Jospair was finishing his business with the river guide who had just escaped in the boat. Jospair, of course, noticed immediately, when the outboard engine had finally started, that his intended target had headed upstream, not down. *Why would he do that?* Jospair wondered. He would consider this more later. Right now he needed to tend to his wounds then dispose of the ranger's body *and* his vehicle, which Jospair knew had to be parked close-by.

Opening the rear hatch of the Jeep, Jospair retrieved a first-aid kit then sat on the rear bumper examining his left lower leg. There were three long furrows in the flesh of his calf. *A grazing wound. That is good*, he thought as he applied anti-biotic cream and gauze dressing to his damaged flesh. With that chore complete, he turned his attention to the dead lawman.

Removing the ranger's keys from his gun belt, Jospair walked back up the four-wheel-drive road, using his small flashlight to illuminate the trail. Within five minutes, he had located the ranger's SUV. He started it and drove it back to the wash. Jospair parked it facing the river, leaving the engine running. He then dragged the ranger's body through the sand to a point where he could hoist the dead man under his arms into the passenger seat, securing his wrists to the dash grab-bar with the ranger's own handcuffs. Jospair then rolled down all the windows. He noticed the hand-written note on the top page of the ranger's notebook. When he read its message, he smiled to himself.

"So, my friend, you were not able to contact anyone on your radio for help, eh?" he said to the dead man.

Seeing the note made Jospair confidant no radio transmission had been sent and no assistance was on the way, at least not yet.

His intention had been to find a large rock to place on the accelerator pedal, but when he noticed the collapsible "Asp" style baton in its pouch on the ranger's gun belt, he smiled to himself a second time. "Thank you, my dead friend. This will work much better."

Jospair extended and locked it into its full twenty-six inch length, wedging it between the seat and the pedal. The engine raced into a high-pitched whine as the tachometer "redlined" at five thousand RPMs. Jospair, standing just outside the driver's door, dropped the transmission shift lever into drive and jumped back lest he be struck by the door frame. The transmission slammed into gear with a loud "Bang!" causing both the front and rear tires of the SUV to throw sand as the vehicle rocketed forward toward the dark swift-running river. A huge splash followed as the SUV hit the water.

For a full ten seconds the engine continued to race, supplying power to the transmission and thus the wheels, driving the SUV out into the river, creating a huge cloud of bottom mud. Finally the tires could no longer touch the bottom and the big V-8 engine sucked in water, stuttering into silence, leaving the SUV floating in the current, steam vapor rising in the cool air.

With the aid of his flashlight, Jospair watched as water poured into the open windows and the vehicle settled. Seconds later it disappeared from sight near mid-stream in the deepest part of the river surrounded by a curtain of huge bubbles. Satisfied with his night's work, Jospair turned and walked back to his rented Jeep. It was time to leave this place and continue his hunt for the boat and the man in it, but first he would tidy the sand up a bit where the tracks of the ranger's SUV led to the water.

CHAPTER 12

EAGLE CLAW

*H*elp!" John called out into the darkness. "Can you guys hear me? Can anyone hear me?"

The only answer was the soft hiss of the water's passage around the hull of his boat. John was certain he was very near the spot where he'd dropped the three men off as he nosed the boat into a cut in the brush at the river's edge. *Damn! They must've hiked up the creek too far to hear me. Now what?*

He tried the boat's horn but it remained silent. Reaching for a small flashlight he kept on the steering pedestal, he shined it on the bell of the horn. It was hanging by a single wire, the diaphragm housing shattered by a bullet.

"Shit, shit, shit, *shit!*" he said out loud then slammed

his hand down on the pedestal temporarily forgetting that he had a hole in his side. His wound reminded him and he grimaced in pain. *C'mon, John, think goddammit! You have to do something or you're gonna die out here!* Suddenly he remembered the 20 mm emergency flare pistol in the bulkhead storage compartment. At first, he was reluctant to use it since a flare could be seen for miles, but he was desperate now. John retrieved the ugly orange and black single shot pistol from its case, broke it open, and dropped in a flare cartridge. He knew that he couldn't shoot the white-hot flare up over the forest for fear of starting a major conflagration, so he chose to shoot it away from him and out over the river. He didn't know if the men would even see the flare if he fired it in that direction, but he was out of options. John pointed the wide muzzle of the flare pistol out over the side of the boat and pulled the trigger.

A loud "POP," followed instantly by a "hiss," were the sounds the flare made as it leapt from the barrel and arched into the sky, trailing orange sparks. Ten feet from the end of the barrel the flare erupted into a blinding red-colored fireball as it continued its ballistic arc into the night sky, bathing the entire section of the river in a red glow. John had never used the flare pistol before and he was shocked by how bright the flare was as it reached its maximum altitude two hundred feet above him. He watched, fascinated. Gravity finally stalled the flare's upward momentum and it slowly fell back into the river where it was instantly extinguished. John repeated the process a second time.

Jackson's warm breath made a cloud of vapor in front of his face as he yawned. Shivering involuntarily in the cool night air, he stood barefoot in his underwear, holding his penis between his thumb and forefinger as he urinated on a small bush. After stuffing himself back into his underwear, he pushed one of the small buttons on the side of his watch. The soft blue light on the face illuminated the time—1:30 am. Jackson had just turned back toward the comfort of his warm sleeping bag when the sky two hundred yards from where he stood turned red.

"What the fuck?" he blurted out, startled, unconsciously reaching for the Glock which was stuck in the waistband of his underwear in the small of his back. Jackson stood frozen as he watched the bright red light fall from the sky and disappear behind the trees.

"Hey, wake up you guys," he called out.

When neither of us responded, he raised his voice. *"Hey, guys, wake up!"*

Startled, I clawed my way out of my bag still half asleep, gun in one hand, flashlight in the other.

"What—what is it?" I asked, trying to find the unseen threat, pointing my pistol and the beam of my light first one way then the other.

Corey was out of his bag now doing the same thing.

"Shit, man! Someone just shot a flare off, right over there," Jackson exclaimed and pointed toward the river.

"Bullshit, you dreamed it," Corey replied, clearly irritated at the rude awakening.

"No, wait—that wasn't—" Jackson said excitedly. "I'm telling you I saw it. Someone shot a flare off right over there by the riv—" Again, he pointed in the direction of the river, but before he could finish his sentence, a second flare split the darkness. The three of us watched it arch across the night sky.

"Assholes and elbows, guys," I whispered.

The three of us quickly threw on clothing and boots. There was no time for socks as we laced up around bare feet. Grabbing our lights, guns, and some extra ammunition, we began to move off through the trees toward the spot where the second flare had disappeared. I used my small tactical light with its red-colored lens for a bit, however, as our eyes became accustomed to the darkness, the small moon shown bright enough that we could see where we were going, making the light unnecessary for the most part.

Fifteen minutes of hiking, stumbling, and some quiet cursing, through the brush and trees brought us to the edge of the river.

"I thought we were farther away from the main river than this," Corey whispered.

"Gotta remember we followed that round-a-bout creek after we landed," I reminded him in my own hushed tone. "Just now we cut straight across country."

Jackson started to speak but I held up my hand.

"Shhhhhh! Let's listen for a few."

We stood in silence for five minutes, hearing only the passage of the water. Then out of the darkness came a quiet "thunk." We all recognized it as the sound of something heavy striking the hull of an aluminum boat. Seconds later the sound was accompanied by a groan. It was close—*real* close. I motioned for the two men to follow me as silently as possible. We crept through the brush at the river's edge, trying to be quiet, but it was an exercise in futility. Each small branch that cracked under our weight sounded as loud as a gunshot to me.

"Who's there?" The weak voice came from the river's edge just ahead. "I warn you, I'm armed and I will fire on you."

"Hold your fire," I replied. "We're not hostile. Are you the one who fired the flares?"

The voice from the darkness asked, "Are you the three guys I hauled in here to fish?"

"John Kimber? Is that you?"

"Yeah—ow! Shit," the voice moaned. "Yeah, it's me. That you, Douglas?"

"It's me. Taggert and Jackson are with me, also"

Kimber moaned again then croaked. "I need help. I'm hurt bad."

I whispered to my two companions to spread out and hang back in the darkness until I knew exactly what was going on. I moved away from them before turning on my light and making a slow approach to the boat, gun in hand.

The river guide was lying on his left side in the prow, his shotgun extended out over the gunwale and pointed in my direction.

"Point that scattergun in a different direction, please?" I asked him.

"Oh, yeah, sorry."

Kimber rolled onto his back and set the shotgun back

down inside the boat, moaning as he did so. I shined my light at his face and was shocked by how pale he looked. As I got closer, I noticed that his entire right side was blood soaked. "Holy shit! Corey! Daryl! Get up here!" I yelled as I jumped into the boat. *Damn, where do I start?* I thought as I looked at his blood-soaked clothing and the blood smeared all around the inside of the boat.

Before I could react, Corey pushed his way past me. I'd forgotten that, amongst his other talents, he was a licensed EMT. I watched as he knelt next to the river guide.

"John. *John*! Do you have a first aid kit on the boat?" Corey asked. "A first aid kit—*John*! Stay with me," he commanded.

The river guide was looking at him but did not reply. Now that he had found help, his body and mind were letting go. He was going into shock.

Corey grabbed his face to make him focus. "*John*, do you have a first aid kit on the boat?" he asked again.

Kimber nodded and pointed to a large compartment under the steering podium, then his eyes rolled back in his head and he passed out. Jackson moved to the compartment and retrieved a large red bag with a white cross embossed on it.

"Good." Corey reached for it. "Looks like a good one and doesn't look like it's ever been used. Jason, I need light here. Daryl, open that bag and pull out anything that looks like sponges."

"Sponges?" Jackson asked. The only sponges he'd ever seen were under his kitchen sink.

"Large squares of gauze bandage, and look for any packs that say 'Blood Clotter' on them. Quick," Corey commanded.

I moved up to illuminate Kimber's side with my light as Jackson retrieved the items requested.

Corey had his own Benchmade tactical knife out now and was slicing the guide's shirt open down the side. "Looks like a bullet got him in his side. I gotta get it cleaned up before I can tell how bad it is."

"What's that nasty shit all over his side?" Jackson asked, referring to a brownish red paste.

Corey picked up a pinch of dried brown granules from the deck beneath Kimber and put it to his nose. "Coffee grounds. Smart boy. He must've had coffee on the boat."

"Coffee grounds?" Jackson asked, not understanding.

I nodded. "Coffee grounds can be used as a coagulant."

"That'll work?" Jackson asked.

I nodded again, not looking away from the work Corey was performing. "Yeah, it'll work."

"Probably stings like hell huh?" Jackson asked

"You can ask him when he wakes up," I replied.

"I need to get this wound cleaned out quick and get this bleeding stopped or you won't be asking him anything." Corey threw the tattered bloody shirt on the deck. "Daryl, see if you can find any clean water on the boat—a canteen or something."

Jackson rummaged around several of the storage compartments and soon handed Corey a sealed one-gallon jug of distilled water. Corey poured the water over Kimber's side and began to gently wipe the blood off with the clean gauze squares. "Okay, it looks like he got lucky. There's a large deep gouge and—wait. There's something stuck in the wound. I need something to probe with."

I handed him the smaller of my two folding knives. "Here, it has a small blade, but if you're gonna do some kind of half-assed surgery, it needs to be disinfected."

I turned to Jackson. "Daryl, see if there's any rubbing alcohol or Betadine or some shit in that kit. Jackson found a squeeze bottle of orange colored Betadine and Corey poured it over the blade and onto the wound. Kimber groaned and moved a bit but didn't wake up. Corey probed and worked at the wound. Thirty seconds later he held up a deformed round-nose copper jacketed bullet and looked at me. "What do you suppose this boy got into?"

"Let me see that." I held out my hand and Corey dropped the bloody bullet into my palm. "Just a guess, but I'd say our guide here was on the receiving end of some of that gunfire last night." That thought provoked my next action. I bent over, picked up the Mossberg shotgun, and put my nose to the action. The smell of gunpowder was unmistakable. "Yup, it's been fired. Probably the first two shots we heard last night."

Jackson offered his opinion on the small lead pellet in my hand. "That bullet looks like a .9 mm."

I nodded. "Probably a good bet." I wiped the blood off of it and turned the bullet over in my fingers to examine the base as the nose was badly deformed. "The diameter is close for sure." I paused, looking at it closely. "Damn thing looks a smidge longer than a normal nine, though. I've seen these bullets before." I cleaned it better with a piece of gauze then examined it closely with my larger flashlight. Rifling striations were visible on the sides, save for one shiny gouge where the copper was missing, exposing the lead underneath. "It definitely hit some hard surface before it hit Kimber. See this shiny gouge in the side?" Jackson nodded. "A ricochet off something harder than the copper jacket. Probably saved his life," I said, waving at the river guide.

"Rock maybe?" Jackson asked.

"No. A rock wouldn't slice the copper jacket clean like that. Had to be something metal, most likely something in the boat here. I can't be positive, of course, but this looks like a bullet from a .30 caliber carbine to me." I held it down for Corey to see.

He looked at it closely. "I think so. Don't see those around much anymore."

Jackson was dubious. "C'mon, are you guys tellin' me you can tell what kind of gun it is just by looking at the bullet?"

Corey and I looked at each other and smiled a knowing smile. "Not the exact *model* of gun, but we're both pretty sure of the caliber and there's not that many different style guns around that shoot this type of round. Ruger made a single action revolver years ago chambered for it, and, of course, the old short military surplus rifle. I'd say by all that shooting we heard we can rule out the revolver."

"Don't forget," Corey interjected, "there's that weird little short thing made from the original rifle...shit what did they call that?" he asked, looking at me

I had to think for a moment. "Explorer? No, wait...it was the same name as that Dirty Harry movie...Enforcer, that's it, 'The Enforcer.'" Jackson still looked dubious so I took a different approach. "Daryl, you've been flying for what twenty-five, or thirty years?"

He nodded. "Give or take."

"Are there things about a plane, or at least certain planes, that you can tell at a glance, just because you've been at that game for so long?" I asked him.

"Of course," he replied.

"Same with us, bud. We've seen so many bullets, cartridge casings, firearms, and bullet holes over the years, we can just tell. Of course, nothing is positive until a micrometer and scale can be used in a lab, but, to both of us, it looks like a .30 caliber FMJ carbine bullet."

Jackson still didn't believe. "Sure doesn't look like an M-1 bullet to me."

"I think you're thinking of an *M-1 Garand.* We're talking about an *M-1 carbine,* or some variation there-of. Two different rifles."

"Ohhhh, okay," Jackson conceded. It had finally clicked for him. "That little rifle with the straight magazine you always see in old war movies."

"That's the one."

"Umm, guys? I hate to cut this discussion short but we need to do something about this wound here to stop this blood seepage." Corey brought our thought train back to John Kimber's wound. "Damn, wish I had something to stich this with."

I snapped my fingers. "We do, but he probably isn't gonna dig it."

Both looked at me quizzically, then Corey winced. "You're not serious?"

"Any better ideas?" I looked at him. He thought for a minute then shrugged. "I'll be right back," I said and, with that, I hopped out of the boat and disappeared into the darkness.

"Where's he goin'?" Jackson asked Corey

"For needle and thread," was Corey's reply. Jackson looked bewildered. "You'll see."

Within twenty minutes, I was back. I handed Corey the items I had retrieved from our fishing supplies—a number eight "Eagle Claw" fish hook, a pair of needle nose pliers, and a plastic covered role of two-pound fishing leader.

"You were serious," Corey said, shaking his head as he took the items from me.

I looked at him and, again, said, "He's a long way from any help. If you've got any better ideas, I'm all ears. There's no cell service up in here, remember?"

Corey let out a long breath. "Okay, but…shit…okay. Mash the barb down with those pliers, then disinfect everything, and hand it all to me. Be sure to disinfect the tip of the pliers too."

I poured a generous amount of my expensive "El Charro" tequila from my flask over all of the items.

Corey took the flask from my hand and took a long swallow, grimacing as the amber liquid flowed down his throat. "Now pour some on my fingers," he said.

He took the items from me and slipped the leader through the eye of the hook, which was now clamped in the tip of the jaws of the pliers. With a wry smile and a bit of dark fisherman's humor, he looked at me and asked, "What do you think? Nail knot or improved clinch knot?"

"Good thing he passed out," Jackson observed as I rolled my eyes at Corey's comment.

Turned out Kimber wasn't quite that far gone. I saw his face flinch as the needle-sharp point of the fishhook pierced the skin on each side of the wound again and again. The guide moaned several times as Corey pulled the fishing line taut, but not too much, lest the nylon line cut right through the skin. Gently he closed the furrow in the flesh an eighth inch at a time. With that accomplished, Corey poured a generous amount of the remaining Betadine over the stitched wound then swallowed a second mouthful of the tequila.

"I thought you didn't drink alcohol anymore," I said.

"I just started again," he replied as he took a third and final drink from the flask.

CHAPTER 13

DAWN

It is said that things always look better in the light of day. That might be so in some instances, but not for the wound in Kimber's side. Frankenstein's monster doesn't look good, no matter when you see it. When I woke at dawn and examined Corey's handiwork, that's exactly what Kimber reminded me of with his ragged looking clothing, blood smeared head to toe, and the rough sutured wound in his side. Definitely something out of a B-rated horror movie. I had to give Corey credit, though. Given the materials on hand and working only by the flashlight I'd held for him, he'd done a good job.

All three of us—well, four if you counted the unconscious Kimber—had collectively fallen asleep in the boat when Corey's work had been completed. Awake now, I could see that the wound was puckered and red, but the bleeding had stopped and, with some luck and the liberal use of the Betadine from the kit, Kimber would survive, at least long enough to get proper medical attention. I noticed he was staring at me.

"Good morning," I said to him.

"Who are you?" he asked, but didn't wait for an answer. "Where did you guys come from? What happened? What the hell did you do to me?"

He tried to pull back from me but then groaned and grabbed for his side. I grabbed his wrist to keep him from touching his wound.

"Here." I offered him the small plastic flask of tequila that I'd brought back along with the fishing supplies. "Drink this, and take these." I handed him three Toradol pain pills from my pack.

The guide gave me a doubtful look but then reached out for the flask. He took in several small sips, swallowing all three pills as I helped him hold it to his lips. I paused as I replaced the cap then began recounting the events surrounding our seeing his flare, discovering his boat, and Corey's treatment of his wound.

"Fuckin' fishing line?" he asked incredulously, sitting up suddenly and craning his neck, trying to see his wound while reaching for it.

I again slapped his hand away. He grimaced from the pain of twisting the flesh around the wound and fell back.

"Take it easy, and don't touch it with your filthy fingers. Corey there is worried about infection enough as it is. We had no choice," I told him. "We had to get the bleeding stopped, and the wound cleaned and closed up. It was either that or risk letting you bleed out."

"Damn that hurts! Guess I should say thanks, though."

"Don't thank me, thank him."

I nodded at Corey who had been awakened by my overly loud voice and was already moving to Kimber's side to check on his handiwork. He bent over to sniff the wound then poked at its reddened edges, making Kimber jump.

"Shit. dude, take it easy, that fuckin' hurts!"

Corey stood. "Quit whining. You're lucky to be alive, and my name is not 'dude.' What did you get into?"

Kimber started a line of bullshit. "Somebody fuckin' shot me when I was cruisin' on the river on my way back and—"

"Nope." I shook my head, cutting him off. "You're gonna have to do better than that."

"What do you mean?" the guide asked, feigning ignorance.

"Don't shit me, pal, I've got a turd in every pocket!" I looked into his eyes. "I've been lied to by the best and, trust me, you're not that good at it," I said sternly. "I've looked your boat over. There are multiple bullet holes in the gunwale and in the engine cover. There's no distortion to the holes." Before he could protest, I held up my hand and explained to him what I meant. "You see, John, when a bullet passes through sheet metal, or aluminum in this case, it leaves a certain shaped hole as it passes through. If it hits straight, the hole is symmetrical. If it hits at an angle, it distorts the soft metal in a very distinctive way. Under the right conditions, a bullet can even transfer the rifling striations from the barrel of the gun to the sheet metal or aluminum as it passes through, but that's another story for another time."

I raised my chin back at the gunfire damage to the boat. "The bullets that made these holes didn't hit at any angle. They hit pretty much straight in, ninety degrees from the side of the boat. Not only that, they're all in a near perfect lateral line. That tells me that your boat wasn't moving, or even bobbing up and down much when it got hit. *However,* John, your wound there is *not* a straight-in hole. In all likelihood, you'd be dead if it were, considering it's about where your liver would be." I gestured to his side. "*And* the bullet Corey dug out of you is not any of the bullets that are stuck in your boat. I've already accounted for all six of them. Your wound is more like a tear, and that tells me *you* were moving when you got hit. Weren't you?" I raised my eyebrows at him. "Running, perhaps?" I saw no reaction. "Diving for cover maybe?" The guide's twitch was almost imperceptible, but it confirmed my suspicion. *Ahh, so that was it!*

I saw a smile briefly cross Corey's lips then vanish just as quickly, as he'd caught it also. I continued to press the guide. "So, John, your boat wasn't' moving, yet you were." I paused for a moment, thinking about the shiny gouge in the bullet from his side and then it clicked. I walked to the left side of the hull, moving slowly from stern to bow, examining the top outer edge of the gunwale closely. Four feet from the bow I discovered a small shiny dent that I'd missed earlier. In the center of the dent, I saw that a rivet head had been flattened. "You were diving back into your boat, weren't you, John?" He didn't respond, but I was putting it together. Now I spoke more to myself than to him. "That can only mean that your boat was probably beached. Whoever shot you was close, wasn't he?"

I was fishing a bit now, for there was no way for me to really know how close his assailant had been, but the guide didn't know that. Once again, his resigned expression gave him away and I knew I was right. Kimber knew now that his story about being randomly shot at while motoring down the river wasn't holding water, no pun intended, and that we were not fools. However, now I wanted him in *awe* of my investigative prowess so to speak. I reached into my pocket and pulled out one of the small copper-jacketed bullets I recovered from the boat while the others were sleeping.

"I found this last night lodged in one of your boat seats. I had to slice the seat up pretty good to get this slug." I held it out for both Corey and the guide to see. "What do you think, Corey? Nine millimeter?"

Corey gave me a quick puzzled glance at my repeating the earlier discussion about the origin and size of the bullets, but immediately caught onto what I was attempting. Surprisingly, so did Jackson. I'd forgotten that he had worked for the NTSB for a short time after his retirement from the airlines, so in reality he had investigative skills in his background too. Corey took the bullet from my hand and feigned a close examination of it.

"Mmmmm. Well, the diameter looks like a nine, but it looks a bit too long," he said, looking at me and winking.

"Just what I was thinking." I grinned slightly at him, hoping he'd run with it, which he did.

He looked from the bullet in his palm to the guide's face then to me. "Thirty caliber carbine," was his simple answer.

"That's what I get out of it, also," Jackson said.

I could tell he was enjoying this. I looked at Kimber. "Now I know you saw the guy who shot you, didn't you, John? A guy with a rifle that fires .30 caliber carbine ammo maybe?"

I took the bullet back from Corey, holding it up to the light with my thumb and forefinger. I prattled on, deliberately trying to goad Kimber with annoying chit-chat "Yeah, these rifles used to be quite common years ago— not so much, anymore. Don't get me wrong, there's still lots of these guns around, especially in third-world shitholes in South America. They seem to love them for some reason, though I don't know why. Pretty crappy round, killing-wise, that is. Just not enough knockdown power. Yeah, the ammo can be hard to find and pretty pricey when you do find—"

"All right, all right! If it will get you to shut up, I'll tell you what happened," Kimber finally said, exasperated by my droning on and on "But first, tell me how the hell could you know all that?"

"Oh, did I forget to tell you?" I grinned to the two

other men standing with me. "We've been in the murder business for years—solving them, of course, not committing them."

I included Jackson in our trio, simply because he was now part of all this. Kimber looked at all three of us, one by one, then it dawned on him and he rolled his eyes.

"Oh, shit! You guys are cops?"

I nodded. "Was—I'm retired. He still is," I said, pointing at Corey.

Kimber looked away, staring out over the river, mumbling to himself. "I can't believe this. First I'm shot, now fuckin' cops"

I knelt next to the guide, placing a comforting hand on his shoulder. "Look, John, we know you're in some kind of trouble." I took a glance around at the heavy forest behind me. "And for all we know, *all* of us could be in danger right now, so we need to know what the hell is going on."

Kimber looked off across the river once again. The reflection of the early morning sun sparkled gold and silver off the turbid surface. The river guide grimaced as he shifted position, then looked down, shook his head, and muttered, "Fuckin' cops."

I could tell that the tequila and the pain medication were performing their magic, as my intent in that respect had been twofold—to both ease his pain and loosen his tongue.

Now I could see, by the expression on his face that I'd seen on the faces of so many suspects over the years, he was defeated. Kimber was about to break and tell us the truth, or most of it, anyway. He just needed a bit more prodding. I took his hand in mine as I gently squeezed his shoulder.

"Talk to me John," I urged him in a low comforting voice.

That was all he needed. Dropping his chin to his chest, the guide began to tell us of the events of the night before. At first Kimber tried hard to omit elements in his story which implicated him in any wrongdoing, but he was dealing with not one, but three experienced investigators. The feeble attempts to hide his own nefarious actions quickly fell apart under our questions. Within an hour, we had all of the details and Kimber was exhausted. When our questions had all been answered, the guide closed his eyes and slept against the bulkhead of the bow as Jackson, Corey, and myself moved to the stern to confer in low voices.

"We've got to get him some medical help and get the authorities in here to find out exactly what happened," Jackson insisted.

"I agree," I replied. "Let's see if we can get the engine started and actually get out of here and get back to Sand Wash."

"Why Sand Wash?" Corey asked. "If this thing runs, why not just head down river and back to civilization."

"The airstrip and the plane are close to the wash. I'm thinking we head there first. Last night while you guys were conked out, I pulled the engine cover on this tub and took a look at that damage. One of the two bullets that hit the cover passed right through it and out the other side without doing any damage. We weren't so lucky on bullet number two. It clipped the ICM and cracked its case. Can't tell if the ICM circuit board is damaged or not. If this thing still runs okay, we can drop Daryl there to fly the plane out while we scoot on downriver with Kimber. If this thing doesn't run right, we can fly Kimber out. He's ambulatory now, so time is on our side, at least for a while, so we need to try for the wash first, just in case. Besides, I want to take a quick look around there and see if we find anything to back up his story."

"What about the holes in the boat?" Jackson asked

"I checked that last night, also. The hull is tight, from what I can tell. The bullet holes we know about are all well above the waterline and, since there's no water in the bilge, I'm assuming there are no holes below the waterline so there's no danger of sinking."

"Said the man who designed the Titanic," Jackson said sarcastically.

"No choice," I replied.

"I'm surprised he doesn't have some kind of radio on board," Corey said. "Even if it was just to contact his dope partners."

"He does—or I should say did." I raised my chin toward the driver podium. "I found that last night also, in the cubby beneath the wheel. Bullet right through the middle—toast."

I stared at the sleeping guide for a moment. "Here's what I'm thinking, and again speak up if you disagree. Corey stays here with Kimber. Daryl, you and I go back and collect our gear. We pile in and get the boat to Sand

Wash and either boat, or fly, our sorry asses out of here. Sound good?"

Both men nodded their agreement and, with that, Jackson and I began our trek back to our camp for our gear. It took much longer than I had thought it would to retrieve and transport all of our gear to the boat.

It was late in the day by the time I turned the ignition key on the boat's podium console. The big Mercury cranked a few times, then caught and began to idle roughly. Jackson waded into the water to his knees and pushed us off. As he hopped into the boat, the current caught us and we began to drift downstream. With the engine at idle I could barely make steerage, so I advanced the throttle a fraction. The engine's RPMs increased for a few seconds, then it died.

"That's not good," I mumbled. Restarting the big Mercury, I tried the same throttle movement, but the engine immediately died for the second time. I started the engine yet again, this time just allowing it to idle.

"Looks like every time I try to give it more gas, it just dies," I said, stating the obvious. "ECM is damaged, I guess. We can just make steerage going downstream, but anything past an idle ,forget it."

Kimber was awake now but in a great deal of pain. I gave him four aspirin from the kit and the last of the tequila.

"Bet you wish you had some of your dope now, don't ya?" Corey sneered.

His only answer was to close his eyes.

"Let it go," I told Corey, then I nodded down the river and spoke to Kimber myself. "Since you know this river, when we get close to the wash you need to let me know. I don't want to expose ourselves if this guy of yours is still around, and I, for sure, don't want to drift past the beach since we have no power to get back to it."

Kimber nodded. "Still don't believe me huh?"

"Time will tell," I replied.

Corey snorted and looked away as we continued to idle down river. It was late in the day when the guide spoke up, his voice raspy, "You need to get over near the shore." He pointed to my right. "We're getting close now," he said as we rounded a sharp bend.

"Let's keep our voices low just in case," I told them all as I turned the wheel to the right.

The boat slowly responded. Kimber motioned silently and I pointed the bow at the shoreline, attempting to ease the boat quietly into the brush thirty yards upstream from the exposed beach. The current was stronger here near the shore, however, and I had no power to counter it. It was obvious the swirling water was going to pull us right past the brush and the beach itself by mere feet, not only losing our landing spot but also exposing us to any danger that might still linger there. I felt helpless. I could do little to alter our path. As my brain desperately tried to seek a solution, I heard a large splash and saw both Corey and Jackson swimming hard together, each with a hand on the bow line, trying to man-handle the heavy boat onto the sand.

Shit! So much for a stealthy approach, I thought, as I jerked my big revolver from my holster, figuring the least

I could do was cover the two men in the water. It was an unnecessary precaution. A few birds scattered from the brush along the shore, scolding us for disturbing them, but, other than that, the only sound to be heard was the sloshing of water as the two slogged out of the river, pulling the bow up onto the sand.

"It's too late today to try it, but first light I'll hike the trail up to the airstrip, get on the radio, and get some help," Jackson offered.

"There's no way we'd be able to get Kimber up to the plane and out of here, not tonight, anyway," I agreed. "And with you being our only pilot, I would prefer you not be stumble-fucking around up on that trail in the dark. Can't chance it. Kimber will be uncomfortable tonight, but he'll just have to be uncomfortable."

Jackson paused, looking first at his watch then at the setting sun. Shadows were already starting to lengthen here in the river bottom and the air was turning decidedly cool.

"Guess we'd better get a fire going, set up camp, and get out of these wet clothes before we lose the light," he said.

I began tossing the few items we would need to spend another night on the river onto the sand next to the boat. It wasn't long before nightfall overtook us once again. Exhausted, we ate a meal of jerky, crackers, and dried fruit by flashlight—none of us having the energy now to fix a proper meal.

"You think we should stand some kind of watches tonight?" Corey asked

"Probably, but do you think you can stay awake? I sure as shit won't be able to," I answered.

"Me neither," Jackson replied.

"Screw it, me neither," Corey said as he lay back on his bag, sliding his revolver under his leg. "Just—have to—chance…" He never finished his sentence. He was sound asleep.

Jackson and I followed suit in seconds.

Sometime during the night as I lay in a deep sleep, I could have sworn I heard the far-off sound of an engine straining, but it lasted only a few seconds and, soon, my dreams swallowed it up.

CHAPTER 14

THE TRAIL

It took several hard tugs, but finally the wiring bundle came loose from under the dash panel of the small airplane. Jospair looked at the bunch of multi-colored wiring in his hand. He didn't know much about aircraft, but he was confident that these separated wires would render the plane's radio permanently out of action. *No one is calling anyone from this radio*, he thought with confidence.

Jospair dropped the bundle on the ground. He'd initially thought about puncturing the planes tires also, but changed his mind and lifted the engine cowling instead, removing the coil wire. After all, he may have use for the plane later and did not want it entirely incapacitated. He stuck the thick black wire into his pocket. With this done, he rummaged through the plane, looking for weapons, but found none. Grunting his approval at this, he turned back to the Jeep which was parked near the hangar. It had been a stroke of luck, his discovering the small airstrip on the bluff—a total accident.

After disposing of the BLM ranger's body and vehicle in the river, Jospair had left Sand Wash in his SUV, intending to drive back along the rough four-wheel-drive trail, trying to spot then intercept the river guide Kimber somewhere between the wash and the boat ramp miles downriver. He was certain he had hit the man with at least one bullet, because he'd seen Kimber flinch involuntarily as he dove into his boat. It was something Jospair had witnessed many times before, thus, he recognized it for what it was. He also knew he had hit the boat and the motor with several bullets, hopefully damaging it severely. *Maybe the man is already dead,* he thought.

Jospair would have preferred not to have killed the man until the guide told him about the money, and he knew the man would have told him eventually—Jospair's powers of "persuasion" being what they were. He shrugged as he thought about it. *If he's dead, so be it, but I need to make sure one way or the other. What was that American term? Ah yes, "tie up a loose end."*

Driving slowly over the rough road in the darkness, Jospair had noticed the off-shoot access road climbing the bluff to the right in the headlights of the Jeep at the last second. He made a snap decision to take the trail upward to higher ground in an attempt to possibly spot the boat on the river in the moonlight.

It was a tough climb for the small V-8 engine and it strained to get to the top, the sound carrying for some distance. When his vehicle exited the timber and brush at the top edge of the plateau onto open ground, Jospair realized instantly that his headlights could be seen for miles. He turned them off, driving slowly with only the light from the moon and stars to guide him. Therefore, he didn't see the hanger or the small plane until he was very close to both. The sight took him by complete surprise, as he'd known nothing of the airstrip.

He quickly shut off the engine and exited the Cherokee, his carbine in hand. Slowly and quietly, he approached the darkened plane and hangar on foot. He surmised the small plane belonged to a fisherman perhaps, or a hunter or poacher. They might be close by and, if it was the latter, they would surely be armed. Immersing himself in a dark shadow, he stood for fifteen minutes in total silence, watching—waiting.

When he was finally comfortable that no one was around, he emerged from the darkness to examine the hanger and the plane. There was always a slight chance that the plane could belong to someone who might stumble upon the injured river guide. Someone who might offer aid to the injured man. True, the odds were small, but Jospair could take no chances and, now seeing the signs of other people in the area, he hoped that the river guide *was* indeed dead. He decided to disable the plane and its radio, making any hope of a rapid exit out of the question for its returning occupants. If he did happen to come across them in this wilderness and they saw him or his vehicle, it could be a problem. Jospair decided that, if that occurred, he would simply kill them and leave their bodies for the creatures of the forest to feast on.

With his reconnaissance of the area and the chore of disabling the plane complete, he walked back to his Jeep and drove slowly from the hanger back to the access road. Just before he began the trek back down to the main four-wheel-drive road, he stopped the SUV and climbed out, picking up his carbine and a pair of Bushnell binoculars off the seat. He wanted to take at least one good look at the river from this height. In the soft light of the moon, he could clearly see the blue ribbon of water snaking for several miles in both directions. Placing his carbine on the ground next to him, he used his binoculars to examine the surface of the water and the edges of the riverbank carefully, but his search was in vain. There was no sign of a boat.

As Jospair turned and stepped toward the Jeep, a dry branch broke with an audible "snap!" on the far side of his vehicle. Years of wartime training and survival instincts took over in him without conscious thought. In one swift motion, he dropped the binoculars from his hand and kneeled swiftly. Using the Jeep as cover, Jospair scooped up the carbine, pointing it in the direction of the noise.

Silently, he listened and scanned the brush on the far side of the SUV, the short black snout of the carbine sweeping back and forth, seeking out any possible threat. *There!* He caught a glimpse of motion.

Pointing both the carbine and his small tactical flashlight at the exact spot, he began applying pressure to the trigger with his right index finger.

There was a mad crunching of brush as the mule deer doe broke from cover and ran from the brush across the open ground toward the airstrip, disappearing into the darkness in no more than five bounds. Jospair let out his breath with a low hiss as he watched her disappear. The doe's speed and agility impressed him, but now he was irritated with himself for violating one of his own strict rules. By allowing his mind to wander with thoughts of the plane, its occupants, and how all of this might affect the outcome of the search for his quarry, he had not paid enough attention to his surroundings and had actually set his weapon down. This could have indeed proved fatal, had the interloper been hostile. Jospair realized his combat survival skills were getting rusty from lack of use. *I will need to be more cautious,* he chastised himself as he started the Jeep and put the transmission into "4WD LOW."

The SUV dropped over the edge of the plateau with Jospair applying the brakes for just an instant as it did so. The brief, bright red flash of the brake lights behind the vehicle illuminated a pair of large yellow-green eyes, looking out from a tangle of sage and fallen branches thirty yards from the spot where the doe had emerged. These eyes, which had watched Jospair's every move since he'd arrived on the plateau, were set in a massive fur covered skull which now emerged from the brush.

CHAPTER 15

HORRIBILLIUS

Ursus arctos horribillius—the binominal name for one particular subspecies of brown bear. It was better known as the North American grizzly. Once numbering in the tens of thousands and sharing its range across western Canada, the United States, and Mexico with its cousins the Kodiak, the mainland, the California, and Mexican brown bears, the grizzly's range today was confined mainly to Alaska, western and northwestern Canada, Montana and northwestern Wyoming.

While the grizzly population in Canada and Alaska was still a formidable one, somewhere between sixteen and seventeen thousand, it was estimated there were only about sixteen *hundred* of these animals left in the lower combined states of Montana and Wyoming. Grizzly bears were solitary creatures, shunning man wherever possible, but they were also unpredictable. Their size, massive strength, and speed over broken ground were a lethal combination when provoked—and they were *easily* provoked. Grizzly had no natural enemies. They were the true rulers of their world and they feared nothing, not even man.

For the second time in two days, a human had disturbed the bear's foraging and he was highly agitated. Human scent drifted over the land like smoke and he didn't like it. He had encountered humans before, of course, and he had learned how easily they died. Two years prior he had attacked and killed a backpacker in the backcountry of British Columbia. The hiker had been unlucky enough to surprise the bear as he raided a mountain lion's cache of a half-eaten elk in the Canadian forest.

The authorities had searched for the missing hiker for several weeks, never finding the remains—and they never would. What the bear hadn't eaten on the spot, smaller forest creatures had feasted on, scattering the bones across the forest floor for hundreds of yards, insects picking them clean. It wouldn't have mattered if any trace of the man had been found, for the bear was long since gone, having wandered south across the Montana border in search of new range and a possible mate. He had roamed this new land in satisfying solitude until yesterday, when humans had once again infringed on his territory.

Normally bears had a short memory for anything that

was not food or mating related. Thus, thoughts of the three men around the campfire the previous night had already begun to fade as the eleven-hundred-pound beast foraged, but tonight the thoughts and smells of the three men came roaring back, triggered by the encounter with this new intruder in a vehicle. This man had acted so aggressively when the doe jumped from the brush, the bear immediately recognized him as a threat, and it infuriated the animal. Just as the bear's muscles tensed to rush the man in a swift and deadly attack, the man turned and re-entered his vehicle, driving off down the trail.

As the taillights dropped over the edge, the bear moved from the tangled brush and stood on his hind legs. Vertically stretching to his full ten-foot-height, he turned toward the trail and the glow of the retreating lights. Arching his back, the animal dropped his head low and extended his huge front paws with their seven-inch-long scimitar-shaped claws out in front of him and bellowed out a loud challenging roar. Anyone who knew anything about bears would have immediately recognized the animal's body posture as a hyper-aggressive "fighting stance," a final warning of sorts. Unfortunately for most who were ever unlucky enough to witness this stance, it was the last thing they ever saw, never getting a chance to heed this warning or even to run.

When the lights had completely disappeared from view, the bear relaxed a bit pointing his ultra-sensitive nose skyward, sorting the passing smells of the man and his vehicle and transmitting them to his brain where they were imprinted. The memory and smell of this man would not fade away any time soon. The bear's brain also sorted through the other scents on the plateau—the fading musk of fear and alarm left by the doe, the musty smell of the sage and soil, the fuel, plastic, and metal of the plane and hangar, even the formic acid of the ants that scurried across the dirt. He also recognized the smell of the three men he'd encountered around the campfire. It was faint now, but he knew they had been here in this place. The fact that their scent was several days old did little to dampen the fire of the bear's hatred for all things that walked on two legs.

When the grizzly was finally certain there was no longer any danger, he "huffed" and again dropped to all four feet. The huge beast would continue his never-ending search for food as he did every day—always seeking the nourishment needed to power his eleven hundred pounds of bone, muscle, teeth and claws, but there was a difference now between today and any other day. Any other day he was just hungry. Today he was hungry, *and* pissed off. His aggressive temper was on a hair trigger and the slightest provocation would certainly set him off. It would not end well for any who crossed the bear's path in the foreseeable future. Fortunately for any and all, the bear was now the sole live occupant of the dark plateau, the doe having bounded a half mile down the side of the bluff into the river basin before slowing to browse once again in her own dark solitude.

CHAPTER 16

TRACKS

The morning started early for the three of us. After looking after Kimber's wound, Corey and I began scouring the wash for signs that this wasn't all some elaborate story made up by the river guide to hide the truth.

Until now my money had been on a drug rip-off, or maybe a drug deal gone south. Jackson had departed an hour prior to begin his hike up the trail to the airstrip at the top of the bluff.

"Found some casings right here!" Corey yelled. He stood in the brush thirty feet or so from the water's edge on the east side of Sand Wash. "Just like we figured, .30 caliber carbine. Found two spent twelve-gauge shells in the sand over there by the boat also."

"Those were mine," John Kimber said from his resting place in the shade of a nearby pine. "I know you don't believe me, but I'm telling you the truth."

"Yeah, after we dragged it out of you," Corey responded testily.

It was somewhat difficult to hear both men from where I stood forty yards north, near the point where the four-wheel-drive trail crossed the top end of the wash. After a quick glance to see where exactly Corey was standing, I looked down again at the sand surrounding my feet. I'd been slowly walking up the wash, examining the ground as I went, when a flash of shiny brass had caught my eye. It was a .223 caliber cartridge casing. It didn't take long to locate several more of the small tubes of brass that littered the sand nearby.

My immediate thought was that many modern rifles were chambered for such a caliber, including those of the military and the police. I reached down and picked one of the casings up, examining the "head-stamp." When I examined several others, I could see they were all the same brand. *All Remington,* I mused. That, in itself, was not telling, but it did plant the seed that whoever fired their weapon here was not just a random shooter, using whatever mixed brands of ammo they happen to have in their pocket. It didn't necessarily mean, either, that the casings *had* to be from ammunition issued to a cop, but being all the same brand, the odds were more likely.

The majority of the casings were scattered near a set of tire tracks. A second set of tracks, perpendicular to the first, were also visible. The first set of tracks looked to have a street or highway type tread pattern. The second was a heavy off-road lug design. I poked at the first set of tracks near the casings with the toe of my boot, moving the sand. Unwittingly, I exposed what could only be described as a hard "brick" of sand mixed with dried blood. Squatting down to examine it, I brushed more of the top sand away and discovered the "brick" was quite large, about three feet in diameter and an inch or so thick. *Well, that's not good. Someone bled out right here. So we have a large pool of blood surrounded by a shit-load of .223 brass and two sets of tire tracks.* I looked back toward the four-wheel-drive trail as I mulled over my discovery. *Mmmmm, both sets entered the wash from the four-wheel-drive trail.*

"Two sets of tracks."

I jumped as Corey spoke from right behind me. I'd been concentrating so hard I hadn't heard him approach and his voice startled me.

"Sorry—didn't mean to scare you," he chortled. "Watcha' got?"

I nodded without looking away. "One set of highway tread," I said pensively, pointing to the first set. "Strange for this rough country. It looks like it pulled in and maybe parked right here—see how the tracks are deep where it settled as it sat for a while? Eventually, it drove out that way." I gestured to the path the tracks made back toward the four-wheel-drive trail. "Also a bunch of spent Remington .223 stuff and a whole lot of blood."

"Brass all the same?" he asked.

I nodded

"Doesn't bode well for someone. You think Mr. highway tread there is the vehicle Kimber said he saw parked when he first pulled his boat in?" he asked

I nodded again. "I do."

Now Corey was intrigued and began to analyze the tracks himself. "That second set looks more like some type of off-road or mud and snow. More aggressive tread—wider track. Looks to me like it pulled down here around this other one, but I don't see where it heads out." He looked toward the trail. "It looks like the tracks just end there in the middle of the wash."

"That they do," I replied, not liking what I was thinking. "I think someone covered the tracks at that point."

"You mean like swept them away, maybe—like you always see in the movies?"

I walked to the point where the tracks ended. "That's *exactly* what I'm thinking. Look here." I motioned him over. "I think these are sweep marks in the sand right here."

Corey looked down at the tracks. "Sure as shit. But why—" He stopped talking as he realized that the tracks had probably been leading toward the river before they had been covered up. He looked at the remaining tracks again, then at me, then slowly turned his head toward the river, and gave a low whistle. "The tracks were headed straight for the water before they were covered up." His words now hung heavy in the air as he raised his chin toward the river.

I blew out a long breath between my lips. "That they were."

"Shit," Corey said to no one in particular.

"That, too," I replied.

Corey turned. The two of us walked slowly toward the water. He was thinking out loud now. "Okay, so for the sake of argument, let's assume Kimber is being straight with us. There's a firefight between the three men—a cop of some kind, according to Kimber, standing right over there by the parked Jeep or whatever it was." He pointed to the first set of tracks. "A second guy was over there in the brush where I found the carbine casings, and Kimber was by his boat—just about where it is now, actually."

I picked up the thought. "So if the cop is standing near the good cover of a parked vehicle, why is he out in the open and not using the solid cover that's right at his elbow? And where did this second set of tracks come from?"

"Good questions, all," Corey said as he looked from the tracks back up to the four-wheel-drive trail. "C'mon, man. We're two pretty smart guys. We should be able to figure this shit out"

A hunch was eating at me. "I'm gonna walk it."

"Walk what?" Corey asked

"The four-wheel-drive trail."

"Okay, I'll come with you," he offered

I shook my head. "Someone has to stay with numb-nuts over there." I raised my chin at the river guide.

Corey paused then nodded. "Yeah, forgot about him for a minute."

He turned with a disgusted look on his face and

walked back toward Kimber and the boat, mumbling to himself.

I moved slowly out of the wash and up onto the trail, trying to follow the tire tracks over the rocks and decomposed granite. . The broken, hard ground made it difficult. I could only catch a small scuffmark here, or a depression there, and was not even sure they were actually marks left there by a vehicle's passage. It took a half hour of slow walking, sometimes having to backtrack, before I found the wide spot in the trail where a vehicle had pulled over. The ground was softer here and the tracks of the heavy off-road tires stood out. Looking at the tread design closely, I was certain they were the same tracks as the second partially swept away set I'd seen in the wash.

"Why park here?" I asked myself out loud as I carefully examined the ground. It was then I saw the boot tracks in the dirt. They were together—a matching set of heavy lug type soles, both a right and left boot—both in the soft dirt at the edge of the trail and both pointed away from the vehicle's tracks and toward the trail itself.

Now it was my turn to think out loud. "So you parked here and walked in. Let's say you *are* a cop. Did you suspect something? See something, maybe?" I said, looking in the direction of the wash through the heavy brush and timber. "There's no way you could have seen anything in the wash from here." Looking around and up, the wall of the bluff behind me caught my eye. "You were up on top, weren't you? You saw something from up there!" *But if that was the deal, how the hell did you get up there? Or down for that matter.* I was baffled. I looked down the four-wheel-drive trail, thinking. *The on-ly answer is there's gotta be an access road I don't know about. Duh—of course, there would have to be some type of access to get that airstrip built.*

Once again, I continued walking the trail, away from Sand Wash, hoping to find an access up the bluff. My watch indicated that another half hour had passed as an-other mile went by under my shoes, without me finding any access up the bluff. "Fuck it," I said out loud as I turned to head back to the wash.

I couldn't know that the access road I sought was mere yards ahead, concealed by a bend in front of me. I was lost in thought as I trudged along and I almost missed the bear track in the soft dirt at the edge of the trail.

I wasn't an expert tracker, but I wasn't a novice, ei-ther. I'd hunted in both the Sierra Nevada and Rocky Mountains for many years and had developed fair track-ing skills. Thus, I was no stranger to the tracks of black bears. I knew instantly this track was *not* that of a black bear—not even a big one. The length of this track, the deep depression it made in the ground due to the animal's weight, plus the depth that the claw tips left in the soft earth, could mean only one thing.

Oh, shit! Grizzly, my brain screamed at me as my head was instantly on a swivel. My hand instinctively reached for the .44 revolver. I knew, by looking at the track closely, that it was fresh. The edges were still sharp and the track had not yet been filled with forest debris. In light of this new development, I decided my hike was over, then and there. Besides, I told myself, other than this one small spot of dirt holding the single bear track, the trail had once again turned to solid granite. *Can't see shit, so I'm outta here.*

I knew it was an excuse, and I certainly was disappointed at not finding the access road to the top of the bluff, but I just as certainly did *not* want to find the bear that made this sized track, .44 magnum or no. I turned to walk back to the wash and the relative safety of our small numbers. Several times along the walk back, I got the distinct feeling I was being watched, but when I would stop and check my back trail, I saw nothing. Once the feeling was so strong, I went so far as to step off the road quickly, standing silently and motionless in the boughs of a large pine, hidden by it's trunk, for a good ten minutes, my hand resting on the grip of my revolver, limbs for climbing within easy reach, but again I saw and heard nothing. *Your imagination is getting the better of you, old man,* I told myself as I moved out from under the tree and hustled back up the trail. An hour later, I re-joined Corey and the river guide. Much to my surprise, Jackson was there as well.

"I'm surprised to see you back so soon," I said to him, walking up to the group under the tree. As I got close I could see the concern on his face. "I don't like that look," I told him. "What's wrong?"

"We're not flying outta here."

"*What?* What do you mean?" I asked, looking up at the bluff.

"The cowling was loose so I checked the engine.

Coil wire is gone and the radio wiring bundle has been ripped out from behind the dash panel. I saw only one set of shoe tracks all around the plane and the hangar, so it was one guy, it looks like. There was also a set of tire tracks that looked a lot like those over there." He pointed to the spot in the sand where the first set of tracks from Kimber's "parked" Jeep were.

"Damn," I blurted out, stunned at this bad news.

It just never occurred to me that someone would find and destroy our transportation and now I silently chastised myself for assuming the plane would be safe.

Jackson looked back toward the top of the bluff. "Whoever it was knew what he was doing. He electively took out the radio and the coil wire. Almost like he didn't want to destroy the plane, but just wanted to deny it to us, the prick!"

Corey spoke then. "You guys do realize this has to be all tied in together don't you?"

"We don't know that for certain," I said

"What's tied in together?" Jackson asked.

Corey filled him in on what we had discovered in the wash in his absence, and I then related to all three what I had discovered up the four-wheel-drive trail, though I left out the part about the bear track and my feelings of being watched.

We had enough *real* problems. There was no room for "imaginary" ones.

Kimber was teetering on the edge of panic. "Man, we are so screwed! What the fuck are we gonna do now, huh? I gotta get to a doctor."

I looked at him but what I said was meant for every-one, including myself. "Calm down. We've got what's left of our food and a river full of fish if we need 'em. We've got water forever." I nodded at the river. "And the boat. All we have to do is put our heads together and make a new plan.

That drew a snort from Jackson. "I think I agree with the doper here. We're pretty screwed."

"I'm not a doper," Kimber fired back. "I don't smoke any of that shit"

"Yeah, you're just an asshole who smuggles it." Co-rey was getting irritated now also.

"All right, that's enough," I interjected. "We need to get out of here. Let's pack all our shit into the boat and we'll drift and idle our way back to the boat ramp."

"So what do you think really happened here?" Jack-son asked as he moved towards his gear.

I motioned to Corey. "Tell him."

"Well, what we *think* happened by what we found, coupled with Kimber's story, is that an unknown man, I'll call him Joe Dirtbag, was waiting for Kimber here in the wash—"

"Or maybe was supposed to meet him?" I interrupt-ed, casting a suspicious eye at the river guide who just looked down and shook his head.

"—then both were surprised by a cop of some kind," Corey continued. "Ranger maybe. Or game warden, something like that. There was a firefight with Joe Dirt-bag coming out on top. Kimber here gets clipped but es-capes, or so he says. Joe Dirtbag then finds the cop's truck or SUV, or whatever it was up on the four-wheel-drive trail, right where the cop had parked it to walk in. Joe drives it back here and ditches it in the river. Since we haven't found the cop's, body by sight or by smell, we're assuming the cop's inside."

"With Kimber having escaped," I added, "Joe Dirtbag tries to cover his ass as best he can around here in the wash. He doesn't do a very good job, probably because it was dark and he didn't want to use a flashlight."

"Maybe he didn't have a light," Kimber suggested.

"This guy?" I asked. "Oh, trust me, this guy had a light, probably more than one. No, he'd gone totally tactical at this point. Joe Dirtbag is very confident about his talents. Without hesitation, he rock-n-rolled with two men standing far apart, one an armed and ready cop, and he got both of them. It follows that he'd have all the right equipment he'd need for a venture like this. He had a light, just chose not to use it."

Jackson looked up at the top of the bluff and tossed in his two cents. "So he gets in his own vehicle and, of course, now we know, he drives up there somehow—" He pointed up to the top of the bluff. "—and wrecks the plane."

"This is all just guesswork," I said with a nod. "But I think we're pretty close. There's a lot of blood over there in the sand that was covered up, so someone besides Kimber got shot here, that's for sure."

"We gotta get out of here and tell the authorities," Jackson said

"Let's move, guys," I told them. "We'll load up

Kimber and our gear and idle down the river to the boat ramp. It's going to take several hours and we need to get going before we have to spend another night here, so let's get started."

Both men nodded and began gathering their gear, with Jackson being the first to get his arms full and move to the boat. I picked up my sleeping bag and turned to see him standing looking down into the hull. The look on his face was not a good one.

"Now what's wrong?" I asked as he stood there not moving.

"You better come see this," he answered.

I walked the short distance through the sand to the side of the boat and looked in. Water had filled the entire rear of the boat to a depth of a foot, and was still slowly rising.

Corey joined us, his arms full with his own sleeping gear. He immediately dropped it and said exactly what I was thinking. "You've got to be fucking kidding me!"

"How the hell did that happen?" Jackson asked. "It was dry just a couple hours ago."

I shook my head slowly as I answered him. "Must've taken a bullet I didn't see."

"Okay, but why is it just now showing up?" Corey asked.

I turned to Kimber. "This boat has a bilge, doesn't it?" But it wasn't really a question, I already knew the answer as I'd noticed a bilge pump switch on the dash pedestal the day before.

Kimber nodded. "Yeah, why?"

I didn't answer, opting instead to step over the side and down into the rising water. Sloshing my way to the pedestal, I turned the ignition key and flipped the bilge pump switch. Nothing.

I tried to start the engine—again, nothing.

"Battery compartment is under water." I looked up into the sky, rubbed the back of my neck. "The reason we didn't see any water until now is the bilge was slowly filling up. Once it was full, the water had no place to go but into the rest of the hull."

"Maybe we could drag it up and find the hole and patch it somehow?" Jackson asked hopefully.

"Never happen—way too heavy," I replied. "With the size and weight of this boat, I doubt the three of us could do it, even if it was empty. Now with the weight of the motor, fuel, all this water? There's just no way."

Jackson started to protest but I already knew what he was going to say so I held up my hand.

"Bailing the water out of the hull won't help. The bilge is full and we can't get to that water and the pump doesn't work because, remember, no batteries now. This boat is going nowhere." The water was almost knee high now, but had stopped rising any farther for the most part. I looked down at my soaked pants and boots.

I urged them to move. "We need to get the rest of our gear outta the boat before it all gets soaked." I began handing the remaining items of our backpacking gear out to both men.

"You should go over and tell him he's gonna need a new boat," Jackson quipped.

"My pleasure," Corey said with a grim smile as he turned toward the shaded area where the river guide lay. He returned a few moments later to help with the remainder of the gear.

"Fuck, man! We're in some real pretty shit now," Kimber wailed.

"Quit whining, asshole," Corey barked. "It's your goddamn fault we're in this mess to begin with."

"How'd he take it?" Jackson asked.

"Not as bad as I'd hoped, about the boat I mean. He's whining about getting out of here, though," Corey replied. "Said the boat was insured, the smug prick." Corey glanced at the sky. "He also said there's a big storm coming in."

"Now how the hell could he know that?" Jackson demanded as he also looked up at the sky above us. "Doesn't look like it to me." There were only a few puffy white cumulus clouds visible against the blue background.

Growing up, I'd spent many days and nights hiking, camping, hunting, and fishing with my father and his father, both of whom never ceased to amaze me with their natural abilities in the wilderness and their knowledge of the Colorado Rocky Mountains. I'd been lucky enough to inherit a fraction of their skills, so I knew mountain weather could change almost in the blink of an eye. I too looked at the clouds overhead and, while I saw nothing threatening, I realized that the high bluff behind Sand Wash blocked our view of the sky to the north. Any heavy weather that might be gathering there was hidden from us totally. One hell of a storm could be moving rapidly toward us from southern Canada and we wouldn't see it coming until it was on us. As if on cue, fifteen minutes later, the clouds over our heads changed to a near solid overcast, and we all heard the rumble of thunder in the distance that shook the ground. It appeared the guide's prediction was turning out to be correct. Soon, another crash was heard, yet this sound was different from the now frequent rumbling of approaching thunder. It was more metallic in tone and sounded closer also.

"What do you suppose that was?" Jackson asked.

The river guide was the first to answer. "Tree fallin'," Kimber said. "Happens all the time up here. Soil gets wet, tree is top heavy and 'boom!'"

"Sounded kind of metallic to me," Corey argued.

I kicked the sand under my feet watching the grains scatter. "This soil isn't wet," I said

"Tree fallin'," Kimber repeated.

"Seems to me if it's going to storm, we should try to find that access road up—" I nodded at the top of the bluff. "—and sit it out in the hangar."

"Be better than tents down here in this loose sand, that's for sure. Tent stakes won't hold here against any strong winds,, Jackson said as he too now kicked the sand with the toe of his boot.

We gathered up our packs and equipment, once again. The metallic crash we'd heard didn't repeat itself and was soon forgotten.

CHAPTER 17

THE BLUFF

The front half-shaft axle on the driver's side was broken at the CV joint. Bowling-ball-sized boulders on the rough four-wheel-drive trail had proven too much for the lightweight Jeep. *So much for those American television commercials showing how rugged these vehicles are*, Jospair thought as he wriggled his ass out from under the front end of the red SUV. He stood and brushed himself off as best he could. Taking stock of his situation, he looked up and down the four-wheel-drive trail. The breakdown was an inconvenience, certainly, but not an insurmountable one. Jospair would, of course, have to change his plans, and possibly even postpone the second rendezvous with the river guide, temporarily, of course. As an experienced soldier, Jospair was well aware that circumstances in these situations were fluid, changing constantly, and one had to adapt. He would now have to hike out of this wilderness, but a look at the sky told him the weather was going to be another problem.

Clouds were gathering to the north—heavy, gray, and dark—and the temperature had taken a turn downward. Jospair knew that he was somewhere just short of six miles from Sand Wash, which meant he was about two miles, give-or-take, from the bluff airstrip. He needed to find shelter and the hangar at the airstrip seemed the closest good cover. Jospair decided he would hike back up the bluff to the three sided building and wait out the storm, but first he needed to get rid of the vehicle. He briefly entertained thoughts of burning it, but just as quickly discarded the notion. While he had once used a large fire in the forests of Serbia to aid in his escape from a Croatian ambush, it had been mere luck. Forest fires were decidedly unpredictable. The flames could easily turn on him, trapping him to roast in the inferno—not a particularly pleasant way to die, not to mention that such a fire would be immediately picked up on satellite imagery, bringing unwanted attention from the authorities

For a moment, Jospair was at a loss as to how best to dispose of the vehicle, then he remembered a sheer rock wall on the downhill side of the four-wheel-drive trail a half-mile back. The Jeep, of course could not be driven forward any farther at all, but if he took the transmission out of its four-wheel-drive position then used its reverse gearing, he might be able to drive it backward, dragging the damaged front end far enough to make the drop-off. There, he would let it crash over the side and down into the timber below where it should be hidden from discovery, at least long enough for him to be away from this place. Fire from the crash would be a risk, of course, but it was one he would have to take.

He climbed in, started the engine, then punched the "2WD" button on the dash and began slowly backing the red SUV over the rough trail, the broken axle and hub scraping badly at first, then groaning, and finally screeching loudly in protest. Several times, Jospair had to gun the engine and rock the SUV back and forth to get the crippled vehicle over a few of the larger granite obstructions and, at one point, the Jeep's differential gearbox almost high-centered itself on a large boulder that Jospair had not seen in the center of the trail. Finally, however, after thirty minutes of torturing the metal of the Jeep, he arrived at the desired spot.

He angled the rear end toward the drop-off as best he could then climbed out. After retrieving items he might need for his hike out and checking for anything else that would connect him to the vehicle, he found a rock heavy enough to mash down on the accelerator, and dropped it into place. The engine raced and the rear tires spun and smoked, dragging the damaged vehicle over the edge of the cliff. The Cherokee tumbled and rolled noisily down the rock wall and into the trees below, disappearing with a loud final "CRASH!"

There was no fire and, as the noise faded, Jospair smiled. The Jeep was totally out of sight of the trail, with only a settling cloud of gray rock dust mixed with yellow pine pollen floating above the Jeep's final resting place. Darkness was approaching once again as Jospair turned and began his hike to the hangar on the bluff.

CHAPTER 18

SEARCH

Women's intuition" some called it. Whatever it was, Sheila Watson knew something wasn't right. The senior female dispatcher keyed her headset microphone for the umpteenth time, repeating the same call sign. "Romeo 16357."

Worry was evident in her voice now. Sheila had been at her dispatch console since 4:00 a.m. She looked at the computer log from the previous day for a third time. After Ranger Tafney's routine first two radio check-ins with the dispatcher from the previous shift, he had not been heard from. As a senior dispatcher, Sheila was aware that the terrain caused reception problems, and the ranger's sleeping hours might figure into the equation. She could *maybe* even forgive his not checking in for his first early morning radio contact before he'd had his breakfast. After all, he *was* a man and men didn't always do what they were supposed to do. But what had her really worried was that, up until a few moments ago, she'd had the ranger's vehicle location pinpointed with the GPS SAT-NAV unit near a place on the Missouri River called "Sand Wash," but now his unit's GPS signal had dropped off the digital map on her secondary computer screen, and he had missed another radio check-in. Of course, it could be a simple electronic glitch, but she'd been doing this job a long time and that little voice in the back of her head was telling her that something was terribly wrong. She punched the auto-dial button for the supervising ranger.

"No, you'll never get a chopper up with this storm coming in," Tafney's boss said in answer to the dispatcher's request to contact air support for a search. "We'll have to send someone in there on four wheels." His mind was already racing, trying to figure how long it would take a second ranger vehicle to get into the area. "Let's wake some folks up at home. Get a double unit staffed, I don't want to send in two vehicles. Oh, and call the sheriff's office. See if they can assist, particularly if they have an S and R boat that can access the area from the river. I'll be in the office in thirty minutes."

"I'm sorry to bother you at home, but I didn't know what else to do," she said.

"No, you did the right thing, Sheila, by calling me at home. You followed protocol. See you in a bit."

With that, the supervising ranger hung up the phone

and grabbed his uniform and duty belt, mumbling to himself, "Shit, Tafney, you'd better not have driven off a cliff or some shit. I'll be backed up with paperwork for a year, not to mention the inquiry that's sure to happen on what the hell you were doing in there in the first place. Jesus H Christ!"

CHAPTER 19

DELUGE

Temperature must've dropped ten degrees in the past ten friggin' minutes," Corey exclaimed.

I nodded and pointed to the dark clouds now visible over the top of the bluff. "Look at those clouds. Christ, we're gonna get hit by a sizable mountain thunderstorm, guys. We need to find some shelter quickly!"

"Maybe we should just go ahead and set up the tents," Jackson suggested.

"Bad idea," the river guide quipped.

"Who asked you, stoner?" Corey said, continuing to antagonize Kimber.

Kimber ignored him and continued. "Look, I know this place. The sand here won't hold your tent stakes, and if the storm is big enough and lasts long enough, water from the rising river will take over the wash in a matter of a few hours. Only good shelter nearby is the hangar on the airstrip."

"We already discussed it and came to the same conclusion." I picked up my pack with all my backpacking gear securely attached. "So let's get up there. We'll have to split Kimber's gear between us. It'll be all he can do just to walk up there."

"Shit, first I have to patch up the doper and now I have to carry his crap," Corey complained.

"I'm not a doper, told you before," Kimber responded.

"Splitting hairs. Either way you're still just another asshole crook." Corey shouldered his own pack as well as some of Kimber's gear, mumbling something about it was no wonder someone wanted to shoot the man, then he began moving toward the four-wheel-drive trail. The three of us followed. As we made the turn out of the wash, a bolt of blue-white lightning flashed across the sky over the top of the bluff, immediately followed by an ear-splitting crash of thunder as the massive sudden release of electrons split the air. This close, the sound was deafening.

"I've flown around and through a lot of storms most of my adult life," Jackson said, looking at the sky. "And I can tell you this is shaping up to be a bad one."

"Gonna piss on us all night, I think," Corey agreed, shaking his head.

"Looks like," I said just as the first large, cold, wet drops of water began to fall from the sky.

We had hiked two miles on the four-wheel-drive trail when we finally came across the access road up to the airstrip. It was fully dark now and the rain was pouring down hard—so hard, in fact, that the beams of our flashlights couldn't penetrate the walls of water on all sides of us. We finally turned them off to save the batteries. The constant flash of lightning splitting the darkness, instantly changing the darkened landscape to bright white for milliseconds, provided all the illumination we needed.

The climb up the access road was a difficult one. Water was streaming down the incline at an ever-increasing rate, making the footing slippery and treacherous. Our gear and clothing were now so saturated that the extra weight made each of us top heavy, adding to the danger of falling. Every step we took was an effort. We climbed single file, no one speaking, as the roar of the rain and the constant crash and boom of the thunder made talking all but impossible.

The climb was less than a half mile, but it took the four of us an hour to reach the summit. All of us had slipped and gone down in the mud at least once, each tumble bringing our foot caravan to a halt. Jackson picked himself up from one such slip. With both hands firmly planted in the rocky mud of the road, he pushed hard and stood, facing downhill just as a fresh bolt lit the sky briefly.

"Hey! Who the hell is that?" he asked, startled, pointing back downhill.

We all turned as the lightning flashed, illuminating our back-trail. There was nothing there.

"I coulda' sworn I just saw a figure down there near the four-wheel-drive trail."

The lightning flashed again and both the access road and trail were lit up brightly, this time for a good three or four seconds. Four sets of eyes searched the landscape, the road, and trail—again nothing.

"Don't fuck around, dude. It's too wet and too dangerous with all this lightning out here without you screwing with us," Corey chastised him.

"I'm not messing around! I really thought I saw someone down there."

The lightning lit up the ground again. Yet the access road and the four-wheel-drive trail below us remained empty.

"You're seeing things, dude. Only the four of us would be dumb enough to be hiking around in the woods, in the dark, in a storm like this. Let's get the fuck outta here before we get roasted by fifty-thousand mega-Jules or whatever the hell it is they measure lightning by!" With that, Corey turned and started up the road again. Kimber followed, then Jackson.

I stood through one more illuminating flash of the landscape below us then turned in behind the others. "Corey's right." I waved my hand up the road. "Let's get the hell off this road and out of the rain."

The others turned and didn't notice me pull my Gortex rain jacket up on my right side, tucking the tail of the jacket *behind* the leather holster that held the big revolver on my hip.

CHAPTER 20

LUCK

Jospair waited under the cover of the trees in the wet darkness for the lightning to flash once again. He wanted to make sure his eyes had not deceived him. It had been pure luck that he'd been looking uphill at the airstrip access road at precisely the right moment that the four men had become visible in those brief seconds of illumination. He had immediately thrown himself face down into the mud as one of the men seemed to be facing in his direction. The sky lit up again as Jospair lay motionless, watching. At first, he was certain he'd been spotted, as all of the men had stopped and had turned in his direction, looking downhill. Soon however, the four resumed their trek uphill in the downpour.

They must not have seen me, Jospair thought. *Either*

that or they didn't believe what that first man had seen after I went to the ground.

Lying there, in the pouring rain and the streaming mud, Jospair was not comfortable. In his homeland of Serbia, he had lain on his stomach in freezing temperatures, snow, and rain, many times for many hours, waiting to spring an ambush on unsuspecting Croat or Bosnian soldiers, but the small river of water cascading down the trail was making it hard to keep his mouth out of the water as the cascade flowed around and under him.

Jospair had to chance moving to the trees. A pause in the lightning gave him that chance and he moved swiftly off the trail. He was reasonably certain that the injured man he'd seen being assisted by the others was indeed his quarry. He could not be positive, of course, until he got close enough to see the man's face, but he knew he had wounded the river guide and, even from this distance, the height and build of the injured man above him looked to be a match. Jospair again marveled at his luck.

Soon the rain and the distance obscured his ability to see the four men well. They were now mere outlines and shadows. Jospair stepped out of the tree line. Remaining in a half-crouch, he began his own climb toward the edge of the escarpment. He moved slowly and cautiously in those moments of complete darkness, remaining motionless with the trees at his back every time the lightning flashed across the sky. The chances of anyone spotting his dark form against the broken background of boulders and trees would be nearly impossible when he was standing still, but Jospair was well aware of the human eye's ability to easily detect motion, so he froze every time the sky lit up. It made for slow going.

Jospair's cautious stalk up the hill remained uneventful with the exception of the sheets of rain pouring from the sky. By this time, he had completely lost sight of the quartet of men. They were at least ten minutes ahead of him and he was sure they had already reached the edge of the plateau—maybe even the hanger.

Jospair reached a point a few feet below the edge and stopped to contemplate his next move. He briefly thought about low-crawling on his belly the last few feet up to the edge to peek over, keeping his silhouette from being visible should the lightning prove uncooperative, but then decided against it. From a prone position it would be impossible to see anything over the sage brush on the flat plain. Instead, he opted for a safer approach. He turned off the road and traversed the hillside laterally just below the edge. The terrain near the top of the bluff was mostly boulders and heavy sage, mixed with course grass. Although Jospair knew the pounding of the driving rain and the banshee shriek of the wind was whipping away any trace of sound, he still winced at even the slightest noise he made passing through the heavy brush.

Finally stopping at a point that he thought must be one hundred or so yards from the access road, he slung the short deadly carbine across his back. Lowering himself to his hands and knees, he crawled up to and over the edge. Ever so slowly, he raised up only high enough that his eyes cleared the sage. Jospair had to wait a full two minutes for a lightning flash large enough to light up the

entire plateau. For a brief instant he could see the plane
and the hangar in the distance. He moved to a sitting position and removed his binoculars from his pack, then it
was back to his knees. For an hour, he watched, yet he
saw no movement nor any lights. He found this curious
since the hangar was an open sided structure, or at least a
portion of it was. On his previous visit to the plateau, his
attention had centered on the airplane. He'd given the
hangar only a cursory examination. Now he wished he'd
paid more attention. *A lesson learned*, he now thought.

Jospair kneeled in the rain with the binoculars
pressed to his eyes, trying to remember the construction
of the structure. Suddenly a dim glow inside the hangar
sprang to life. Jospair smiled to himself. His first thought
was that the men were fools, using a light or lantern that
could be seen from a distance, but then he remembered
that it was possible that only the river guide knew the real
danger, and the other three might just be fishermen, at-
tending to an injured man. *They may not even know yet
that their airplane has been rendered useless*, he thought.
*In this heavy storm, they probably won't even look inside
until it gets light enough to fly. I'll need to make sure that
we conclude our business while it is still dark.* It was only
then that Jospair realized what a blessing the heavy storm
was.

If the rain continued like this, there would be no
trace of his footprints, and if he could lure the men out
into the open, there would be no trace of blood to be
found on the rain soaked ground either. He smiled for the
second time as he stood and stretched the stiffness from

his legs and arms then began a slow stalk toward the hangar.

This will be easy. Jospair then abandoned his usual caution, stood upright, and began walking swiftly toward the light.

CHAPTER 21

TORRENT

The rain came in sheets. The water pounding on the tin roof and against the sides of the hangar created an overwhelming roar. With no rain gutters to control it, the torrent cascaded off the eves on each side like four separate waterfalls, hammering troughs in the ground on all four sides of the hangar and splattering mud in every direction six feet from impact.

Corey shook his head as he watched it. "The water falls in Yosemite got nothin' on this," he told Jackson who nodded his head in agreement.

"Gonna be damn hard to get any shuteye with this racket," Jackson replied.

"Doesn't seem to be keeping the doper awake." Corey pointed to Kimber, who was already snoring, despite the hard wet floor, his head propped up on his duffle of gear from his boat.

Both men were standing around a small fire they had built in the center of the concrete floor, the dry wood coming from a stack in the corner of the hanger which someone had had the foresight to stockpile. The two men had also swapped their soaked clothing for some extras they carried in the waterproof bags in their backpacks.

"Where the hell did Jason run off to do you think," Jackson asked.

Corey shook his head and shrugged. "Got me—said he was going to go check on something before drying off, then he just took off in this wet mess that way." Corey waved a hand back in the direction of their approach.

Jackson looked out into the darkness. "Maybe he's havin' a flashback. Thinks he's back in "the Nam" or some silly shit like that."

"I'm thinking forty-two years is a little late for PTSD to take hold. It was strange, though, for him to just take off like that. Maybe he had to take a crap." Corey dismissed *that* unpleasant theater of the mind and busied himself preparing a place to sleep near the fire. He was aided by the light of his small LED lantern.

Jackson began to do the same. It would be a noisy and uncomfortably damp night, but both men knew it was better to have the hangar roof over their heads than not. For a brief moment, Jackson thought about sleeping in the plane, then he decided against it. There it would be no less noisy and far more cramped.

"Well, I'm not going to get any warmer—or dryer,

for that matter—than I am, so I'm getting into my bag," Jackson said as he climbed inside the mummy-style sleeping bag he'd unrolled. It was wet, but he was so tired, it didn't matter.

Corey mumbled his agreement and made preparations to do the same. "I'll pile some more wood on the fire and leave the lantern, but Jason'll have to feather his own nest. I ain't waiting up for him or tucking his ass in, that's for sure."

Jackson didn't hear that. He had fallen asleep as soon as his head rested on his pack. Corey soon followed.

Neither of them could know that, at that moment, sleep was the farthest thing from my mind, and that both of them would be wide awake again in *very* short order.

CHAPTER 22

RODS AND CONES

E volution has provided human beings with a wondrous window on the world—the human eye. The cells that allow us such vision—rods and cones as they are normally referred to—are located in the retina of the eye. Connected to the brain through the optic nerve, rods and cones allow the eye to take in multiple dimensions, see a wide array of colors and shades, determine shapes and contrasts, detect the smallest of movements, and, given time to adjust, see fairly well in near total darkness. The time it takes for the human eye to adjust to darkness varies from person to person, of course, but generally speaking, within five minutes the pupil begins to dilate and a person's night vision begins to improve, reaching its maximum ocular range in darkness in approximately fifteen minutes. It usually surprises people how good they can see in the dark, when given the time and proper conditions.

Any soldier could tell you that in night combat training, they were taught to enhance their nighttime vision by never staring *directly* at whatever object was out there in the dark that interested them. Soldiers were taught to look just *over* the top of the suspicious object or person, in order to see it better—something to do with the shadow cast by the iris on the retina. Sitting in the mud and pouring rain at the edge of the plateau near the trail where we had come up and over, I was staring just over the top of *my* object of interest out there in the dark. It was a man moving slowly away from me, fifty yards distant.

When the four of us had stopped to rest earlier on the access road climb, just like Jackson, I'd been fairly certain I had seen the shape of a man standing on the road below us when the lightning flashed. When another bolt lit up the sky seconds later, the shape was gone. At first, I dismissed it as just a figure of my imagination and, of course, I said nothing to the others, lest they think I was seeing things. After all, as Corey had pointed out, who but us would have been out there? However, the blue-white incandescent scene had been burned into my brain and haunted me until, finally, after reaching the hangar and dropping my gear, I decided to hike back and have one more look. I had been standing in the waist high sage near the edge no more than a minute, shivering in the downpour, watching the lightning light up the surrounding timber and looking back down the road. *Guess I was just seeing things* I thought, turning to walk back to the hangar. It was then I saw the figure illuminated, not on the trail below me, but on the flat of the plateau only fifty yards distant. The figure was walking nonchalantly toward the hangar as if he was out for a Sunday stroll. I could see he would pass in front of me fairly close. The sight of the man had taken me by such surprise, that I hesitated before dropping to one knee in the mud and jerking the big Smith from its holster. Both actions were really unnecessary, especially the latter. The tall brush behind me at the edge of the bluff would not have allowed my silhouette to be seen even at half the distance that now separated us, and the four-and-one-half-inch barrel on my revolver made it pretty much useless at that range, even for a .44 mag. In that brief instant of light, as I dropped to one knee, I saw there was an object in the figure's hands. The distance was too great and the illumination too brief for me to see for sure what the object was, but I knew instinctively it was a weapon, and it was a good bet that it was an Enforcer .30 caliber carbine.

Although we were fifty yards apart, the distance between the two of us and the hangar was about the same. I knew I had to warn the others but if I took off at a run, the movement would surely draw the man's attention. *Well, you need to do something. Move! There's no other options here!* I turned and prepared myself to run for the hangar, thinking that even a brief warning would give the three men I was with time to get to their weapons, but then something strange happened. The next lightning flash illuminated the figure on the plateau turning away from the hangar and moving *away* from me at a ninety degree angle. I was puzzled for a moment until I recognized this for what it was. The man was turning to encircle and approach the hangar from the side. *This guy has had some sort of tactical training or maybe experience. Both, maybe? Be just my luck!* I instantly realized that the figure turning away was the break I needed. *This end-around approach of his will give me the extra time I need to get back to the hangar and warn the guys!* It was only my good fortune that the man had decided to approach from the far side of the hangar as opposed to turning directly toward me. Had he done so, the outcome would not have been pleasant for one of us, maybe both.

Not one to wait on providence, I took off for the hangar as fast as my sixty-year-old body could move, muddy water splashing with every step. I didn't care about the noise I was making, as long as I made to the hanger in time.

CHAPTER 23

WET DARKNESS

Jospair had covered half the distance to the hangar. Each time the lightning flashed, he would freeze, then move on when darkness descended again. After the fifth such stop, he decided there was no need to use this type of caution. *These are common fishermen, not experienced adversaries.* He smirked. His disdain for any night fighting skills these fishermen might have pushed his normal cautious nature aside, and he kept walking upright through the next round of illumination. When he was still seventy-five yards from the plane, Jospair once again stopped to watch, and listen. He could not hear anything above the noise of the large raindrops splattering the mud around him. There was no movement from inside the hangar that he could discern, and the flickering glow from the fire had not changed in intensity. Nor were any shadows moving about. He could now barely see the light from a small lantern near the far wall of the hanger where the men lay, their inert forms barely visible only as black lumps on the floor.

Jospair briefly considered turning right, cutting across in front of the plane, and hitting the men from the opposite side of the hangar. The solid tin wall on that side of it would certainly block him from the men's view, should one of them be awake, but it would also block his view into the hangar until he was able to look around one end of the wall. Shaking his head, he decided against that move. Instead, he would swing out to the left another hundred yards or so before turning to come in on the men's flank through the open side of the structure. Between the darkness and the noise of the rain on the tin roof, he would be upon the men before they knew what hit them. When Jospair was satisfied that no alarm had been raised, he turned left away from the hangar, smiling to himself. *So easy.*

CHAPTER 24

RAGE

Even at the storm's height, it had no physical effect on the brown four-legged behemoth. His thick layer of fat and heavy fur completely negated the effects of the cold and wet weather. The lightning and accompanying thunder had moved to the south now and the wind was slowly abating. The rain was also easing up a bit as the main part of the storm slowly passed overhead, yet the cloud cover still blocked any ambient star or moonlight. Near total darkness had settled over the plateau, save for the flickering of light from the lantern in the hangar. The bear would pause occasionally, to shake the water from his face, more out of annoyance than an actual need to see the dim glow, now less than one-quarter mile ahead. Once again his eyesight was not one of the senses he relied on as he moved silently over the wet ground, his large paws sinking almost two inches into the mud.

Earlier, the tumultuous sound of crashing thunder and the roar of the rain pounding the ground had somewhat reduced the beast's ability to hear, but he wasn't relying on his short stubby ears, any more than he was his poor vision. He was following his nose, *the* most important of the beast's senses. Not only had the bear's sense of smell not been affected in the slightest by the storm, but now the heavy moist air combined with only a slight breeze, actually magnified his olfactory abilities. The bear was aware of everything within the half-mile diameter circle of which he was the center. As the animal moved forward in the darkness, his brain instantly identified every individual scent—the wet sage and grass, the residual traces of ozone lingering in the air from the lightning, the five mule deer and the single coyote—all of which had taken cover in the nearby heavy brush.

The bear also recognized the scent of the same three humans from the camp down river which now emitted from the hangar. The animal voiced a low growl and turned to move in the direction of these three interlopers who now once again angered him so.

The bear shuffled only a few yards, then stopped suddenly and lowered his nose halfway to the earth, momentarily confused. He now detected the very fresh scent of a fourth human.

Already in a state of agitation, this new scent poured gasoline on the smoldering fire of his rage. It took only seconds for his brain to recall the challenge and threat from the scent of *this* man.

One thousand, one hundred pounds of highly pissed-off muscle, teeth, and claws immediately turned away from the hangar, temporarily forgetting the first three men, in order follow the fresh scent across the muddy wet ground.

CHAPTER 25

ESCAPE

Mmmmphhh!" Corey's startled yell was muffled by my hand clamped hard over his mouth.

"Shhhhhh—no noise," I whispered urgently. "Get up. We gotta get outta here quick!" I heard a soft "swish" behind me and I slowly turned my head. The muzzle of Jackson's .40 caliber Glock looked as big around as a fifty-five gallon drum pointed directly at my face.

"Shit, man! I almost shot your ass! What the hell's going on?" he asked, a bit too loudly

"Shhhhhh." I put my index finger to my lips. "Get up, grab your packs and coats, and be sure you've got your weapons and ammo. We've got trouble and we don't have much time. Move!" I urged them both. Corey reached for the lantern. "No! Leave it on or he'll know something's up."

"Who'll know?" Jackson asked

"I'll explain later," I whispered with urgency. "C'mon. Move like your life depends on it, because it does! Help me get Kimber's ass moving, and don't forget his shotgun."

Maybe it was the urgency of my voice, but no more questions were asked. The three of us scooped up the coats, weapons, and John Kimber, and started for the wet darkness.

"Head that way." Still whispering, I pointed in the direction of the edge of the plateau past the plane, near the point where I figured the access road crested the top.

"I *think* not." The monotone voice from behind us stopped us all in our tracks.

"Stand very, very still, my friends. Do not try to turn around or you will only hasten the inevitable," the man said in a quiet, chilling voice, totally lacking emotion.

Jackson shot me a quick glance. I knew what he was thinking. If we all turned swiftly, it would confuse the guy just long enough for one of us to get a shot off. But I knew better. Instinctively, I knew this was the voice of an experienced killer and that he was expecting *just* such a move. There was no way we would take this man by surprise. I was actually rather shocked that he had not killed us all outright. I gave Jackson an almost-imperceptible single shake of my head.

"One at a time, starting with you on the left," the man said, addressing Corey, who stood hunched with his left arm supporting Kimber and his pistol in his right hand. "Place your weapon on the ground and kick it away."

There was nothing to be done. We'd been caught by surprise and were now helpless. I silently cursed our bad luck. We'd been mere seconds from the relative cover of the plane, and the safety of the darkness. Cory looked down at his feet, contemplating.

"Do it Corey," I told him. "You'd be dead before you turned halfway around." Again I wondered why we were still alive.

"*Fuck*," Corey exclaimed as his revolver hit the concrete and he kicked it three feet away.

"That was sound advice," the man said. "If it makes you feel better to have only moved your weapon such a short distance away, so be it. It might as well be one hundred feet away, for all the good it will do you. Now you big man in the black parka," he said to me.

I stooped, letting the big Smith .44 clatter to the hangar floor.

"That is a big gun. A big gun for a big man, I take it?" I didn't answer. He snorted. "Or maybe you think you are...what was his name?...Dusty Harry?"

"Dirty Harry," I corrected him.

"Yes, that's it, Dirty Harry." He chuckled. "Kick it."

I did.

"Now, you in the center with the shotgun."

Jackson let the shotgun drop.

The man clicked his tongue. "You Americans all think you are cowboys. My friend, I know about the pistol stuck in your belt. Do not try for it. You will never make it."

Jackson sighed and reached for the Glock stuck in his front waistband.

"*Slowly,*" the guy barked as Jackson moved a little too quickly for the his comfort.

The sound of our last weapon hitting the concrete echoed across the hangar like a death knell.

"There now, we can all be friends. Turn around slowly and keep your hands where I can see them."

The four of us turned, Corey helping Kimber limp in a half-circle. The man stood at the very edge of the concrete at the open side of the hangar. The circle of light given off by the fire and the small lantern cast his shadow behind him into the darkness beyond. I looked him over quickly, calling once again on the powers of observation learned from years as a cop. He was a man of medium height, somewhere on the upper side of forty. His dark hair was just long enough to be plastered to his head by the rain that he'd come through. He wore only jeans and a long-sleeved shirt. Obviously, the cold and the rain did not bother him. He was conditioned to it. In my mind this made him a native of someplace where cold and snow were the main weather features. It was impossible to tell the color of his eyes. In the dim light of the lantern they looked black, like a doll's eyes. From what I could see, he looked to be in good shape—lean, yet with defined muscles. His hands looked large as they gripped the short carbine with the ugly snout that was pointed at us. The muzzle never wavered. It was rock steady in his hands.

Yup, we were right. I almost snorted as I thought, *We are about to be killed by a shorty M-1 carbine.* I then noticed the weapon was actually pointed directly at Kimber. *Experienced,* I mused. *He only has to swing the muzzle from left to right to cut us all down, instead of back and forth had it been pointed in the middle of the group of all four of us.*

"BANG!"

The sound of the single shot fired from the carbine was as unexpected as it was deafening under the tin roof of the hangar. It made me jump. A wisp of smoke rose from the end of the barrel, a small red hole appearing in Kimber's forehead just over his right eye. Bright red arterial blood and small bloody fragments of bone and gray brain matter splattered on the left side of Corey's face as well as across the concrete floor behind both men as the 115 grain FMJ bullet blew out the back of Kimber's skull. He instantly collapsed to the floor like a deflated balloon.

Corey had no time to let go of the dead man and was dragged to the floor with him, where both were now covered in the gore that a moment before had been John Kimber's head.

As Corey attempted to untangle himself from the corpse, the killer swung the smoking muzzle of the carbine toward me. The three of us were stunned with surprise and shock. Our ears rang. The sulfur smell of cordite and the strong copper smell of blood filled the hangar. I knew I should move, dive out of the way, run, do something to try to save myself. *All that running for nothing.* I smiled at the fact that this would undoubtedly be my last thought. *Here goes.* I tensed my muscles to make a dive for the Smith, knowing I wouldn't make it.

What happened next occurred at such speed, it froze me in my tracks. My brain, jolted by the sudden massive shot of adrenalin to my system when the shot rang out, was moving a thousand miles an hour and I could comprehend everything unfolding in front of my eyes as if in slow motion.

"REEEOWWOAAR!"

A horrible ear-splitting roar came from the darkness behind the killer. It was a sound that I never thought a living creature could make. Even with my ears still ringing from the gunshot, the sound seemed the loudest, most terrifying I'd ever heard. I'd read somewhere that a grizzly could outpace a Quarter Horse over a short distance. I believed it, as I saw a thousand pounds of raging bear rocket out of the darkness.

The killer spun, and it said much for his own speed, as his reaction to the bear's presence was lightning quick, but it was a mismatch from the beginning.

As the huge brown shape hurled across the last few feet separating the bear from the man he hated, the carbine begin to spit fire, but the little 115-grain bullets were no match for the bear's muscled girth. It was akin to hurling golf balls at a speeding car, as it bore down on you. You might put some dents in it, but you sure as hell were not going to stop it.

It was these gunshots however, that finally jolted me out of my shock.

"R*un, goddammit, run*," I shouted as I kicked hard at the wood in the campfire.

Flaming branches, embers, and sparks flew in every direction. I scooped up my revolver and pack, running for all I was worth out the doorway of the hangar and into the safety of the darkness. I could only hope Jackson and Corey had done the same, for I surely couldn't take the time to stop and look back for them. Somewhere behind me, I thought I heard several more gunshots. My own labored breathing was so loud, *it* was the only sound I was sure of, however.

I ran across the plateau as fast as I could, but it seemed I was running in a sea of molasses. The mud sucked at my boots and the brush seemed like wicked hands, grabbing to hold on and purposely slow me. Time stood still. My leg muscles burned like fire and my lungs felt as if they were going to burst, but still I ran. I had been operating on pure adrenaline up to this point, but the effects of it were fading now. I was involuntarily slowing and I felt it. I knew my legs would probably give out any second, but I couldn't bring myself to stop.

Then, without any warning, the ground disappeared under my feet and I was falling. I'd run right off the edge of the tabletop mountain. My arms and legs flailed at the empty air for several seconds, then came the jarring impact as I hit.

"*Ugh*," I exclaimed as I landed on my side on the slope, ten feet below the escarpment, and rolled, my pack flying one way and my revolver the other. It was my good luck that my fall had been somewhat broken by the large thick bush I'd landed in. It was my bad luck that this particular species of bush I'd landed in was scientifically named *Urtica Incisia*, commonly known as stinging nettles. The thousands of tiny spines pierced every inch of my exposed skin, depositing their painful toxin. As I lay there, I began to laugh quietly, realizing that I really didn't care about the discomfort the toxic plant was causing me. I was just damn thankful I was still alive to feel it. At some point, I began to recover from the shock of the past hour's events and drifted off to sleep. Actually "passed out" would be a more descriptive term. I lay as I had fallen, feeling nothing.

CHAPTER 26

DAWN

*J*ason! *Jason!*"

The urgent whisper dragged me from my unconscious bliss. A hand shook my shoulder.

"Ouch! Fuck, Jason! Wake up, man. I can't get any closer to you. You're in some kind of sticker bush. Wake up, dammit. Ouch." Corey jerked his hand back from the aggressive nettles as I cracked open one eye.

"C—C—Corey?" I stammered, trying to right myself.

"Shhhh." He put his index finger to his lips, looking first at the top of the plateau some ten feet above his head, then downhill in the three directions that were visible in the low light of dawn. Steam vapor rose from his mouth in the cold air. "You're gonna have to drag your ass out of those stickers 'cause I ain't coming in there to help you. The little fuckers are nasty." He continued to whisper, referring, of course, to the nettles.

I finally got my bearings, regaining enough of my wits, and began to extricate myself from the thorny plant. When I had done so, I immediately plopped to the muddy ground and groaned.

"Man, every square inch of me hurts—inside and out" I looked up at Corey. "Holy shit, Corey, if I look half as bad as you..." I let the sentence trail off, looking down at the dried blood on my clothing and hands, then at the muddy, wet, gore-splattered mess Corey had become.

"Take my word for it," he replied. "You look a hundred times worse."

"Why are we whispering?" I asked, taking a look around for myself.

"Because I don't know if we're the only ones left alive or not and I don't want whatever that was last night to find my sorry ass. What the fuck was that thing last night, Jason?"

"Only caught a glimpse of it, but it had to be a grizzly—either that or Big Foot," I answered, trying to work up a smile.

"Nothing to joke about, dude," Corey said seriously. "The Reaper reached out for us last night."

"That he did, but he missed, didn't he? Not sure he did us any favors, though."

He looked at me incredulously. "What the hell is *that* supposed to mean?"

"Thirty carbine round to the forehead beats slowly dying in bed of cancer, don't you think?"

He shook his head. "Not right now, thank you very much. Man, you're—"

I held up my hand. "Just trying to lighten the mood and take focus off how truly *fucked* we are right now. Did you see what happened to Jackson?"

Again, he shook his head. "When whatever that was came roaring out of the darkness like a damn freight train and you yelled. I ran like hell. I think we all went in different directions, man."

"How the hell did you find me?" I asked him.

"You were snoring. It was so loud at first I thought it was a bear, but after moving in this direction—" He glanced at the nettle bush. "I knew it had to either be you or Jackson. What do you think we should do?"

I paused for a moment, thinking. "We've gotta go back up there." I raised my chin at the plateau, of course meaning the hangar.

"Fuck that!" His whisper almost turned into a shout. "In case you're not keeping track of current events, we just got our asses kicked up there, pal. The two of us barely got out with our lives."

"Shhhhh, bud. Calm down. I'm not saying we're gonna walk back up there with our pants around our knees saying, 'thank you, sir, may I have another,' but we've got to know if Jackson survived and who won the man-versus-bear-death-match."

Corey started to protest once more but I cut him off. "Jackson could be up there, hurt. If he's not, *and* we can find that coil wire, I'd sure rather fly outta here than walk, wouldn't you?"

Corey still didn't like this idea at all. "Yeah? And what about the shooter or the bear? What if they both survived?"

I shook my head. "Odds are, one, or possibly even both, are dead. Hell, they might both be lying up there next to each other hard as a carp.

And if one, or even both of them, did survive, they gotta be messed up bad." I pulled my arms loose from the grasp of the mud. "Help me find my pistol. I dropped it when I fell."

"Here." Corey held out my .44. "I found it right over there when I came up." He pointed to a clear patch of wet dirt fifteen feet from where I sat. "Your pack is right over there." He pointed in the opposite direction

"Were you able to get yours?" I asked him.

He shook his head. "Went the other way out, but I did scoop up Jackson's Glock. Only has the one magazine that's in it, though."

I smiled at him. "See? Piece of cake, bro."

He didn't find any humor in my comment. "What I see is us, either buried in a shallow grave or turned into bear crap."

I reached out for his hand. "Help an old man up and we'll go."

After getting to my feet, I wiped the mud from my Smith revolver then walked over and retrieved my pack

"You must be crazy, man, and I must be crazy to let you talk me into going back there," Corey said as he helped me slip my arms through the straps of my back-pack.

As the two of us started climbing back up the hillside, I knew what he was thinking. *This crazy old bas-tard is gonna get me killed, for sure.*

CHAPTER 27

RETURN

Sunlight slowly crept across the wilderness that surrounded us. Purple shadows cast by the higher peaks kept its warmth from the plateau and the two of us shivered as we lay side by side on the wet ground beneath a large sage bush thirty yards from the plane. We had used the cover of the remaining minutes of dawn's twilight to jog across the plateau to this spot. As shards of sunlight finally began to spread around us, wisps of steam lifted from the moist earth. Nothing stirred in the morning light, save the flittering of several small birds as we watched in silence.

"Looks deserted, but I still think this is a bad idea," Corey whispered.

My eyes darted from side to side, taking in everything within the one hundred and eighty degree arc, which included the plane, the hangar, and the sage of the plateau that was visible on both sides of the structure.

"We have to know," I replied in an equally quiet voice. "You cover everything from the hangar right, and I'll do the same to the left. Let's go."

He nodded his reply and we both rose up from our hide beneath the sage bush. Had anyone been watching, I was sure we must have looked like apparitions rising from the grave. I moved slowly forward in a low crouch, holding my revolver in a "Weaver stance" grip, its barrel pointed slightly downward, the index finger of my right hand extended along the frame just above the trigger. My eyes darted from the plane, to the hanger, out to the left, then repeated the cycle over and over. Out of my peripheral vision I could see Corey moving forward in the same manner, keeping pace with me to my right, his head on a swivel.

Ten feet from the plane, I heard a faint "click-click," which froze me in my tracks. It was the unmistakable sound of a weapon being cocked.

"I figured you both were dead." Jackson's familiar voice came from behind the tail of the plane.

At the sound of his voice, Corey and I both dropped to the ground out of pure reflex. We had been whispering all morning and the normal volume of Jackson's voice seemed to boom across the quiet landscape.

"Relax, there's no one around," he said as he emerged from cover behind the plane.

The two of us rose.

"I see you made it," I told him as we approached each other near the tail.

Corey's .357 revolver was in Jackson's right hand. There was another audible double click as he un-cocked it.

"Really? No one around?" I turned my body 360 degrees, surveying everything within sight.

"Near as I can tell," Jackson replied.

We all shook hands then, grateful to have survived the night.

"I've been holed up right here all night. Jesus, what happened to you two?" he asked now that he'd gotten a good close look at us—wet, covered in mud and, in my case, blood. "You guys look like you've been dragged through a knothole backward."

"Close encounter of the worst kind," I replied. "Not as bad as it looks. I'll tell you about it later. First tell me what happened with you."

Jackson shrugged and looked back at the hanger. "When that giant friggin' bear barreled into that asshole and you yelled, I took off just like you guys did but got a late start scooping up Corey's revolver and *my* coat. I tried to catch up to at least one of you, but as soon as you guys hit the darkness, you disappeared. So I just hunkered down here, hiding in that little ditch behind the plane. I tried not to move around much in case our friend with the ugly little carbine survived, but I don't think he did. I had just climbed out when I heard you guys hoofin' it across the frozen tundra out there. I was pretty sure it had to be you, but still had to be *really* sure, so I went to

ground back in that ditch right there." He pointed to a
narrow furrow in the earth that was about two feet wide,
two feet deep, and ten feet long, near the tail of the plane.
"Never did see that when I taxied up here. Blocked by the
sage I guess—pure luck I didn't dump the nose wheel
into it. Anyway, I damn near froze my ass off waiting for
you guys to move again." He then nodded at the hanger.
"It stayed pretty noisy in there for a while, as you can im-
agine, but haven't heard anything for hours now."

"Well, no time like the present to take a look," I said

"Just what I was getting ready to do when I saw you
two walking toward me." Jackson extended the revolver
to Corey. "Here, trade me guns. I'm not used to the way
this thing feels and I don't like having only six shots."
The two exchanged weapons.

"How you want to do this?" Corey asked.

I gestured at the hangar. "You two go around to the
solid wall side to the door. I'll work toward the open
side."

Slowly and cautiously, our weapons at the ready, the
three of us crept toward the hangar spreading out, Jackson and Corey moving away from me to the right. I
reached the wall near the open side and put my back to it,
standing silently, listening for any small sound that would
convey a threat. *Well, here goes.* I cocked the hammer
back on the big Smith, something I rarely did—way too
easy to get startled and accidently shoot something you
don't intend to with the light trigger pull—but then I was
already scared shitless so I figured what the hell? I spun
around the corner, swinging the barrel of my revolver

first one way then the other swiftly. After a quick glance inside to confirm that I was in no immediate danger from within, I turned my attention to the surrounding sage on my side of the exterior and spun that way, repeating the movements with my weapon, should anything come at me from behind. *Clear*.

At that moment Jackson and Corey burst through the doorway of the hangar, Jackson covering right and Corey left.

"Clear!" Corey said

"Clear!" Jackson repeated.

CHAPTER 28

MISSING

The meager contents of the hanger looked the same to me. The gear we had brought with us lay strewn on the floor where we had placed it the previous evening in our haste to bed down. Smoke drifted up from the ashes of the fire, now scattered around. Even the small lantern, still sitting upright, continued to glow. Corey and Jackson moved to the center of the hangar.

"Where the hell is Kimber's body?" Corey asked.

"I was wondering that myself." I'd immediately noticed the river guide's corpse was missing as I'd spun around the corner of the wall. A foot wide smear of dried blood led from the spot where Kimber had fallen to the open side of the hanger.

Jackson walked the length of it looking down at the

long brownish smear. "Guys, you better come see this," he said as he stopped halfway to the edge of the concrete.

Corey and I crossed the short expanse of floor that separated us and came up behind Jackson. He pointed at the floor.

There, on the concrete, in the same rust-brown color of Kimber's dried blood, was the unmistakable fifteen-inch long track of the bear's hind paw.

"Guess we know now who survived the fight," Corey offered.

"Yeah, but where's our shooter?" Jackson asked. "His body isn't here either."

"Another good question," I replied.

"Blood spatter along the floor," Corey noted, pointing to the small circular shapes at spaced intervals on both sides of the long smear. As was usual for blood dripping from an open wound onto a hard surface, all had the spiked jagged edges from their impact with the concrete floor.

"From Kimber you think?" Jackson asked, already suspecting the answer—an answer he did *not* want to hear.

"No, not from Kimber." Corey shook his head and squatted to examine one of the drops more closely. "Bear was dragging him so his body wouldn't have been high enough off the floor to make these, not to mention he was dead before he hit the floor so his blood quit pumping almost instantly. Look at the difference in color." He pointed between the rust color of the drag smear and the dark burgundy of the droplets. "The drops are fresher. Totally different source."

I nodded my agreement as I bent down to get my own close look at one of the small serrated brown circles. The tiny spikes surrounding the outer edge of the droplet, were longer on the side closest to the open end of the hanger, indicating that whoever, or whatever, had been bleeding, it had been moving in that direction as the blood dripped from the wound.

"Let's see what we can find outside." I stood and raised my chin at the open side of the hangar. "But since we don't know who, or what, might be hanging around, let's stay together—standard triangle: two forward, one back to cover." The three of us spread out with Jackson and myself forward. Corey held back about five feet to cover our advance. Together we began to walk slowly toward the open side of the hangar. As if on cue, all three of our weapons came up, barrels pointed ahead of us.

CHAPTER 29

REMAINS

O ver here," Corey called, his voice only slightly raised.

We were now spread ten yards apart, so it wasn't necessary for him to shout his discovery of John Kimber's remains. Jackson and I both turned in his direction.

"Holy Mary Mother and Joseph!" Jackson exclaimed as the three of us gazed down upon what was left of the river guide. Having witnessed a lot of death by violent means in my life, I was hardened to the sight of a severely damaged human body, but looking at Kimber's mutilated corpse still made me wince. Blood had saturated the dirt surrounding the body, and several large paw prints were clearly visible in still soft mixture.

"He's looked better," Corey stated flatly. "Bad way to go if you're still alive—when something starts to eat you, I mean. He's lucky he was already dead."

I shook my head. "That's a fact." I picked up a near-by stick and poked at the man's shredded carcass. "Doesn't look like the bear ate any of him, just ripped him apart."

Muscle, sinew, and flesh had been ripped away from nearly every part of the body, exposing skeletal bone. Even the flesh from the skull and face was shredded like so much paper. The discolored hole that was the fatal bullet wound was visible in the exposed bone of the skull above Kimber's eye. Had we not known it was him by the tattered remains of his clothing, what remained of the guide would have been unrecognizable as the person we'd spent the past couple of days with.

"That was one truly pissed off animal." Corey raised his chin in the direction of the tracks leading away from the corpse. "Tracks lead off to the South."

"Waste of good leader," I mused.

"Huh?" Jackson asked.

"Corey's patch job on Kimber's bullet wound," I replied referring to the fine suturing Corey had done, using the fishing line. That wound was now nowhere to be seen in the mess that had once been Kimber's side.

"Humph!" Corey snorted. "No shit."

"Shouldn't we look for his wallet or something? You know, to take back with us?" Jackson asked.

"You can poke through that mess, if you want to." I shook my head. "Me? I'll pass. There's gonna be plenty of people here at some point to investigate all this shit. Let them do it."

"Should we bury him?" Jackson continued.

"Fuck that," Corey exclaimed. "I didn't even like the guy."

It suddenly dawned on me that we had been so focused on the remains we had not bothered to keep track of our surroundings. I silently chastised myself for the oversight and put my head back on a swivel again. "We need to police up the rest of our stuff and beat feet outta here," I told them both. "Odds are, that bear is still around. They usually don't go far from a kill. We need to assume he's wounded and, if so, he'll be more dangerous than before, if that's even possible. Just for kicks, Daryl, take one last look at the radio in the plane."

Jackson nodded but continued to press about Kimber. "We gotta at least say something over him."

No one move or spoke for a few seconds.

Exasperated, I finally nodded. "Oh, hell, if it'll get us moving any quicker, I'll do it." I turned back toward the corpse. "Life is short. Shorter for some than for others. There's accidents in life. John Kimber met with a bad one and it's gonna happen to all of us if we don't get the fuck outta here. Ashes to ashes, dust to dust—"

Corey broke in. "Amen, let's go." He immediately turned toward the plane

"Very touching," Jackson said dryly, taking a final glance at the mess that had once been our river guide, then he too turned away.

"We're gonna need to tell someone about all this,"

Corey offered half-heartedly as he walked. "Not that they'll believe it. Hell, I don't believe it now and I've lived through it…well, so far, anyway."

"Humph," I mumbled as I turned toward the plane, thinking, *I just wonder if we will live through this.* For thirty minutes Corey and I stood guard, one on each side of the plane, while Jackson contorted himself in the small confines of the plane's cockpit on his back, muttering a stream of curses that would make a sailor blush. Finally, he crawled out and announced that there was no way the radio was fixable without the proper tools, and additional wire.

"Looks like we're walking outta here," I told them. "Let's get started."

Keeping a wary eye on the open side of the hangar, the three of us gathered up our remaining gear from inside. Ten minutes later, we were walking, one behind the other, packs on our backs. We crossed the plateau and started down the same access road we had hiked up only hours before in the rain. It seemed so long ago now. Corey was in the lead while I brought up the rear, once again constantly checking our back trail for any sign of danger from man or beast.

CHAPTER 30

GODS OF WAR

When he opened his eyes, Jospair saw that he was surrounded by large pine trees. The sun was fully up and the sounds of water tumbling over rocks was loud, so he knew he was lying next to a stream. He also knew he was injured, but not how badly. Jospair had been wounded in battle twice before and, thus, was no stranger to pain, but this was different. Nearly every part of his body screamed, and his thirst from shock and the adrenaline dump he'd experienced was overpowering. With great difficulty, he rolled over and slowly dragged himself into the flow of the tumbling water. This stream was one of many that were considered "seasonal," only running with water when rain or snow made its presence known in the high country. The previous evening's storm had raised the water level to knee deep, and the water ran clear and cold.

He laid his weapon on a rock next to him then cupped his hands, bringing the cool liquid to his lips. He drank until he thought his stomach would burst, then he splashed water on his face and neck repeatedly, washing away the mud and coagulated blood that had dried there. With his fingertips he examined his head and face. He could feel several deep puncture wounds in his scalp and forehead, as well as deep lacerations on the back of his neck. His right ear was partially torn away, but the good news, if there was any, was that the bleeding had stopped, for now.

Grimacing with the effort, he straightened his right leg into the flow, letting the water wash the blood from his torn right pants leg and the wounds beneath. He lifted his tattered clothing to look at the deep lacerations in his upper thigh. *You were very lucky, Jospair Yakif, that the femoral artery was not punctured*, he thought. He lifted his shirt to examine the torn flesh along his left ribcage, grunting with the pain the movement caused. Massive bruising and some smaller lacerations were visible there, He was sure that several of his ribs had been fractured. *How long have I been here?* he wondered. *How did I get here and, more importantly, why am I still alive?*

Jospair remembered firing the shot that killed the river guide and he would've killed the others immediately after had he not heard the roar behind him. He remembered spinning to face the largest, most ferocious animal he had ever seen and thinking how it's open jaws and the teeth within seemed to fill the sky. Although he couldn't remember actually pulling the trigger, he remembered the little carbine in his hands spitting fire over and over and then the bear was on him. After that, nothing. No matter how hard he tried, he couldn't remember how he got to this stream, or even at what point he'd passed out.

With the greatest of effort and a lot of painful grunting, Jospair climbed out of the stream and unbuttoned his bush-pants, letting them drop onto the ground around his ankles so as to more closely examine the damage to his leg. Several large puncture marks, obviously from the bear's canine teeth, were visible in his upper thigh. Blood still oozed from two of the deepest. "Why am I still alive?" he repeated his own question, out loud this time, as he plucked dry moss from a nearby tree trunk and stuffed it in the two holes that were still seeping blood, shutting off the flow. *Why didn't the bear finish me?*

Jospair couldn't know, of course, that several of the small .30 caliber bullets he'd fired had found their mark in the bears tough chest and neck muscles, one even striking the beast in the face. While not nearly powerful enough to kill the animal, the bullets had stung him. That coupled with the sudden unexpected commotion inside the hangar as the three other men shouted and fled had caught the bear by surprise. It was enough to make the animal momentarily turn his attention away from Jospair, just long enough for him to regain his footing and flee as the others had done.

Although Jospair remembered none of it, he had run in a state of primal terror out into the darkness and across the plateau until he too fell off one of the steeper edges of the escarpment, stumbling and rolling down the steep slope, where he slammed face first into the four-wheel-drive trail at the bottom. Crawling on his hands and knees across the trail and through the timber, he'd finally collapsed, injured and exhausted next to the stream, where he'd immediately passed out.

Jospair now noticed his pack ten feet away on dry ground. How the pack had stayed attached to him was a wonder, as was the fact that he had retained his weapon. He stood slowly, scooped up his carbine, then limped over to his pack. Removing a large first aid kit, he sat once again and used the contents to disinfect and treat his wounds as best he could. With that chore done, he greedily chewed and swallowed two protein bars as he looked through the remaining contents of his pack. He had enough food, and now water, to last him several days. He was glad his extra magazines and spare ammunition were still there. Removing the magazine from the carbine he refilled it with five cartridges from one of the boxes in his pack.

"So I shot you four times, my big hairy friend, eh?" Jospair said out loud to himself. He was sure all four bullets hit their mark. How could they not with the animal so close? "But did I kill you?" *Probably not*, he thought, *not enough gun.*

He knew the animal might die from his wounds later, of course, but at present it was probably still alive, wounded, and, thus, *more* dangerous than before. He had never seen such a creature and wished he knew more

about these large North American bears. It just never occurred to him to do any research on them before he came
to this wilderness. After all, who gets attacked by bears? *I
guess the answer is...me, and I survived.* He smiled at
that thought, but the movement of his face made him
wince and reminded him that his ear needed attention also.

Yes, Jospair had survived and, as a bonus, he had
killed the man he'd come to kill. It was unfortunate that
the others got away, but no matter. They didn't know him
or enough about him to be a threat at this point. He would
rest here for several hours then cut himself a crutch from
a pine bough and begin his trek out of this place. He
smiled at his good fortune as he stretched out on the forest floor to rest and heal. The gods of war had smiled on
him once again.

CHAPTER 31

BLIND

The bear didn't know why the world on his right side had gone dark. He couldn't understand the concept that he was now blind in his right eye. One of the bullets fired from the human's gun had torn across the front of his snout at an angle, losing most of its energy as it furrowed through the half-inch thick flesh and fur just behind his nose, yet still it retained enough power to destroy the bear's right eye as it came to rest in the back of the eye socket, against his thick skull. Four other bullets had struck the animal in the chest and neck, but all four we're stopped short of piercing anything vital by his heavy breastbone plate after penetrating only three inches into fur, heavy muscle, and fat. None of the wounds would prove fatal. The chest and neck wounds were annoying and stung the animal as he moved, but eventually the flesh would heal around the small copper and lead projectiles and the bear would not notice them. It was the eye wound that was causing him the most agony. Given enough time, even the injury to his eye would heal, though the blindness would be permanent. The *pain* from the eye wound was a different matter entirely and he sought relief from the agony.

It had actually been more the sudden blindness in his right eye, accompanied by pain that followed, and the scattering flames that had brought the bear up short in his attack on his hated enemy. The shouting of the other three humans was a contributing factor to a small degree as the bear did release the vise-like grip of his jaws on the his enemy's thigh to turn and face what he'd assumed was a new threat when the shouting started, but seeing the other men flee, the animal turned back to destroy his original target only to find that the man had fled also. The bear could have easily run him down—the tracking skills of his nose were not in the least bit damaged despite the bleeding groove across the top of his muzzle, but his skull ached terribly.

With the scent of human blood in his nostrils and the taste in his jaws, the bear screamed a howl of pain and rage then rushed into the hanger scattering the belongings that stank of the humans. He sank his three-inch long fangs into the prone dead body of Kimber, dragging him as if he were a child's doll out of the hangar by his shoulder into the sage where he proceeded to rip the man's body apart with his teeth and claws. This did nothing to ease the bear's pain, of course, but the physical effort it took to destroy the corpse and the unexplained satisfaction it gave him did release some of his pent-up anger.

In real agony now, the bear could only think of rubbing his face in the soft moist earth in an attempt to get some relief. This was of no help however, as scraping the injury in the dirt only increased the pain. Instinctively, the animal knew he needed to find water to help ease his pain and clean his wounds. The grizzly turned, stood on his hind legs, and put his nose into the air. Upon catching the scent of the stream, the animal moved across the plateau to the north, then over the edge, shuffling down-slope toward the water and relief. The bear finally crossed the four-wheel-drive trail, maneuvered through the trees, and waded into the shallow stream. Lying on his belly, he lowered his face into the running water, which cooled and soothed the fire in his face.

Three-quarters of a mile east, Jospair lay resting and nursing his wounds on the bank of the same stream.

Almost directly in between those two, three muddy, exhausted men, with packs on their backs, took their last few steps on the downhill slope of the dirt access road. As the three stepped out onto the four-wheel-drive trail, the sound of rushing water was clearly audible.

"Stream across the trail there in the trees somewhere," Corey said, though both Jackson and I had already heard it.

"Let's take a break for a few, eat, and drink and fill our camelbacks," I replied.

Corey nodded and moved into the trees, followed by

Jackson then me. I stopped just inside the tree line and stood silently listening and looking up and down the four-wheel-drive trail.

Jackson walked back to me and whispered, "What? You see something?"

After a pause, I shook my head. "Nothing, I guess. Thought I heard the sound of an engine but was probably just the wind in the trees. Let's go."

I motioned for him to catch up with Corey. Five minutes later, we dropped our packs and sat down next to the running water.

CHAPTER 32

ECHO

R omeo 16788 to dispatch," the BLM ranger driving the Ford Bronco said into the hand mic. One
of two rangers sitting in the front seat who had
been sent out to search for the missing Ryan Tafney, he'd
been busy struggling to control the four-wheel-drive Ford
as it slowly made its way over the rocks, shale, and gravel of Trail 79.

"Romeo 16788, this is dispatch. You are breaking
badly, copy?" the female dispatcher answered.

"Ten-four, dispatch. If you can copy, we have just
crossed Winter road and are proceeding up Trail 79. No
sign of 167. Any word on your end?"

"I have you Lima Charlie now 788. Negative. No
word and no hit on his pinger."

"Ten-four, dispatch. Proceeding North up Trail 79 from Winter road."

A stern male voice came on the air from the dispatch end. "Romeo 16788. Make your check-ins on time. You were late with that one."

The driver looked at his partner and rolled his eyes.

"You pissed off the boss," the other ranger told him.

The driver nodded. "Ten-four, boss. Fighting the rocks. Won't happen again." Then he repeated, "Proceeding north up Trail 79 from Winter road."

The female voice returned. "Ten-four, 788."

"Considering the circumstances, I'll probably get a letter in my file over that one," the ranger driving mumbled at the thought of being "counseled" over not following procedure.

"Mmmm-hmmmm," his partner replied in his best "Mommy" voice.

"Blow me," the driver fired back.

The ranger riding in the passenger seat made repeated calls on the radio in an attempt to contact the missing Tafney, to no avail. Both men kept a wary eye out for tracks leading off the trail, or broken brush or trees—anything that might indicate the missing ranger had driven off the trail by accident.

The ranger in the passenger seat looked down at the "topo" map in his lap then glanced up through the front windshield at the bluffs on the left side of the Bronco. "According to the map, we're getting fairly close to the airstrip up there," he said, jerking his chin at the bluffs.

The ranger driving just nodded his head in acknowledgement. The trail here was too narrow to drive around several large boulders. He was concentrating on powering over them without tearing a hole in the oil pan. The bottom of the Bronco thumped the gravel hard as one of the tires dropped off a rock, back down to the gravel.

"Shit, wish this damn thing had a skid plate," he said.

The engine revved and whined as the Bronco sped up and slowed down, navigating the rough terrain. The sound of the straining engine, echoing off the canyon walls, could be heard for a mile or more along the river canyon.

CHAPTER 33

THE CHARGE

There it is again. You heard that?" I said, cocking my head. "Sounds like an engine."

"I don't hear anything," Jackson replied. "'cept the water, that is."

Corey cocked his head and listened for a few seconds. "Nope, me neither."

I stood and cupped a hand behind each ear. Opening my mouth slightly, I turned my head slowly, first one direction, then the other, like some bazaar-looking radar.

"What *are* you doing?" Corey asked. "And what's with the open mouth?"

"Trick I learned in the army. Helps your ears work better. Now shush for a minute," I told them both. "Nope, gone now, but I'm pretty sure I heard an engine. You guys stay here where I can find you. I'm gonna walk up the road a little ways and see what I can see—or hear rather. Maybe we'll get lucky enough to stumble across someone with a ride and won't have to hike out of this place, after all."

I moved back through the trees to the four-wheel-drive trail and stopped to listen again. *Nope, nothing.* I walked another few yards north, paralleling the stream. I stopped for the second time. The sound was barely audible but was gaining in volume. *There! I knew I heard an engine goddammit.*

The faint sound drifted in and out of the trees, but it was the unmistakable of a straining engine, and it had to be a vehicle on the trail, coming our way. Had it been the motor of a boat on the river, which was only a quarter-mile away, the tone would have been a steady drone, not the ebb and flow of the sound I heard echoing off the canyon walls.

Seriously thinking, now, of the possibility of rescue, I moved even farther north. The sound seemed to be fading. *Shit, the noise must be coming from the south. I've been walking away from it.* I turned to walk back along the trail and immediately froze.

It was fortunate for most people that, during the course of their lives, they never had to endure stark, paralyzing, mind-numbing fear. I was talking real primal terror stuff. The kind of fear that shut down all rational thought processes. The kind of fear that was so strong it could override a human's instinctual fight-or-flight impulse and make them literally "frozen with fear." The kind of fear that could make someone unconsciously lose control of their bodily functions. *That* was the kind of fear that I was experiencing, at this very moment, for, you see, the injured grizzly had heard the sound of the engine also and had come out of the comfort of the water to investigate.

The behemoth now stood on his hind legs with his back partially to me, water dripping from his muddy fur, his nose in the air. Cognizant thought finally returned to me, fed by adrenaline. My heart was racing as thoughts flashed through my mind at incredible speed. *Shit. My .44 is in my holster, snapped down. Why don't I have it in my hand? Stupid! You knew it wasn't safe here. I've been careless and now I'm going to die for my carelessness. The pistol is perfectly capable of killing the bear, but he's only fifty feet away and, with his speed, I'll never be able to draw and fire with any accuracy before he's on me. I'm going to die right here, right now. He's going kill me and rip me apart just like Kimber.* It seemed an eternity of thought, but it was mere seconds as I waited for the bellow and the charge that would be the last thing I ever heard—the last thing I ever saw, but the charge never came. Momentarily confused, I finally realized why. *I'm downwind. He can't smell me.*

The bear was actually turning away from me now to face completely in the opposite direction. I could see his head clearly now. Half of it was covered with blood, flies circling his snout.

I quickly glanced at the ground, lest I step on a dry branch and give myself away, then back to the bear. Ever so slowly, so as not to make a sound, I sidestepped three feet to the large trunk of a downed tree and quickly knelt behind its cover. With my right thumb and forefinger I quietly unsnapped my holster and pulled the heavy weapon free with my right hand. It seemed to weigh twenty pounds, though its actual weight was only two and a half. My heart was pounding out of my chest and blood hissed in my ears. Suddenly everything seemed to go dark around me, the bear being the only thing I was aware of. It was as if the two of us were in a tunnel, he at one end, and me at the other. I heard no sound, except that of my own breathing. I had experienced this phenomenon before—both in combat in Vietnam, and as recent as a year ago in the southwest Texas desert. *How the hell did it come to this?* my mind screamed.

Extending my revolver in front of me with my left hand supporting its weight under the butt, I took a solid rest on the tree trunk. The bark was rough against the back of my left hand and, somewhere in the back of my mind, I knew I would pay the price for firing a weapon with such massive recoil with my hand pressed against the log, but the thought was only a fleeting one for I now felt nothing. I was in "the zone," total concentration on my weapon and the target. I didn't want to shoot unless forced to, but I was going to be ready, regardless. I slowly thumbed back the hammer. The double "click-click" as the cylinder rotated into place and the hammer locked back seemed as loud as two gunshots. I centered the orange ramp of the front sight between the white slotted blades of the rear sight, then lined both up with the area just behind the left shoulder of the standing animal. If I could punch the "Buffalo Bore" 270 grain jacketed hollow-point bullet into the bear's chest cavity from behind, missing the heavy bone and muscle of the shoulder, it would probably drop him—probably. Synapses in my brain began to fire and told the nerves in my right index finger to begin applying slow steady pressure to the trigger.

"Jason?" Corey's voice came from behind me and a bit off to the side.

My finger instantly relaxed, but I dared not move or take my eyes off the bear. Walking up the four-wheel-drive road, Corey was thirty feet behind me. He was able to see my back as I knelt in the small clearing just off the trail, but he couldn't see the bear from where he stood. I frantically waved my left hand behind me to get him to stop, but it was too late. The sound of his voice surprised the grizzly and it whirled. In seemingly one motion, the animal roared in its wounded rage, dropped to all four paws, and started for Corey at full speed, crashing through the brush and breaking down small trees like a semi-truck in its charge. To his credit Corey, did raise his revolver with only a second's hesitation and got off all six rounds. Again, as if in slow motion, I saw two puffs of dust rise from the bears left shoulder, but the short barrel of the Ruger just didn't allow the bullets to generate enough energy to slow, much less stop, the beast.

Corey dropped the pistol and ran for a large pine tree halfway between himself and the bear, but I could see he wasn't going to make it. The grizzly was up to full speed now, somewhere in the vicinity of thirty-five MPH and, even as adrenaline-pumped as Corey was, he was making thirteen MPH, at best. It was an equation of death, and the answer was a simple one to figure out. I had only seconds to find an alternate solution. The bear was still unaware of my presence as I suddenly realized he would pass within ten feet of me—almost broadside—a childishly easy shot had he been standing still, or even walking, but the raging animal was galloping flat out. His huge body—moving up and down, powered by those immense muscles—was covering the distance swiftly. He would be on Corey in mere seconds. I quickly shifted my body and, once again, placed my left hand under the rubber Pachmayer grips. Aligning the sights of the big Smith revolver at the spot where I anticipated the bear *would be* in two seconds, I prayed I was guessing correctly. It wasn't the best way to shoot at a moving target, but I was probably only going to get one shot off before the bear was on Corey, and I didn't trust myself "tracking" a target moving perpendicular to me this fast. Had I opted for that, I knew I would hit the bear *somewhere*, but it just as easily could be in the stomach or haunch as in the chest, and that wouldn't help either of us. My breathing was deep and fast now as the sound the bear created, as he crashed through the brush, seemed as loud as an approaching train.

Time once again stood still as I took one last deep breath, let half of it out, then held it. The silent black tunnel descended on me once again. My finger tightened on the trigger.

Aim small, hit small…aim small, hit small…NOW!

Now I could hear the ragged heavy "huffing" of the bear's breathing and smell the foul musty odor of his fur—he was *that* close. Foaming saliva flew in all directions from his jaws as he vaulted over the downed tree which concealed me. Just as the front edge of the brown fur on the animal's heaving chest touched the edge of my front sight, I squeezed the trigger.

Instantly, my heart sank as I heard only the loud metallic "CLICK!" of the hammer dropping onto the firing pin. *Oh my God, a misfire! I blew it and now Corey's dead,* my brain screamed at me. Then it suddenly felt as if someone had *punched* me in the center of the forehead. Yellow and orange fire blossomed from around the cylinder and leapt four feet out in front of the barrel. Two jets of white-hot flame shot upward from the Magna-port vents, all of which combined to produce flashbulb-like retina shadows floating around my eyeballs.

I heard no muzzle blast, initially, but my ears now rang like the bells of St. Mary's. My mind was struggling to come to grips with the assault on my senses from the massive flash and concussion.

Jackson would later tell me the blast of the big pistol firing echoed off the canyon walls up and down the river for miles.

"All I heard was a 'click,'" would be my reply.

CHAPTER 34

ON THE MOVE

B oom—oom—oom!"
Jackson wasn't the only one who'd been surprised by the echo of the .44 down the canyon.

Jospair immediately jumped to his feet. *That shot was close*, he thought. He swiftly threw his first aid kit, uneaten food, and canteen into the heavy brush nearby and took note of a nearby rock pile as a landmark, lest he not be able to find this spot again. Grabbing his extra ammunition and magazines from his pack, he moved quickly and quietly through the trees in the direction of the single shot, his carbine at the ready. Now his mind quickly worked through several scenarios, none of which made sense to him at this point.

Who shot and why? How many were there? Were they

the same fishermen I confronted in the hangar? Or is this some new player of which I am unaware? Deep in thought, he didn't see the tinder-dry, one-inch thick branch beneath his right foot and stepped on it with all his weight.

"*Snap!*" The noise of the branch breaking was unusually loud in the now quiet forest and a dead giveaway to his position. Jospair froze but the damage had already been done.

Jackson knew the only pistol that would have made the heavy booming report he'd just heard was Jason's big .44 Smith. He'd been moving toward the location of the shot when the branch snapped off to his right. He immediately dropped to one knee, watching the trees. *Whatever had made that noise was close—VERY close.* Using his hunter's experience, Jackson turned his head ever-so-slowly, making no sudden movements, his eyes examining every inch of nearby foliage. In under a minute, he spotted the silhouetted outline of a man standing slightly hunched and unmoving.

Jackson also spotted the outline of the small deadly carbine in the figure's hands. *Oh, shit. Not this guy again. Just my luck this asshole is still alive and, damn, he's right there.*

Now it was Jackson's turn to have a racing heart as he stared at the figure not thirty yards into the trees to his right and slightly ahead of him. Before he could decide what to do, the man moved forward silently and disappeared into the forest.

Jospair stood perfectly still for thirty seconds after

the branch had broken under his weight, but soon realized he was too exposed in the spot where he stood and decided to move into heavier cover. He crept forward thirty feet, making no noise, then again stopped to listen. After five full minutes, he was convinced the broken branch had given his location away to no one, so again he moved forward, stopping to listen and even to smell the air every few feet.

At one point he thought he's heard the slight sound of rustling in the trees to his left, *or was it just that of the rushing water in the creek?*

Jospair cautiously moved on.

Jackson knew he must find his two companions and warn them of the intruder's presence. He moved forward, angling to the left back toward the creek. *Okay, this guy is being cautious and moving slow.* Jackson's mind raced. *I'll backtrack to the creek and use its sound to cover mine and I'll get past him, then angle back to the trail and pick up Jason and Corey, or at least, hopefully, their trail.*

Parallel to the creek now and only a few feet from the rushing water, Jackson moved swiftly, confident that no one could hear his footfalls. The ground was still moist and his boots made no sound that would carry more than a few feet as he moved at a near trot along the bank.

Ten minutes at this pace brought him to a small alpine meadow that opened to his right. He decided this would be the spot to cut back to the trail. Turning away from the creek, he held to the far edge of the clearing next to the tree line, figuring it was safer than walking across the center of the open area.

The adjacent trees would also provide quick cover should he need to dart into them. Jackson was halfway across the clearing when I stood up from behind the downed tree thirty feet in front of him.

"Daryl," I said quietly, my voice shaky.

I saw him jump and raise the Glock in my direction, obviously startled at my sudden appearance. I raised my chin in the only form of greeting I was able to muster as both my hands were still gripped like a vise to the butt of my revolver. Both were shaking badly as the adrenalin bled out of my system. I opened my mouth to speak but Jackson quickly drew his left index finger to his pursed lips, then violently gestured a slashing motion back and forth across his throat with the same hand.

No sooner had he motioned me in this manner, than the sound of boots scraping on bark to his left startled him a second time. He swung the Glock in that direction only to see Corey emerge from behind the trunk of a large pine tree where he had taken what little shelter he could find from the bear's charge. Corey had already seen the gesture Jackson had made, so he attempted no conversation. Both men moved toward me at the far end of the clearing, Corey pausing to retrieve his Ruger from the dirt where it had fallen.

As they neared, both stopped to stare at the massive inert form laying on the forest floor in front of them. It looked as big as a small mountain.

CHAPTER 35

AGAIN

The 270-grain copper-jacketed bullet had jumped from the muzzle of the four-and-a-half-inch barrel of my .44 magnum surrounded by Hades's fire at just under 1400 feet per second, crossing the short distance from the muzzle to the bear in one thousandth of a second—about half a heartbeat. The bullet struck the animal just behind the left shoulder with no less than twelve hundred foot pounds of energy, instantly shattering the bear's left ribcage. As the bullet passed through the pulverized rib bones and side muscle, the diameter of the bullet expanded to just over .60 caliber, the lead core and the copper jacket expanding halfway back the bullet's length.

Well over a half-inch in diameter now and still spi-

raling, the bullet blew a three-inch hole in the bear's left
lung, exploding his heart as it continued through the animal's thirty-inch-thick chest cavity, exacting the same
damage to the right lung as it passed. The projectile then
penetrated the right rib cage, breaking ribs on that side in
the process. It rapidly lost its remaining energy, retaining
just enough to punch a large hole through the skin and fur
on the bear's right side, disappearing into the organic debris on the forest floor twenty feet beyond.

In the animal's enraged state, it felt no pain, just a
terrific impact in its left side. Blackness descended upon
the bear as it died in mid-stride, but the animal's mass
and forward momentum carried it another fifteen feet before the huge body collapsed with a tremendous thud in a
cloud of dust, pine needles, and dry branches.

I continued to kneel, not believing that I had just
made what any hunter would deem "the shot of a lifetime." I would've liked to think I could have repeated
such a shot at my leisure, but truth be told, it was, in actuality, a small amount of skill and a whole lot of luck
that allowed me to bring the raging animal down, saving
both our lives.

I stared through the brush at the furry heap, feeling
saddened somehow. Oh, I knew the animal had to be
killed, especially since it had already been wounded. It
was true that all of our lives had been in danger from
him, but it was we who had intruded into his domain, not
he into ours and, as a result, a magnificent animal was
now nothing more than a pile of dead flesh and bone.

Shaking these thoughts from my head, I stood.

Movement caught my eye and, for the first time, I noticed a small clearing to my left. Jackson raised first his Glock then his hand, recognizing me. He did the same to Corey as Corey emerged from behind a large pine. I started to call out to Jackson, but he silenced me with his alarmed gesturing. I walked toward him, as did Corey. When we were within a few feet of each other, Jackson spoke in a low tone.

"I'm sure I just saw our shooter from last night. That asshole survived somehow and he's headed this way," he said, pointing back through the timber.

"How far?" I asked, looking where he pointed.

"Not more than five minutes behind me," Jackson replied. "He must've heard your shot, same as I did, and he's coming to investigate. We need to split, right now."

Before I could answer, a loud voice emitted from the trees on the far side of the clearing. "So we meet again, eh?"

The three of us jumped at the unexpected voice then whirled in that direction. It was apparent that Jackson had underestimated the amount of head start he'd had as the killer stepped out of the tree line, his deadly little carbine leveled at us.

Oh shit, not again, I thought then quickly realized how different the circumstances were now as compared to last night in the hangar. The shooter was at least forty yards from us across the clearing and *we* had cover close at hand this time. I whispered out of the side of my mouth to my companions, "When I move, you guys dive for that downed tree."

The killer must've realized the circumstances had changed, also, for he began to edge closer to a large pine tree to his right. After two steps sideways, and without another word being said, he opened fire on us.

CHAPTER 36

FLANKED

With a few exceptions, high velocity bullets travel faster than the speed of sound. If you are unlucky enough to have them fired in your direction and they pass relatively close to you, a loud whining "buzz" sound can be heard, not unlike that of a very large, very angry insect. Of course, what you are hearing is the sound traveling *behind* the bullet, the little pellet of death having long since passed you by. However, when that whining buzz is accompanied by a loud "crack," the bullet has passed *very* close indeed— the "crack" being the noise of the sound barrier being broken, which can only be heard a couple feet away, due to the relatively small size of the bullet.

The three of us dove for the cover of the downed

tree. As we ducked down behind it, we heard a lot of the whining, buzzing, *and* cracking around us as the killer fired round after round in quick succession. Chunks of bark flew from the tree trunk that provided us cover as, a flurry of .30 caliber slugs dug deep into the wood. Without exposing ourselves, the three of us raised only our gun-hands over the trunk as we returned fire from our pistols in the general direction we had last seen the shooter. My return fire was relatively worthless, as anyone who has fired a .44 magnum revolver with one hand can attest to. I was repeatedly squeezing the trigger, simply hoping that the ultra-loud bark of the big revolver would at least worry our attacker.

Corey was in the same position with his short barreled .357. Of the three of us, Jackson was probably the biggest threat to our antagonist as he had more control over the .40 with one hand and more than six shots in his weapon.

"Loading," I shouted to the others as Jackson slowed his rate of fire, lest all three weapons be out of ammunition at the same time.

As I started firing again, it was Corey's turn. "Loading," he repeated.

Then Jackson in succession. "Loading."

"Hold it! Hold it! He's not firing!" I yelled above Corey's revolver banging away.

Total silence greeted us

"Think one of us hit him?" Jackson asked.

"I doubt it. Would be just dumb luck if we had. Why don't you stick your head up and see?" I taunted grimly.

"Yeeeah, I just might but I kinda' fuckin' doubt it," he snidely replied.

I quickly glanced at the trees and brush both to the left and right. The meadow clearing opened to the right. *No cover for him in that direction*, I thought as I turned my attention to the more heavily wooded left.

"He's gonna try to flank us to the left," I told the others.

"How do you know that?" Corey asked.

"Because that's what I'd do. No cover on this side." I jerked my head in the direction of the clearing.

"If he gets sideways to us, our shit is weak," Jackson said, using a term I hadn't heard since my army days.

"That's a fact," I said rapidly. "We gotta move while he's moving. Across the meadow to the far tree line in one fast dash. Zigzag but not too wide—three second in-intervals. Dump your packs but keep your ammo *and* your camelbacks. We're gonna need the water. Daryl, you first. I'll cover. Then you, Corey. When you get to the trees, turn and cover my run. Ready?"

They both nodded as their packs hit the ground. Both were breathing fast and labored now, their bodies pumped for the umpteenth time with adrenaline.

I moved out of their way, dumped my pack, pointed my revolver at the trees behind them, and simply said, "Move."

Jackson sprinted out from behind the cover of the log, zigzagging back and forth, his legs pumping. I fired twice. "BOOM! BOOM!"

Without taking my eyes off the forest area I was

watching, I counted out loud, "One…two…three, go!"

Corey jumped up and was gone. I fired again and suddenly felt very alone and vulnerable as I silently counted to myself. *One…two…three.*

My boots kicked up dust as my sixty-year-old legs drove me across the open space toward the safety of the trees. My breath came in rapid gasps as my lungs tried to take in enough oxygen to power my body through the exertion at this altitude.

"BUZZ-CRACK! BUZZ CRACK!"

I instinctively ducked my head as I recognized the sound of bullets narrowly missing me. I was fifteen feet from the safety of the trees, running as hard as my legs would carry me, when something slammed into my back spinning me to the ground. Jackson's Glock barked four times as Corey broke from the tree line toward me. I was already regaining my feet when he grabbed my arm and we both dived the final five feet to safety behind two separate solid pine tree trunks only a few feet apart.

"Jason, you hit?" Corey asked urgently.

"Shit, not sure. My back is all wet and it must've been a bullet that knocked me down. Doesn't hurt yet, though." But I knew that was very normal with gunshot wounds. My brain just hadn't registered the damage and the pain that would accompany it in a few moments. Corey stood, fired two shots from behind his tree at an unseen target then dived for *my* tree. Jackson's Glock continued to bark every few seconds.

"Roll over and let me take a look, but stay low," Corey commanded.

As if I needed a reminder, two more carbine bullets sliced chunks of bark from the edge of the pine just over our heads, scattering bark dust on us.

"Guy's a good fucking shot," I said, as I rolled onto my stomach, closing my eyes and gritting my teeth against the pain that I was sure would come. When it didn't I opened them again.

Corey ducked and gave me a grim smile as another bullet slammed into the tree above us. "Getting shot seems to be a habit with you, it would seem," he said, smiling grimly.

I cocked an eyebrow at him. "My getting shot is funny to you?"

"Relax, you ain't' hurt." He drew his knife, shaking his head. "Man, today you gotta be the luckiest motherfucker in the world—hold still," he commanded as he cut the straps that held my Camelback. "Check it out." He flipped the empty water pouch onto the ground next to me. "Hole in both edges—one going in and one coming out. Went clean through sideways. That must've been what spun you around."

Just then two of the killer's bullets whacked into the ground next to the Camelback. While he couldn't see us or the pouch itself, he'd obviously noticed the motion of the pouch being tossed. It was a stark reminder, as was the continued pop-pop-popping of Jackson's Glock, that this was not the time to sit and ponder my good fortune.

I gained my feet behind the cover of the tree and called out to Jackson, "Can you see him, Daryl?"

"Not really," he replied. "I've seen his muzzle flash a

couple times but every time I find a new place to peek from, the cocksucker shoots at me, and he's damn good. Last time I peeked, he damn near shot me in the face. I've worried him a couple times, though. Asshole's got a lot of ammo."

"More than us, I'm sure. How you doing?"

"I'm getting low."

I looked at Corey and he nodded his response. "Yeah, we are, too." The lengthy conversation drew more fire from the woods. Nine shots in rapid succession ripped bark from the trees around us. "We gotta get outta here or this guy is gonna clean our clocks," I said, more to myself than Corey.

He nodded and pointed to the trees behind us. "We could get to the four-wheel-drive trail through there."

"Not sure how much good that'll do us." I shook my head. "It's much more open up there. He'll know we pulled out as soon as we stop firing and, if he hustles through the trees, he'll catch us on the open trail or hillside. We'll be truly fucked then, because *he'll* still be in the cover of the trees."

Two bullets whizzed by us. "BUZZ-CRACK! BUZZ-CRACK!" Both of us instinctively, yet uselessly, ducked our heads. "*Goddammit*," I blurted, as I once again fell to my stomach.

"Any suggestions," Corey asked as he fired two more rounds from his prone position at the base of the trunk. I stuck my hand out from behind the tree and fired three times also—the deep "BOOM!" of the .44 sounding very different from the other weapons.

Corey raised his revolver again, but I waved him off.

"Save your ammo," I told him. "We can't hit shit from here. Only way I see it, we're gonna have to try to flank him and kill him before he does the same to us." I spoke in a voice just above a whisper. "Daryl, can you hear me?" I saw his thumbs up from behind his tree, the movement immediately drawing fire. Continuing in the low tone, I told Jackson, "Corey and I are going to try to flank him. I need you to keep popping rounds at him occasionally to keep him focused on this position, but don't run yourself out of ammo."

"Got it," came the low reply, followed by the "POP! POP!" of the Glock in his hand.

I swung open the cylinder of my revolver, ejecting three empty casings and loading three fresh one. Corey followed suit. I pursed my lips and blew large chunks of sage and dirt from the revolver, where they had lodged during my fall.

Keeping my voice low, I said, "We're gonna low crawl that way." I pointed out to both men the path I wanted to follow. "When we're out of his line of sight, we'll stand and work our way around to the left. Hopefully, this asshole will keep firing at Daryl's tree and we'll be able to locate him."

"And what if he doesn't?" Corey asked as he reloaded his revolver. "What if he moves toward Daryl and figures out what we're doing, or sees us or hears us or some shit? This guy's no dummy."

"Well then, the odds are, that your kids are going to be calling someone else 'Daddy' and Sonya's gonna have to find herself a new ol' man," I whispered as I crawled off through the pine needles on my stomach.

"Thanks for that rousing pep talk, Jason," Corey mumbled as he slithered behind me. "With a positive attitude like that, how can we lose?" he said quietly to himself.

CHAPTER 37

FUSILLADE

Five minutes had passed since the two rangers had heard the single nearby gunshot off to the left in the forest and braked their four-wheel-drive Ford Bronco to a halt.

"Hunter?" said his partner.

"Poacher, most likely. Nothing in season that I know about and, if it was just a recreational shooter, he would have fired more than one shot by now." The ranger driving cocked his head as he shut off the engine and rolled his window down all the way. "Pretty close," he said, looking out into the trees, resting his hand on the butt of his sidearm.

"Check it out?" his partner asked.

"No doubt."

Both doors opened and the men stepped onto the rocky four-wheel-drive trail. The men stretched their muscles from the hours in a rough-riding truck. One adjusted his gun belt and was about to speak when a fusillade of gunfire broke out from the same general direction as the first shot. It was obvious to both that several different weapons were in use. The shots were in such close proximity, that both rangers ducked and took cover behind their vehicle, not knowing whether or not *they* were the target. Several minutes passed before the rate of fire died away into spaced shots from each of the four weapons they had identified so far, each muzzle blast distinctively different.

"I think whoever it is, is shooting at each other," the senior of the two said.

"How can you tell?"

Listening carefully to the shots now, the senior ranger said, "Listen.—As soon as there are shots from that one higher-pitched gun, the other two or three respond."

"Is that louder one a rifle of some type?" the younger man asked, peering over the hood.

His older partner jerked him back. "*Never* look over the top of your cover. Always look around one end or the other. Makes your silhouette harder to spot." He paused a moment. "Hard to say, 'bout the rifle, I mean. Doesn't really sound like a rifle, though. I think they all might be pistols. One of them, I'm sure, is a Glock—sounds just like the ones at the range. Could be wrong, of course, with the trees and brush distorting the sound, but I don't think I am."

"Shit, that loud one sounds like a fuckin' cannon!"

"Shhhh." The older man held up his hand. "Two of the guns have stopped firing."

"What do you think that means?"

"Well, if they *are* shooting at each other, then two are either out of ammo or dead."

"Hopefully the latter, if we're gonna do what I think we're gonna do?" the younger ranger retorted.

"Yup, we're going in there." The older man nodded toward the trees. He was obviously the more experienced "senior" ranger of the two. "Get the M-4 and the shotgun outta the truck and grab as much ammo out of the back as we can carry. I'll call it in!"

Without exposing himself, the younger ranger opened the passenger door, handed the older ranger the microphone, then retrieved the long guns from the cab. The older of the two conversed with his dispatcher then scuttled around to the rear of the vehicle and retrieved two olive-green ammo cans from the rear cargo area. Both men crammed as many magazines loaded with .223 caliber "green tip" ammunition and twelve-gauge 00 buckshot shells into two camouflage day packs as would fit.

The younger man held out both long guns. "Which one you want?"

"I'll take the shotgun and lead out. You stay back and cover me with the M-4, and be careful where you point that damn thing. I'm too close to retirement to get shot today, from the front *or* the back."

Both men moved around the front grill of the Ford

and into the trees in a low crouch, slowly heading toward the now-sporadic gunfire.

As it turned out, these two rangers weren't the only lawmen zeroing in on the sound of the gunfire. White water, splashing high on both sides of the bow of the speeding twenty-three-foot aluminum boat, covered most of a large star decal and logo beneath it which read *Garfield County Sheriff's Department.*

However, the flashing blue lights mounted on the top of the windscreen frame, not to mention the gold-colored reflection off the badges pinned to tan shirts, made it clear that the two armed men riding to the sounds of the gunshots were sheriff's deputies.

The radio transmission from the two-man ranger unit about shots being fired had indeed stirred up a hornet's nest of law enforcement activity. Sixty miles to the northwest, a blue and white US Customs and Border Protection helicopter made a U-turn in the sky, diverting from its normal patrol activity, and raced toward Trail 79 at full speed.

In Glasgow to the north, several additional sheriff's deputies, and even three game wardens, pointed their four-wheel-drive trucks south, mashing their accelerators to the floor.

Sitting behind his desk in the federal building in downtown Billings, Montana, FBI SAC James Nelson sat at his desk, working on the endless mountain of paperwork generated by the field agents he supervised.

The phone on his desk rang. Picking up the receiver, he spoke into the mouthpiece. "Nelson." Listening to the caller on the other end for a full minute without speaking, he finally asked a few questions concerning the manpower of local response, then simply said, "All right, keep me posted," and hung up.

He immediately dialed another number. "Hey, Connie, this is Jim Nelson, Is Frank in?" he asked, referring to FBI Special Agent Frank Smitheson. The two had been friends since the academy at Quantico, though Nelson had just recently been promoted and assigned to the Billings office.

A voice came on the other end of the line. "Smitheson."

"Frank? Jim. We may have something going on up north. Not sure quite what yet—may be something, may be nothing. There's a BLM ranger missing up there and now the two rangers they sent to look for him are reporting gunfire in the area. Nelson paused as the man on the other end of the line spoke.

"Hell, everyone up there has a gun and they all shoot stuff," Smitheson told his boss.

"Yeah, I know, every cowboy and shit-kicker up there has a gun and shoots at shit, but evidently the ranger reporting it was pretty excited and their dispatcher said it sounded like a war going on in the background."

"Are the rangers involved in the shootout?"

"No, as I understand it, they themselves are not involved in any gunfight at this time, just investigating the shots. Couple of local boat deputies are enroute on the river also."

"What river?"

"The Missouri River, of course."

"I thought the Missouri River was in Missouri."

"Oh, you did, did you? You lived in New York too long, buddy. Go buy a geography book and expand your horizons, will ya?"

Smitheson snorted.

"Okay. Listen," Nelson continued. "We probably won't have to get involved but I wanted to give you a heads up, just in case, since you're the sweet soul I'll be sending up there if this pile of shit lands in our lap."

"So where is this place?"

"I don't know, some remote place up north called Trail 79. Better alert any forensic guys you might want to take with you." The SAC tapped his pen one the desk, thinking, then continued. "Shit, I better alert HRT and pull a chopper crew together also, just in case."

The voice on the other end of the line began to voice his displeasure at the prospect of hiking around the remote Montana mountains, but Nelson cut him off. "Yeah? Well, complain to your union."

"Nice. Thanks a lot."

"Uh huh. Your welcome, Frank, and I love you too," Nelson said as he hit the disconnect then dialed two additional numbers, speaking briefly to men on the other end of those two lines. When the short conversations ended, the SAC dropped the receiver back into its cradle. Satisfied that the men under his command were prepared, he returned to his paperwork. While his men may have been prepared for what came next, SAC James Nelson was most definitely not.

CHAPTER 38

HIT

Jospair had not stayed alive in the war-torn hell of Serbia by being stupid, and it didn't take him long to realize that not only had the rate of fire being returned in his general direction had slackened, but now there was only one weapon firing when there should have been three. *Out of ammunition? Or hit maybe?* he wondered as he fired three more shots at the sole remaining man behind the tree. Either could be the case, but Jospair knew he could not chance making that assumption. If the men behind the other two guns were not dead or wounded, and they had *not* run out of ammunition, then it could only mean one thing—they were trying to work their way behind him. He tried to remember how long it had been since either of the other two weapons had fired. *It*

couldn't have been more than a few minutes, he thought.
How close could they be by now?

Jospair raised up slightly, in an attempt to get a better
view of the most likely avenue this new threat might
come from, and was immediately slammed backward to
the ground by a .40 caliber hollow-point bullet from his
enemy's gun. It entered his left shoulder, breaking his left
collarbone before it exited through the flesh of his back
just above his scapula. He lay there stunned for just a
moment. He'd been shot before, and the realization of
what had happened came swiftly. He knew he had to get
the bleeding stopped. Grabbing his combat knife, he cut
two large pieces of cloth from the tail of his shirt, feeling
for both bullet holes with his finger. Fortunately his right
arm was long enough to allow him to reach the damage in
his back. Jospair stuffed the cloth pieces in each hole,
then tore off several more pieces and stuffed them in each
hole. The pain was so intense he wanted to cry out but
immediately gritted his teeth to silence himself. Although
his lower left arm and hand were still useable, his left
shoulder would support no weight, making his left arm,
for the most part, useless to him now.

Still crouched behind the cover of a brush covered
tree stump, Jospair removed his belt and used it to form a
crude sling for his arm, then lengthened the carry sling of
his carbine so it would hang and be supported by his
good right shoulder, where he could fire it from the hip
with his right hand. It wasn't the best arrangement, but it
would keep him in the fight. Replacing the magazine in
the rifle with one of the full ones in his pants pockets,

Jospair picked up the carbine and fired two more shots in the general direction of the lone shooter, then scooped up his knife and water bottle making his way noisily through the brush to his right.

CHAPTER 39

ANTS

It was pure coincidence that Jackson had been looking directly at the tree stump the killer was using as cover when the man fired three shots in close succession "POP! POP! POP!"

The muzzle flashes were bright orange against the contrast of the green foliage surrounding the stump. Up until then, Jackson had known the man had to be somewhere in that general area but he didn't know exactly where. With his ammunition getting low, Jackson wasn't just tossing out stray shots anymore. He held his fire and, although it was risky, he kept his head up, hoping he might get lucky. The three muzzle flashes were just what Jackson was hoping to see as he leaned out for a look. He was tired of this cat and mouse game that accomplished nothing, except biding time until he ran out of ammunition. This time, he ignored the "BUZZ-CRACK!" of the bullets as they whizzed by his head and didn't duck back behind the tree. Instead, he put his sights slightly just above the spot where he'd seen the flashes and waited, holding half a breath. *There! Something's moving near the top edge of the stump.* Jackson squeezed the trigger then heard the sound he'd heard many times before when on a successful hunt. It was the hollow "THUMP!" of a bullet striking flesh, followed instantly by a muted "Unh!"

I hit you, didn't I, you prick? The question in Jackson's mind was rhetorical, for he knew the answer. There were no answering shots this time and, after two minutes had passed, Jackson stepped out from behind the tree, smiling at both his skill and the luck—mostly the luck—it had taken to hit such a small target with a pistol at the 40-plus-yard range. With the Glock extended in front of him, he took two tentative steps toward the stump when two more shots rang out from behind it. He nose-dived into the dirt. Shocked, his mind raced. *Fuck, I know I hit that asshole.* Suddenly he heard brush cracking and breaking under foot near the stump, then silence. Jackson lay in the dirt for another two minutes before slowly raising up for a look.

Seeing and hearing nothing, he moved swiftly across the open ground, zigzagging from bush to bush, using the sparse sage for concealment. He finally reached a vantage point where he could see behind the stump. The shooter was gone but Jackson had been right about his hit.

Crouching and keeping a wary eye on his surroundings, he moved behind the stump and looked down at the spent .30 caliber casings at his feet. He saw the blood smeared on the stump and surrounding sage. There was also a large pool of blood slowly soaking into the dirt.

"I knew I hit him. There's no mistaking that sound," Jackson said quietly to the ants that were already working at the edges of the red stain. Attracted by the coppery smell, they were eating and carrying away minuscule amounts of the protein-rich liquid. He knelt and examined the ground closely. Several broken branches, a single boot track, and three drops of blood pointed out the direction the shooter had taken as he'd fled into the trees. It took Jackson only a few seconds to realize the shooter's path would intersect Jason and Corey's, if it hadn't already.

Shit! This is like a nightmare that you just can't wake up from, Jackson thought as he began to follow the shooter's trail.

CHAPTER 40

SILENCE

My right palm went up as I knelt down on one knee, cocking my head. Corey moved silently up along my right side.

We'd been lucky. The ground over which we'd been creeping was bare of any dry brush and the soil itself was moist. The combination allowed us to pass through this area of the forest as silently as any creature could. Corey leaned close to whisper but my index finger went immediately to my lips, silencing him. I pointed to my ear then to the trees ahead of us. He immediately understood the meaning—that I'd heard something to our front. Both of us strained to catch any sound.

Finally, the sound came to us again. It was the soft "crunch" of twigs under a boot moving slowly, cautiously, accompanied by the "swish" of cloth rubbing against foliage. Soon there was a soft "clink" that I instantly recognized as the buckle of a rifle sling hitting the stock. These were sounds from my haunted past—the sounds of an armed man moving slowly and quietly in my direction, intending to do me harm. Looking at Corey, I held up two fingers then made a walking motion with them. Corey nodded that he understood and agreed that there were two sets of boots coming toward us. I pointed at Corey's chest then to the forest on my right, made the walking fingers again, held up all five fingers, closed my fist, and repeated the five-finger gesture.

Again he nodded, turned, silently moved out ten yards to my right, and took cover behind a tree.

I lay prone on my belly, my arms extending the big revolver, the front sight now centered on the trees and brush to my front. Cover was sparse where I lay, but I had a clear view of the approach and a good field of fire. I knew I was all but invisible, lying on the ground as I was, as long as I remained motionless. Ever so slowly, so as not to make any sudden movements that might catch the eye of a potential enemy, I turned my head in Corey's direction. He had found cover behind a large tree and gave me a thumbs up. We were ready and waiting for whoever was coming.

The minutes ticked by. My heart pounded as it had so many times in these past days. Once again, we were playing a deadly version of "hide and seek," and it was beginning to take its toll on all of us. My mind wandered for a moment. *How long would our luck hold o—there!*

Movement to my front snapped me back to the moment. The outlines of two men in a crouch, moving slowly, were visible only for a few seconds as they made their way through the trees—one several feet behind the other. Both were carrying long guns, angling more in Cory's direction than mine. Like wisps of smoke, I would see them for just a second or two, then they were gone again hidden by the forest. They were close now. I could clearly hear the soft crunching of pine needles beneath their boots as the two carefully placed their feet before putting their full weight down. *These guys seem to know what they are about,* I thought uncomfortably, *but who the hell are they?*

I cocked the hammer back on my .44. The cylinder rotated and the hammer locked back with its usual double "click-click."

Sunlight streamed between the overhead branches, casting beams of light on a small clearing between the trees. Maybe the two men heard the sound of my revolver cocking, or simply sensed something was wrong. They froze as they stepped into the open area, probably not realizing how fully visible they were in the broken beams of directed light. Their weapons were at the ready. They looked first one way, then the other. *Damn foolish place to stop,* I thought as I centered my sights on the upper torso of the first man. He carried what looked like a shotgun. The deadliest of the two weapons at this range.

My right index finger slid off the side of the revolver's frame and into the trigger guard. Just as my finger touched the trigger, one of the beams of sunlight reflected off of a piece of gold metal above the man's left breast pocket. I instantly relaxed. Both men wore the gold badges of cops—BLM rangers to be more accurate. An audible sigh of relief escaped my lips as my chin dropped onto my outstretched bicep. I took a few seconds to consider the least lethal way to announce my presence, knowing better than to jump up, waving a pistol, and yelling, "Hey," in front of these two armed and obviously apprehensive souls.

Upon later reflection, I realized that this brief pause undoubtedly saved my life, for just as I opened my mouth to announce my presence, came the loud, triple "POP! POP! POP!" of three shots fired not five yards from where I lay. My head whipped around.

Maybe it was my position on the ground that kept me from hearing the approach of this *third* set of boots, or maybe I'd been concentrating so hard on my initial contact with these two nervous lawmen that I'd ignored the fact that there was still a very bad man around, or maybe—just maybe—I was getting old and my senses weren't what they were at a younger age. Whatever the reason, the appearance of Kimber's killer stepping out from behind a tree mere feet from where I lay caught me totally by surprise. The man's left shoulder was a bloody mess and that deadly little "Enforcer" carbine in his right hand was again spitting fire. I flinched involuntarily as the shots from behind continued to flay the tree all around Corey.

Bark and moss flew from the sides of the tree as Corey desperately tried to dive to the opposite side of the trunk. I couldn't tell from where I lay if he'd been hit, but to his credit he got two shots off with his Ruger in mid-dive, before disappearing from my view. I saw dust fly from the shooter's shirt and saw him stagger under the impact of at least one hit from Corey's small magnum revolver, though it didn't seem to have much, if any, effect.

Both rangers spun to face the sound of the shots, the motion attracting the attention of the killer, who had not noticed the two men until they moved. Both dived for cover themselves as the killer turned his carbine on them in a literal hail of bullets. They fired wildly in return, neither one hitting their mark. I could see shredded leaves and pine needles rain down on the killer as 00-sized buckshot and .223 caliber bullets of the M-4 shredded branches high over his head.

I jumped up to one knee, swinging my revolver in the killer's direction. I saw his eyes widen in surprise at my sudden appearance from seemingly out of nowhere. He smiled then as the ugly black snout of his carbine swung my way now, still spitting fire and spewing those deadly .30 caliber lead pellets, one after another.

Here came the molasses again—my arms bringing up my revolver way too slowly. I was going to lose this fatal race. The muzzle of the carbine was centered on me a full second before my front sight finally found its place in the center of his chest.

I couldn't understand why he hadn't fired, then I noticed that his eyes were wide with a look of total shock and surprise. Blood erupted in a geyser toward me from

his sternum and his stomach. The guy took two stagger-
ing steps toward me as I pulled the trigger on my big
Smith.

His feet came completely off the ground as he was
first pitched forward by the two shots he'd taken in the
back then thrown backward by the impact of the bullet
from my revolver. His human bone and tissue might as
well have been cardboard for all the resistance it offered
the 270 grain "bear-load" from my magnum. The ballistic
bubble of air surrounding the .44 caliber bullet as it penetrated his chest cavity pulverized his sternum, left lung,
and heart, blowing pieces of all three, along with a large
section of his shattered spine, in a tremendous spray of
blood and tissue out the three inch exit hole in his back,
the bullet hardly slowing as it spun off into the forest.

A man with no conscience or compassion—a killer
who showed no mercy to anyone—now lay dead at Jackson's feet, his blood soaking into the forest floor. It had
all happened so fast that I hadn't been aware of Jackson's
presence until the killer had fallen. To now see him
standing twenty feet in front of me, his still smoking
Glock in his hand was a shock. He walked slowly forward until he was standing over the dead man, as silence
once again descended on the forest around us. I glanced
at the Glock now dangling loosely in the fingers of Jackson's right hand. The slide was locked back, the magazine empty.

It was then that I realized that the two shots that had
struck the killer in the back and had propelled him toward
me, leaving him with such a stunned and surprised look

on his face—those two shots that had undoubtedly saved my life—were the last two shots Jackson had in his Glock.

"Well, that was exciting I must say," Corey said dryly as he rose to his feet from behind the tree to join us. Jackson and I both jumped, startled by the sudden break in the stillness.

"You okay?" I asked him

"A little worse for wear, but yeah." He looked down at the large wet stain on the front of his pants. "Think I pissed myself, though."

"It happens." I turned my attention back to the dead man. "If it's any consolation, I think you hit him on the fly when you dove for the ground."

Corey nodded, looking down at the bloody, bullet-riddled corpse. "Did I? Well, either way he's smokin' a turd in hell now."

CHAPTER 41

OLD FRIENDS

Freeze! Federal officers," came the shouted command from behind us.

A few seconds later, accompanied by some crashing through the brush and pine boughs, a similar command was repeated by the two newly arrived sheriff's deputies. There were four guns on us now, with four nervous fingers on triggers.

"Take it easy, fellas," I said evenly. "We're the good guys."

"Shut up," replied the older ranger. "Keep your mouth shut and don't you so much as twitch, or I'm gonna blow you to Mars! Very slowly now, place your weapons on the ground."

The three of us dropped our pistols into the dirt.

"That's it, now extend your arms straight out and turn your backs to me."

Again we complied.

"Kneel down, cross your ankles, and interlock your fingers behind your heads."

When the three of us were in this controlled position, the two deputies walked forward, handcuffed us, then stood us up one by one and walked us back through the trees to the rangers' SUV, where we were unceremoniously crammed into the back seat.

"Jason," Corey whispered. "Shouldn't we tell them we're cops?"

"Not just yet." Corey looked at me with skepticism as I continued. "They'll figure it out when they get into our wallets. For now just dummy up and follow orders until they calm down some."

After a brief discussion between the four lawmen at the front bumper, it was decided that the two deputies would stay with the body, and the two rangers would take us up to the hangar. Both rangers climbed into the front seat, started the engine, and pointed the SUV up the incline of the airstrip access road. No sooner had the vehicle reached the top of the grade than the older man was on the radio, advising that no further assistance was needed and that three "suspects" were in custody. The ranger driving parked near the plane and the three of us were led into the hangar, ordered to sit on the floor, our backs leaning against the wall.

The younger of the two kept watch on us, while the older man walked back to their SUV and commenced what could only be described as a very long conversation on his satellite cellphone.

Two hours after the ranger completed his call, two black Euro copter EC153 helicopters flared for a landing near the back side of the hangar, throwing up dust, gravel, and sage in a great cloud. Both had the seal of the United States Department of Justice painted on their nose. Large white letters stenciled on the sides spelled out *FBI, HRT*. I immediately recognized the initials of the Hostage Rescue Team, having trained with them in the past when I was on my own department's Special Weapons and Tactics team. Out of the first helicopter to land poured seven well-armed men in black tactical jump suits, complete with body armor and Kevlar helmets, faces covered by balaclavas. The armed men spread out and established a secure perimeter surrounding the choppers. Only two men stepped from the other helicopter. Both wore suits and aviator style sunglasses. As the HRT men trained their weapons in a 360-degree circle, the two men in suits walked into the hangar, removing their sunglasses and stood over us.

The taller one spoke directly to me. "When I got the phone call and heard the name of one of the assholes who was in custody here for being involved in a gunfight with two BLM rangers in the backcountry of Montana, I said to myself that it just can't be." He turned to Jackson. "Then I was told the name of the second involved asshole and I knew I had to come see this dog and pony show for myself, just to see if it was true."

I looked up at the FBI man. "Well, actually, G-Man,

we were in a gunfight with the *real* asshole. The rangers showed up after the party was over. Hello, Duane. Bet you thought you'd never see me again."

"That was my hope, Jason." He looked at Jackson. "Daryl."

Jackson nodded at the FBI man. "Hello, Agent Johnson."

Turning to the older ranger standing behind him, the FBI man asked, "Ranger, where is the identification you took off of these men?"

"Right here, sir," the ranger replied as he handed over our driver's licenses and fishing licenses. "They each had these in their shirt pockets."

"Uh-huh." He waved the small documents away. "What about their wallets?"

"They told us their wallets were in their backpacks, sir." The ranger jerked his chin toward the back of their SUV in which they had thrown our packs. "But we didn't need them since they had their IDs on them."

Johnson closed his eyes, paused and shook his head, then looked at me. "You didn't tell them?"

I shrugged. "They didn't ask."

Turning, he said to the two rangers, "Find their wallets, please. Oh, and I want to see their weapons also."

The younger ranger walked to their vehicle, rummaged through our packs, and came back with three wallets.

"Bring their wallets to me," Johnson said.

The younger ranger walked over, carrying the three wallets and a small duffel which contained our weapons.

He placed the wallets on a rusted metal workbench that was bolted to the floor.

"Which one is yours, Jason?"

I nodded at a thick, worn, black leather wallet in the center of the three.

"Ranger, open the wallet in the center and tell me what you see."

The ranger complied with the FBI man's request. "Oh, shit," he mumbled.

In the center of the wallet, covered by a thin flap of leather, was a silver badge in the shape of a seven-point star. An official ID card bearing the likeness of me was opposite the badge under a clear plastic sheath.

"Tell me what the badge says, Ranger," the FBI man said.

"Er—um—it says 'Police Officer City of Vista California, Retired,' sir."

"Okay, now open that other brown wallet there—no the thick one—and tell me what that *badge*, the one I can *see* from here, says."

The young man reached for the wallet, as if it were a poisonous snake, and opened it. "California Department of Justice, Special Investigator."

Duane Johnson was not a happy man right now. "Remove their handcuffs, please."

Both rangers looked stunned. "Sir they didn't tell us—"

Johnson cut him off. "Do it now, Ranger."

The three of us stood, rubbing our wrists and stretching our legs. Agent Johnson extended his hand, first to

Corey, then to Jackson. "Daryl, I'd like to say good to see you again, but it's really not."

"Likewise," Jackson replied sheepishly.

Both rangers were baffled, not just at the verbal exchange, but at the handshakes.

Johnson reached into the satchel and removed the Ruger revolver and the Glock, examining each to make sure they were unloaded. He then held them up one at a time. Corey and Jackson acknowledged which belonged to whom.

When he pulled my Model 29 from the pouch, he whistled and looked at me. "Yours I take it." I nodded. "Should have figured," he snorted, placing all the weapons back in the duffle and handing it back to the ranger. "You'll get them back after we figure this mess out."

Looking around the hangar, then out across the plateau, he asked the rangers several questions about the scene below and who was securing it.

"The boat deputies agreed to stand by until we got someone else down there," the younger ranger replied.

Johnson nodded to the commander of the HRT team who was standing a few feet away. The ominous-looking black-clad figure walked over to two of his men who, after brief instructions, set off across the plateau and down the access trail at a jog, their tactical holsters and vests, filled with the tools of the trade, slapping against their bodies as they ran.

Johnson turned back to me and was about to speak when a third FBI helicopter roared overhead and flared for landing, noisily coming to rest on its skids, once again stirring up a maelstrom. This one carried an FBI forensic evidence response team. Simultaneously to their unloading, two sheriff's department four-wheel-drive SUVs crested the access trail on the far side of the plateau, followed closely by two additional BLM ranger Jeeps.

Johnson turned back to me with a frown. "This is going to turn into a circus here, real soon, Jason. The three of you need to tell me about all of this before the clowns and jugglers show up."

"Well, Duane, I hope you brought your sleeping bag and hiking boots. This is going to take a while, especially since we're gonna do a *lot* of walk and talk. Oh, and you're gonna have to drag the river also."

"Jesus Christ, Jason, it's 2015. The FBI doesn't 'drag' rivers anymore. Now it's all done by side-scan sonar—and just why would we need to do that?"

"Because I'm ninety-nine percent positive you'll find your missing ranger, or at least his vehicle, at the bottom of the Missouri, somewhere downstream from Sand Wash."

Johnson frowned and gazed out at the approaching vehicles then motioned for me to come closer. "You really do like to make trouble for me, Jason," he said quietly.

"How the hell did you come to be in Montana, Duane?"

Johnson paused for a moment, then without turning, reached into the side pocket of his coat for a pack of cigarettes. Placing one between his lips, he lit it and inhaled deeply, then slowly blew out the blue-white cloud of smoke. "Goddamn, that's good. Wife won't let me smoke at home, you know, so I have to sneak one when I can." There was another pause and another drag. "After your little wing-ding in Texas, I got promoted. Seems that surgeon's family had a friend that was a senator who dropped a dime to his golf buddy who happens to be the Bureau director—my boss, in case you're not following—about what a bang-up job I did recovering the good doctor's body. Thanks for that, by the way."

"Anytime."

"Anyway, the only two slots open for SAC were Anchorage and Billings. I chose Billings, or maybe I should say, my *wife* chose Billings." He finally turned toward me. "Now I'll ask *you* the same question."

I shrugged. "Hell, all I wanted was to go fishing, get in some male bonding, and all that shit."

Johnson stared at me for a long minute, reading my face and body language, then looked across the hangar at Jackson and Corey. Finally, he nodded. "Okay, I'll buy that. Let's take a walk so you can get to the rest of this fairy tale."

I smiled inwardly. He was good, I'd give him that. The FBI man was putting on his best "we're old friends" façade while, in actuality, breaking me away from my two companions so they could not hear what I was saying. Undoubtedly, he would question them separately and see if our stories were the same.

We walked around the plateau for nearly two hours while I recounted the events that had unfolded over the past three days. He examined the hangar, then the damaged plane, the bloodied sage and dirt, and of course the ravaged body of John Kimber, which was in the process of being photographed and picked at by half of the forensic team, the other half having already moved down the hillside to the carcass of the bear and the body of the killer. Finally, we stood overlooking the river. I pointed out the area of Sand Wash.

Johnson frowned. "First light, I'll have the sheriff's boat take us all upstream. I'll need to see where this whole thing started."

I nodded and rubbed the back of my neck. The razor's edge events of the last several days were starting to catch up to me.

"Do you need me to call your wives?" Johnson asked.

"Hell, no!" I replied. "We're not expected back for three more days. No sense worrying them for nothing."

He looked me up and down then shook his head. "It'll be dark soon. You look like shit, Jason. Go get some rest and have Jackson come talk to me—then Taggert. You know the drill, no exchanging stories beforehand."

I nodded and turned away, realizing how totally exhausted, sore, and generally beat up I really was. I entered the hangar and noticed that our packs, sleeping bags, and coats had been placed at one end. My companions had already rolled out all three sleeping mats and bags and were stretched out on theirs, napping. I kicked Jackson's boot sole.

"Yo, s'up," he asked sleepily.

"Fee-bee wants to talk to you guys. Daryl, you first,

then you, Corey." I flopped down on my bag as Jackson climbed to his feet, yawning.

"Where is he?"

"Out by the plane."

Those were the last words I spoke as my eyelids slammed shut. I slept long and hard, not moving even to climb inside my bag in the cool night air.

Just after dawn, the three of us were shaken from our exhausted slumbers by the FBI man.

"Drop you cocks and grab your socks!" Johnson did his best Drill Sergeant imitation. "Let's take a boat ride shall we?" he said, smiling with way too much energy for this early hour. "C'mon, c'mon, the day is wasting. Hot coffee waiting for you outside. A couple of the HRT guys are going with us to provide any security we might need."

I stood up and stretched out the stiffness in my muscles. As I stepped from the hangar, I yawned, then froze as my mouth stayed open in shock. What had once been the sage covered plain of the plateau had been converted into a large camp. Two large green MH-53 Army National-al Guard helicopters, affectionately known by those who flew them as "Jolly Green Giants," sat near the center of the plateau, their huge rotor blades drooping, seemingly almost touching the ground. Four olive drab colored "GP Medium" tents had been erected between the hanger and the choppers. Men and women in blue colored wind-breakers, with *FBI* stenciled on the back in bright yellow, hustled from tent to tent. No less than ten BLM ranger and sheriff's four-wheel-drive vehicles were now present. There was even a green HMMWV with bright red crosses painted on both doors and the hood, parked near the plane.

Duane Johnson pressed a hot cup of coffee into my hand.

"This all happen overnight?" I asked. "I must've been sleeping real hard not to have heard those big-ass helos come in."

"You were dead to the world. I came by to get another word from you but I just couldn't bring myself to wake you up. Let's go," he said as a second black HMMWV that I hadn't seen pulled up to take the four of us to the boat. The Hummer ate up the rough terrain as the FBI man handed me an eight-by-ten photograph of a man's face.

"Recognize him?" he asked, watching my face closely, looking for any clue I might be lying.

"Nope, should I?"

"This is the man the three of you shot to pieces yesterday."

"Never saw him before. Wouldn't know him, anyway—only time I saw him up close, he was shooting at me, so I wasn't paying much attention to what his face looked like." I handed the picture back.

Johnson showed the picture to Corey and Jackson, getting head shakes from both.

Johnson looked at the photo for a long moment then slipped it back in his satchel. "Got results on his prints from Interpol last night. Seems you guys may have done the justice system a favor. His name is—or was—Jospair Yakif, a former Serbian soldier turned enforcer for his mobster uncle. Wanted by Interpol for murder and by the new Serbian government for war crimes. This guy was a *very* bad man—total psychotic killer. Women, children— no conscience at all. Raped and tortured most of his victims before killing them—men, too. Seems he liked fucking men and boys as much as women and girls."

Johnson held up another photograph. "What about this guy?"

All three of us nodded. "That's our river guide John Kimber"

Jackson spoke first. "You gonna tell us he was wanted also?"

Johnson shook his head. "Not by us or any other law enforcement agency that we know of. So far it looks like he was a legit licensed guide and outfitter, but DEA was looking at him. They seem to think he was supplementing his income running marijuana up and down the river for one of the cartels. He probably had no direct cartel connection—just a sub-contractor, so to speak. Word is he had quite the gambling problem a while back and borrowed some money off of a loan shark in Vegas, then welshed on the loan. Guess who's money it was."

"The mobster uncle's," I offered.

"You guessed it." Johnson held up a surveillance photo of Jospair's uncle.

"You guy's gonna hook him?" I asked.

Johnson shook his head. "Oh, someone will, eventually, but not right now. Both ATF and the DEA have him under surveillance for some possible gun and dope smuggling activities in his beloved homeland. Our OCU is tapping him, trying for a RICO conviction, so he's under the microscope. Only a matter of time."

Twenty minutes later seven of us were in the sheriff's boat speeding upriver.

CHAPTER 42

CLEANING UP

By mid-morning, Duane Johnson had seen all he needed to see, both at our original campsite on the fishing stream and at Sand Wash. I'd shown him where we had first encountered the wounded Kimber, then it was back in the boat to the wash to look at the damage to Kimber's partially sunken boat. The wash was a hive of activity with the FBI's forensic team scurrying to and fro, taking photographs and collecting shell casings. The information Johnson was receiving on a regular basis, both in person here at Sand Wash and via his radio from the other field agents and his forensic people scattered across the plateau and the forest beneath the bluff, seemed to corroborate our stories.

When Johnson was satisfied that all was moving as it

should be with the investigation, he herded the three of us to the Hummer, instructing the driver to take us back to the hangar. Johnson himself climbed back into the sheriff's boat. A thirty-two-foot "Metal Shark" US Coastguard patrol boat, equipped with a side scan sonar ROV had just arrived on the scene and was slowly circling off shore awaiting instructions. After a brief meeting mid-river of both crafts to confirm the search area with the FBI man, the patrol boat lowered the ROV into the water and began a grid search of the river channel.

The three of us arrived back at the hangar and climbed out of the Hummer, returning to the make-shift FBI field headquarters now set up inside the hangar. Two hours later, Johnson joined us. Late in the day, he told us that the missing ranger's vehicle had been located a half mile downstream from Sand Wash in twenty-three feet of water.

The coastguard had put a rescue swimmer in the water and confirmed that Ranger Tafney's body was indeed inside, handcuffed to the interior. A chartered salvage and recovery barge was on its way from Fort Benton, but wouldn't arrive until the next morning.

Johnson pulled the three of us aside. "Okay, you three. It looks like everything you guys told us is on the level. I think I'm going to cut you lose, for now, but stay available. Is everyone just going home?"

"If I can get the hell out of here, I sure as hell am," Jackson said. "This has been enough excitement to last...well, you know."

"Really no other choice, is there?" Corey added.

Johnson looked at me. "What about you, Jason?"

"I don't know. Might hang around Buffalo for couple more weeks before we head south again."

"You're not going back to Texas again, are you?" the FBI man queried.

I shook my head. "Sonya and I are going to head down to Yuma for a while. I hear it's pretty nice down there this time of year."

Johnson nodded. "Well, I have your number so I can call you if I need to, I guess, but let me know where you end up, in case I need to talk to you again. Like I said, I'll be keeping your guns for a while for ballistics, but I'll personally see they get returned to all of you. You won't get the ammo back though. Speaking of that—" He looked at me. "No promises but I'll try to run interference for you on the killing of that bear with fish and wildlife, although that's one federal agency that even I don't like to cross—real assholes over there and they'll sure be looking to hang someone over killing an endangered species. By the way, my head forensic ballistic guy tells me that was one hell of a shot you made."

I shrugged. "Tell the fish and wildlife that I said the perp killed the bear. I'm sure the carcass has some .30 carbine holes in it," I told him.

Johnson looked skeptical and mused more to himself than to me. "They've got a couple of their agents on the way here now. They'll never believe it was killed by a .30 carbine, not with the size of the exit hole in the hide, but what the hell? With no bullet to trace, what can they prove." It wasn't a question.

I smiled at that. "First rule of police work, Agent Johnson. It's not what you believe, it's what you can *prove*. No bullet to match to *anyone's* gun."

Johnson chuckled. "I bet you were a pretty good detective, Jason, you know, before you got old and decrepit."

"I had my moments."

The FBI man handed each of us one of his business cards. "Oh, almost forgot." He reached inside his left coat pocket and pulled out a section of short thick black wire, handing it to Jackson. "We found it in Yakif's pants pocket. Couldn't figure out what it was for a minute but then I remembered you said the plane was missing its coil wire—gotta be it."

Jackson smiled taking the wire and turned for the plane.

"Wait a minute, I'm not done."

Jackson turned around.

"The FAA will have my ass if I were to let you fly outta here without a radio, so I...um....*borrowed* this hand-held from one of the army pukes' helicopters. They don't know it yet. Just keep it."

"Shame on you," I told him. "You, an upstanding agent of the FBI, swiping an army radio from your fellow soldiers," I said as I extended my hand.

The FBI man shook it. "Fellow soldiers, bullshit! I was a marine. Besides, what was that you told me down in Texas? Oh yeah. 'If you don't have pictures, it never happened.' Let's just consider it a tax refund. I'll square it with the bean counters. Now all three of you get out of my sight before I change my mind. I'll get these guys to move their trucks off the strip."

CHAPTER 43

FISHING

The engine of the Mooney howled in acceleration as the plane bounced down the rough dirt strip in a cloud of dust. The tires lifted off the earth and seconds later the plateau fell away beneath the belly of the plane. It had taken Jackson almost thirty minutes sitting in the cockpit to figure out how to program the digital hand-held aviation radio, but he finally got it working and was now talking into the mouthpiece, radio in one hand, the other on the yolk. When he was satisfied with the altitude and attitude of the craft, he manipulated the throttle and the fuel mixture until he was satisfied with the drone of the engine, as well, and had the plane at a proper cruising speed. We were silent as we stared out different windows at the greenish-brown Missouri River snaking its way through high bluffed canyons and timbered valleys eight thousand feet beneath us, all of us trying to process the events of the past few days.

It was Corey who finally broke the silence. "I really just don't know what to say about all this."

Jackson blew air out through his pursed lips, "That's a fact."

Gazing at the winding river below Corey continued. "Sure fucked up our fishing trip. Dammit, still can't believe that you caught the biggest fish."

That statement finally broke through melancholy mood and we all laughed.

"I sure wish we could have finished that fishing trip," Jackson said.

Corey nodded. "Yep. Sure don't like being upstaged by a novice."

I looked at both of them. "Well, why can't we?"

Both looked at me with questioning faces.

"Look," I told them. "We're not expected back for three more days."

"What about what we told Johnson?" Jackson asked.

"Are you kidding me?" I retorted. "It'll take 'em weeks to sort through that mess. Hell, they won't get off that mountain for at least three more days. Right now the FBI doesn't know whether to shit or go blind."

Jackson consulted the fuel gauge in the dash then his Aviation GPS. "Well, I do need to gas up and there's a paved strip and fuel at Loma, and Loma *is* right on the river. You know, just saying."

Neither Corey nor I said a word. Our expressions

told him everything he needed to know. Always, in his mind, Jackson was still a fighter jock. He turned the wheel on the yoke and pushed it forward, kicking the pedals and opening the throttle at the same time.

The Mooney responded like a horse that had just been spurred. The nose snapped to the west and the engine howled. We *were* going to get another chance at the river.

EPILOGUE

His white lab coat was far too easy to spot in the greens and browns of the forest so he slipped it off, rolled it neatly and laid it behind a rock where it couldn't be seen by the others. His group was some distance away working near the dead man's body. He had lingered behind, telling the others he wanted to collect two more hair samples from the bear. No one questioned it.

When he was sure none of the other members of his team nor any of the assisting FBI Agents were looking his way, the FBI forensic team specialist slipped thirty yards through the trees and brush until he reached a small clearing free of overhead branches. Reaching inside the equipment pouch he wore around his waist, the man removed a satellite cellular phone and dialed the number he had been given. The man was nervous, and the pause until the phone connected seemed like an hour, even though it was barely twenty seconds before a voice on the other end answered.

"Si?"

"It's me. Your man for the river is confirmed, and the plane just left."

The voice on the other end of the line paused before continuing in English. "Which direction"

"To the east but it turned south"

"Was he on board?"

"I am told he was. I did not actually see him get on, but I'm sure he is."

"Why did you not see him?"

"I was given an assignment far away from the plane."

"Where is the plane going?"

"I was told that two of them are going home, but Douglas is going to Yuma."

"Do you know when he will arrive?"

"No"

"Very well."

"CLICK!" The line disconnected. The forensic specialist put the phone back in his pouch then cautiously retraced his steps to the place he had hidden his coat. After putting it back on, he returned to the tree line. When he was certain no one was looking, he nonchalantly stepped out of the trees, walked past the carcass of the bear, quickly joining the others near the Serb's body.

One thousand, four hundred miles to the south, another phone rang.

"Yes?"

"I have been told we lost our Montana river connection"

"How did it happen?"

"We are not totally sure of the series of events, however, we do know that the same man who caused us problems in Pecos and El Paso last year was involved."

"Are you sure it was the same man?"

"Yes. It was the retired policeman, Jason Douglas."

"How do we find this man?"

"I do not think it will be a problem. He is coming to Yuma."

"Call me when you know more of this man and secure additional services for us up there quickly. We cannot have that operation down for long."

"Very well."

"CLICK!"

About the Author

Douglas Durham was born and raised in the Central Valley of California. After serving in the US Army as a military policeman, both in Southeast Asia and in the United States, he ended up in the San Francisco Bay Area where he worked as a police officer. Remarried now, Durham moved to the coast of California near San Luis Obispo, but the Central Valley was not yet ready to turn loose of him. In the late 1980s, he and his wife returned to Fresno, California, a city of over half a million people, where he worked in the Investigations Division of the Fresno Police Department as a Crime Scene Investigations Supervisor, assigned to the night shift for twenty-two years, retiring in 2011. Always the aspiring writer, Durham kept notes over the years of his adventures and real life cases, and, finally, upon retirement, had the time to start his writing career. His first novel *Death in the Desert* (Black Opal Books) was released in 2014. Durham resides the majority of the year in Yuma, Arizona. He and his wife travel during the summer months in his RV and on his motorcycle, both for new project research and just to see America. He is still married to his wife of thirty-one years and has two grown daughters, one living in Hollywood, the other living in Yuma. Be sure and look for the third novel in the Jason Douglas series, *Steel Horses*, out next year.

Made in the USA
Lexington, KY
09 February 2018